The
Gypsy

A Romantic Thriller

by

T.J. Jones

This is a work of fiction. All the characters, events, and most of the places are creations of the author's imagination.

The Gypsy

Prologue

I awoke, disoriented and in the dark. The darkness of a tomb, or a cave far underground. A complete and silent darkness. It wasn't like those shrouded moonless nights on sentry watch. Those nights in that faraway desert when slivers of gray cast fleeting shadows along the horizon. Those nights when the chills running down my spine belied the sweat on my forehead and made me reach out for my rifle. It was much darker than that. Devoid of form and motion. Where was this place? Was I back in that high desert?

I took a few quick breaths as reality came flooding back to me. How long had I been unconscious? Minutes? Hours? Had the sun set in the drill yard? Day or night, I must still be in the interrogation room. I peered toward where I thought the door should be, searching along the floor-line for the slightest glimmer of light from the hallway I knew lay beyond. Still nothing. Was this what it felt like to be blind? In a moment of panic, I blinked rapidly, reassured by the flutter of my eyelids. Despite the depravation of my senses, I was reasonably sure my sight was intact.

I tried to reach out and assess the damage done to my face, but both my hands were bound, my arms stretched up and out to either side. I gathered myself, fighting the pain tearing at my shoulders and attempted to pull one of my arms free. The straps binding my wrists were beyond my strength and I stopped short of dislocating a shoulder.

Disoriented by the blackness around me, I fought the fear and held my breath, listening. In the distance I could hear the sound of measured footfalls and the bark of someone counting cadence. Grown men playing at being soldiers. It wasn't them I had to fear. I listened again. More footsteps, and these were closer. If the three from before returned, it would be to kill me.

I felt motion. I'm told the blind use their remaining faculties to locate and identify the movements of people and objects close at hand. I didn't need to see or hear the Gypsy to know she was near. I could feel the heat of her skin when she leaned over me. Her scent enveloped me, an exotic oil I'd yet to identify. I searched the inky space in front of me and whispered her name.

"Gabriel?"

She hissed, surprisingly close to my ear. "You know I hate that name."

"You shouldn't have followed me here. It's you they're after. Did they hurt you?"

She lowered her voice. "He would kill them if they did. He's saving that pleasure for himself. But they made me watch when they beat you and blamed me for your suffering."

"You shouldn't have come," I repeated, "not alone."

"You came for her, I had to come for you." She paused, then qualified her response. "We all have our parts to play, Cain, and I'm not done with you yet."

"Touching," I said dryly, "and cryptic as usual." I waited for her to say more, but sarcasm seldom swayed her. "I don't think they give a damn what their boss says. They're going to kill me, then torture you until you tell them what they want to know. You always know more than you say, Gypsy. Tell me you've seen a way out of this."

"Seen?" she said peevishly. "It's completely dark."

"This room," I asked, "or our combined futures?" Despite our predicament my lips turned up. It hurt to smile.

She wasn't amused and I didn't need to see her to know that. There wasn't the usual banter in her voice. "I do know that more people are going to die here today, for someone who couldn't care less about their cause. Can you hear them? They're coming back. Those three won't be enough, but they aren't alone. The others might try to stop us."

Her sigh whispered against my cheek. "I'm tired of all the killing."

A warm hand settled on my forearm, then I felt the touch of a blade on my wrist. Her fragrance overwhelmed my senses as she cut the second strap, then her lips ghosted up and touched mine. It was surprising, fleeting. She pulled away quickly and I knew she was listening.

"I cut the leather nearly through. Just give a good tug when the time is right. I'm going to let them think I'm still tied to the chair, but you'll need to distract them until I can use the knife."

The sliver of light I had expected at the base of the door appeared suddenly and I heard footsteps again, much closer this time. There was no rhythm to indicate the military precision from before, just the shuffle of feet, sharp voices, and a harsh laugh from beyond the door. The air stirred against my face as the Gypsy pulled away from me and returned to her bonds, or so they would think.

I guessed that she was on my right and that the door was in front of me. I tipped my head up and waited, staring roughly in the direction of the overhead light. Acclimating my eyes quickly would be important if we were to have any chance of leaving this room alive. The footsteps stopped and the latch creaked. Then the door swung open...

Chapter One

I met the woman who changed everything for me on a cold and windy day in January. The third of January, to be exact. It's an easy date to remember because a lot happened on that day. It was the day my girlfriend called it quits, the day the Gypsy came into my life, and the day I got shot. Only two of those things were unique. I never was worth a damn at long-term relationships.

Jenny and I had been together for a little over a year. She met me at the door of my apartment that morning with her bags already packed. I had walked out in the middle of a fight the night before to go to work. She told me I wasn't the right guy and that she didn't think I ever would be. She said that she'd had enough of a man that would never be emotionally available or able to commit to her. I suspect it was a New Years' resolution that she'd been putting off. It said a lot that she didn't cry, and I guess it said something to her that I didn't beg for another chance.

Emotionally unavailable might seem vague to some people, but I knew exactly what she meant. Committing had never crossed my mind. That's not to say it didn't hurt, because she was a warm and funny girl that was generous in every aspect of our relationship. But it didn't tear my heart out the way it should have, and she saw that too. None of our friends, and we shared very few, were surprised that she'd given up on me.

There were things she couldn't carry, and they were all stacked in a neat pile next to the door. She said she'd pick the rest of her stuff up that night after I left for work and leave her key on the kitchen table. She slammed the door a little harder than she needed to, even though the lock was shitty and tended to stick if you didn't give it a good yank. I sank into the couch and stared at the small pyramid of books and dishes stacked up like a shrine to our failed relationship.

The pair of crystal wine glasses I'd gotten her for Christmas were perched precariously on top of the pile, and as I kicked my shoes off and stretched out for a nap, they toppled onto the hardwood floor. The fragile long-stemmed flutes smashed against each other and disintegrated into razorlike shards with a single melodic finality. It felt orchestrated and intentional. The thought made me smile as I drifted off to sleep. It seemed like something Jenny would do.

When I woke up, I called in and asked for the night off. Security guards are a dime a dozen in Vegas and I knew they could cover my shift. I called it a personal emergency, but really, I just wanted to get drunk. Then I did what any emotionally unavailable and recently single man that lived in Sin City would do; I filled my pockets with cash and headed to the strip club. But I didn't want a girl. I just wanted to see a friendly face and not think about my latest failure.

Strip clubs are plentiful in Las Vegas, which was where I'd landed after ten years in the Army. I didn't expect to stay long, but I had nothing better to do and no plan. My best friend from my unit was there and he made some calls. The job came first, and then one night a pretty blonde smiled shyly at me from across a crowded bar. It was cold that winter too, and just before Christmas. It wasn't long before Jenny had most of the closet space in my apartment.

Now it was a year later, just as cold, and I was alone again. The cold didn't bother me. The mountains of Afghanistan had been colder, and I'd spent the first dozen years of my life in upstate New York, where summers lasted a few weeks and winters forever. But, as I was soon to learn, there are times when Las Vegas can be the coldest place on earth.

I went all the way up north to the older, seedier, part of town. As drunk as I planned to get I needed someone to watch my back. What happens in Vegas stays in Vegas, but there are plenty of opportunities for trouble, and I had no intention of waking up in jail or worse because of my latest rejection.

It was a Monday night and relatively quiet in the club. The doorman recognized me and waved me through without the price of admission. Mickey was behind the bar. Mickey was my best friend from a different life. We'd served together in Afghanistan before the Army politely asked me to find a different line of work. Truth be told, it wasn't polite at all, but the discharge papers said Honorable and by then I was happy to go. The upgraded discharge didn't prohibit me from getting a permit to carry, and I needed that to find security work.

I picked a quiet spot close to the far end of the bar, leaving just enough room for the bar-back to do her job. Most of the girls knew me. They smiled and gave me little waves but kept their distance. They were all working girls, and a security guard with a steady girlfriend wasn't likely to pay for fifteen minutes in the VIP room. Sex in the club was strictly forbidden, but as everyone learned in the nineties, sex is a word open to interpretation.

"Mickey, I plan to get shit-faced tonight," I shared as he handed me a cold one.

"Yeah? I heard Jenny bailed. You had to know that was coming. Justine was on the phone with her half the morning."

11

"Was she upset? She didn't seem too broken up about it."

"Sounded like it to me. I could hear her bawling on Justine's phone, and I was clear across the room trying to watch the news. Justine is ready to give you a good swift kick, so consider yourself warned. I don't think Jenny was expecting a proposal for Christmas, but it's been a year. Saying I love you doesn't cost a thing."

"That's a matter of opinion. She's been talking about the future, as in our future. She wants us to move back east together. She even talked to her brother about a job for me."

"I forgot you're both from the same place. New York, right?"

"Big state, and it's not like we were neighbors. She's talking about moving into the city, and I'm a country boy. I have to go home sooner or later to clean up the old man's mess, but I plan to go alone. She and I were always going to be temporary. I made that clear when we started. Very clear."

"Women are poor listeners when it comes to that kind of shit," Mickey observed, reaching out for a handful of popcorn from the big plastic bowl that was sitting between us. "She figured you'd change for her."

"That's Jenny, always the optimist. People don't change, Mickey. We are at eighty who we were at eight. And I don't do permanent."

"Just saying, girls like Jenny don't come along every day. I think you screwed up."

I reached for the popcorn. "Not the first time and it won't be the last."

I had always used the Army as an excuse not to put down roots. The next deployment was never far away, and I didn't want to be attached when it came time to leave or explain that I wasn't planning to return. My father had said my mother was leaving when I was eleven, and somehow I got the impression she would be coming back. She didn't. We put her in the ground on a dreary day in November, just before my twelfth birthday. My father cried, and I did because I knew it was expected of me. But the concept of her never returning didn't settle in for a long time.

I went to live with my grandmother after that, because my dad was a lifer in the Navy and always gone. I found out later he kept volunteering to get deployed overseas. My grandmother said that it was what he was good at, running away when things got difficult.

My grandmother was an oversized doting woman that hugged me more than I liked and reeked of the cigarette that always hung from her bottom lip. She coughed continually like my mother had right before she died. I was sure the old lady was going to follow her youngest child to the grave at any minute, so I kept my distance. She was eighty-nine when she passed. I was deployed and couldn't get back for the funeral.

The club Mickey worked at wasn't the biggest on the strip, and it sure as hell wasn't the nicest. It did have a well-deserved reputation. If you got into a cab and told the driver you were looking for a sure thing, he dropped you off at the Exotic. Finding a hooker in Vegas isn't difficult, and generally speaking a certain percentage of the girls in any strip club are willing to turn a trick if the money is good and the conditions are right. At the Exotic, the conditions were always right. It was guaranteed. There were two rules at the club, and the first was that saying no to a customer wasn't allowed.

A guy by the name of Alex Gainey owned the place. He was a small-time wannabe bad man that thought he could steal the lion's share of the strip club business by making sure his girls were always available for sex. He didn't force anyone into the business, per se, unless you considered the fact that most of the girls had kids to feed or a drug habit to support. There was a time when I thought of prostitution as a victimless crime, but it was hard to look at Gainey's Girls and not rethink that notion.

Still, it was safer for them than working the streets. That was Gainey's second rule. No rough stuff. If you hurt one of Gainey's Girls, the least you'd get would be the beating of your life. Hurt one of them badly enough and they would find your body parts strung out across the Mojave. It was common knowledge. Gainey was a loyal guy. An honorable pimp. Ironically, most of his girls adored him for it.

"Is Gainey around tonight?" I asked Mickey.

"He's in the VIP room. Don't worry, he likes you. He's fine with you hanging out as long as I'm not giving you free drinks."

I tossed a small pile of twenties on the bar. "Is he okay with me getting your discount?"

Mickey grabbed one of the bills and dropped it into his tip jar, then grinned at me. "He is now."

"Whatever works." I pushed the stack in his direction. "There's more in it for you if you make sure I get home in one piece."

He nodded and walked off to take an order. "I'd see to it anyway."

By ten o'clock the Exotic was filling up with patrons: horny college kids that gave the bouncers fits by putting their hands where they shouldn't, and fat balding car salesmen from the mid-west looking to check a Vegas hooker off their bucket-list. I sat there pouring down beers and watching the stream of clients disappearing into the VIP room, some with girls that were probably their granddaughter's age. All those girls were someone else's granddaughter. It made me want to punch Alex Gainey in the face, along with every one of those lousy car salesmen with their bucket-lists.

After a while Mickey slid down the bar. "You okay, buddy? You've been pounding the beers and you look pissed-off at the world."

"You're right," I admitted. "I'm drunk. You know what else you were right about?"

He pushed the popcorn in my direction and grinned. "Jenny?"

"She wasn't asking for a lot. I'm a dumb ass."

"A dumb ass that's had too much to drink. And you've been looking at naked women all night, so that could be clouding your judgment. Tomorrow morning, if you still want her back, call her up. My money says she hasn't really given up on you. Just don't do it tonight when you're drunk. That would be a dick move."

"You really think she'd take me back?"

"This is Jenny we're talking about, Cain. You said it yourself, she's the eternal optimist. Just don't jerk her around or I'll turn Justine loose on your stupid ass. Here, drink this. You're cut off for a while."

I hoisted the tall glass of water he pushed in front of me. He was right. I was drunk, and I was an idiot. Jenny deserved better.

Alex Gainey came out of the VIP room and walked over. He flipped up the bar-hatch and walked behind the bar, then pointed at my glass. "Are you drinking water? Have a real drink, on me."

"Maybe later," I said. "I think I've had enough for a while." Pimp or not, he was pleasant enough. It's hard to dislike a guy when he's offering you free booze.

"Mickey, Cain's money is no good in here tonight." He reached out for my hand. "Good to have you in here, Adam. Big guy like you, you can back Mickey up if there's trouble. My bouncers can handle about anything, but Mickey tells me you're a good guy to have around if there's a fight. Downright dangerous is what he said."

I shrugged it off. "Only if you're someone that's trying to kill me."

He chuckled. "Well, there's always a job here for you if you're ever looking."

I motioned toward a drunken twenty-something that was pushing a reluctant stripper toward a dark corner of the room. "Too many college kids out of control in here. I don't have the temperament for it."

Gainey followed my gaze, then waved a hand at one of his three hundred-pound bouncers. He pointed at the frat-boy. "He's out of here, right now."

The drunk objected loudly and tried to resist. A second bouncer joined the fray, and they pushed and carried the kid out the front door. The first man followed him out. I was pretty sure he was going to get more than cab-fare and a warning to play nice the next time. Gainey gave me a pointed look and grinned. "I don't have the temperament for it either."

After a nod to Mickey, Gainey disappeared into his office in the back. Within ten minutes he returned with two bags of garbage and unlocked the padlock that secured the service door. Mickey's bar-back picked the wrong time to walk up. Deloris was on the backside of thirty and the only woman in the place with all her clothes on. Without being asked she picked up the bags and leaned a shoulder against the door.

"How about I walk you out there?" I asked. "I could use the fresh air." The back lot was dark, and it was quite a distance to the dumpster.

She glanced at Mickey, who nodded. She shrugged. "Suit yourself. I've been going out there every night for three years and nothing bad has happened yet."

"Still, I'll walk you out." I grabbed the bigger of the two bags and stumbled through the door ahead of her.

She looked at me warily as we crossed the lot. "You have a girlfriend, don't you?"

"Pretty sure I don't, not after the fight we had this morning," I admitted.

"Well, I have a husband. Mickey says you're a good guy and all, but don't get the idea I want to hook up."

I nodded. "That's not what I had in mind, honest. I just wanted to be sure you didn't get mugged."

"Want a cigarette, long as we're out here? Cold as hell, but I can't smoke inside."

"I don't smoke, but I'll hang out while you have one." I wanted to share my distaste for the nasty habit, but I held my tongue. She lit up and took a long pull on the cancer stick. The glow illuminated her face. She was decidedly pretty. "Three years?" I asked. "What's Gainey like to work for?"

She leaned against the wall and flicked some ashes into the night air. "Moody bastard, and he doesn't pay me for shit. But he's okay for the most part."

"What's a bar-back do at a strip club?"

Her eyes narrowed a little. "Same as any bar. I don't take my clothes off if that's what you're asking. Sometimes I let the girls cry on my shoulder when they get their fill of it. Some of the clients are real pigs."

"But it's not like they have a choice. It seems like the hooking should be optional."

"A lot of things in this world should be optional," she mused, "but we all have to eat." She took another pull on her cigarette and smiled, savoring whatever satisfaction it is that smokers crave, then flipped the butt into the night. "Life doesn't always turn out like you figure it's gonna, does it? Most of these girls are out of options or they wouldn't be here."

I held the door open and followed her in.

Chapter Two

When we walked back inside, I discovered that my spot at the bar had been taken. The person sitting on my seat was wearing what I took to be a hoodie, and presumed that one of the college kids had displaced me. A closer look revealed that the hoodie was more of a coat that stretched halfway to the floor and exposed the bottom third of some decidedly feminine legs. An exotic scent drifted my way. My water glass had moved, and I slid onto the barstool in front of it.

"You stole my spot," I explained when the hood shifted in my direction. I caught a glimpse of a high cheekbone and a dark meandering eyebrow.

"Sorry," she said. "I like to hide in the corner and people watch. Warmer over here too. I'm still cold from being outside."

The voice was decidedly feminine, rich, and surprisingly deep. There was a hint of an accent. Mickey walked up with a glass of wine and put it down in front of the woman. A slender hand reached out and the glass disappeared for a moment into the folds of cloth that surrounded her face. Mickey stood there gaping until I pushed a twenty in his direction. The folds shifted again as the woman turned her head.

"You don't have to do that. I should buy you one for taking your spot."

"You can get the next one," I said, then slid a hand along the edge of the bar. "Adam Cain, but my friends just call me Cain."

The hand came out again and slipped into mine. Her fingers were long and her grip was firm. "Cain? Is that a biblical reference? Or is it, Cane, like a sugar bush?"

"I don't think sugar grows on a bush," I said, then nodded toward the room. "Or was that a Freudian slip?"

She laughed lightly at my failed humor. "Okay, not a sugar bush. Cain, like in the bible."

"How about you? Do you have a name to go with that face? Not that I've seen much of your face."

She chuckled again. "It's embarrassing, my name. But I'm finally getting warm so I guess the coat can go." She opened the top button of her wrap then lifted her hands to the edge of the hood and pushed it away from her face.

Mickey hadn't moved, and when the woman tipped her head back and shook the torrents of raven hair away from her face, he made a choking sound and started coughing. He covered his tracks quickly.

"Damn popcorn," he complained, then gave me a furtive look as he walked toward the other end of the bar. "Holy shit," he mouthed quietly and rolled his eyes.

In a town filled with beautiful women, my unnamed bar-mate was still likely to turn heads. Her black hair tumbled off her shoulders in waves and her eyes were the darkest brown I'd ever seen, several shades darker than her skin-tone. I couldn't hazard a guess at her ethnicity. Her face was sharp and angular, her lips full and red.

"My friend thinks you're attractive," I pointed out. "He doesn't gag and turn that shade of purple for every woman he sees."

She offered a grin. "That's sweet, but I really think it was the popcorn."

"What brings you to a strip club? Are you looking for your pick of guys, or does your girlfriend work here?"

She raised a brow. "Freud again, or are you fishing? I like men, generally. There was that one time in college..."

I laughed. "Now you're just messing with me."

"Every guy alive wants to hear that story. Really, I'm too busy to date, and relationships are hard."

"Tell me about it. My girlfriend just walked out this morning. I was drowning my sorrows until Mickey cut me off."

"That sounds like a line. Am I'm supposed to feel bad now, and sleep with you?"

"That would only work for a little while, because I'd wake up and still be my stupid self."

I shrugged and reached for the popcorn. "But if you think it would help..."

She laughed again. "I can tell you for sure that isn't going to happen, not tonight."

"That's indefinite, but not a no," I pointed out. Her laugh was genuine and guttural. I kept it going. "Honestly, Mickey just got through convincing me I should try again with Jenny, so don't get your hopes up."

She eyed me skeptically. "I'll be sure to temper my expectations."

"Just so you know, I'm a catch. I have a glamorous job as a security guard at one of the casinos."

She played along. "Good-looking and gainfully employed. You are a catch."

"I'll ignore the sarcasm. What is it you do?"

"Futures. Stock futures and analysis. We're always trying to figure out the next big thing and make someone rich. I'm actually pretty good at it. That's how I got my silly nickname."

"The face did not disappoint; what kind of a name could be that bad?"

"I had a good run of luck when I first started at the firm, and some of the guys were kidding me that it was more than just being good at my job. They started saying I must be able to see the future. Then there was a bunch of nonsense about crystal balls and tarot cards, and one thing led to another. Pretty soon they started calling me the Gypsy. Fits too, because I'm always traveling. Truthfully, I kind of like it."

"*The* Gypsy?"

She made a face. "Just Gypsy. It's a nickname, not a statement. I'll admit, I look the part, and I actually have some of that heritage on my mother's side. Anyway, the name stuck, and I like it better than the alternative."

I studied her features. "I think it suits you. You do look kind of dark and mysterious, in a good way. Can we still call people Gypsies? "

She waved a hand. "They're my people, and I'm not offended."

I rolled it around in my head. "Yeah, I like it. But what's your real name?"

She looked around, as if about to reveal a deep dark secret, then leaned in. "Gabriel," she said and scowled. "I've always hated it. I was named after my grandmother, and she's a spiteful old tyrant."

I asked the obvious question. "Why tell me, if you dislike the name so much?"

Her smile came easily. "Friends should know each other's secrets, don't you think?"

I grinned back at her. "We're friends?"

She put a warm hand on my forearm. "I think we're going to be very good friends, Adam Cain."

Despite my claim of heartbreak and my intention to call Jenny the next day, I found myself drawn to the beautiful dark-haired woman that sat beside me. There was no denying that she was incredibly attractive, but there was more to it. Every movement, every smile, every laugh, exuded an undeniable force: a gravity pulling at me, as if she was a newly formed sun and I was a wayward planet being yanked into her orbit. I could feel her heat burning its way into my flesh each time she touched me, and her scent flooded my nostrils with a combination of exotic perfume and what I imagined to be pheromones working their magic somewhere deep inside my hypothalamus.

True or not, I imagined that it wasn't purely sexual, and that the attraction wasn't one-sided. At every turn we connected. I told her about growing up in New York, and she told me about Boston and traveling all the time because of her job. Hers were vague stories that were unusually short and lacked specifics. She told me more about getting her name and about how knowing what was going to happen in the markets didn't always work out the way she hoped.

She explained. "Sometimes I know when things are going to happen that will cost people a lot of money and possibly ruin them. I offer them options to mitigate the damages and make the best of a bad situation. That's a big part of what I do, mitigating damage. But sometimes people won't listen, and that's hard for me. Especially when I know I'm right. And I'm almost always right."

She finished her wine and stared thoughtfully at the empty glass, growing suddenly somber. After a moment she reached out and slid an elegant fingertip around the rim, stroking it lightly until the crystal started to vibrate melodically. Despite the background noise the oscillations reached my ears; the hum of the glass brought her smile back.

"But sometimes the market is like everything else in life and there aren't any good options. Sometimes, everything just turns to shit, and there's nothing anyone can do about it."

I nodded toward the nearest table where two young girls were disrobing in front of a crowd of chanting thirty-somethings.

The smile fell from her face again. "Good example. Kids like that get swept up by circumstance and then make some bad decisions. And sometimes the choices don't matter. Sometimes it just comes down to being in the wrong place at the wrong time. Then all a person can do is try to mitigate the damage."

I searched her face. "Are we still talking about the stock market?"

She shrugged. "I wish."

It was still Monday, twenty minutes before midnight. In that moment everything went to hell and the Exotic became the latest name attached to a long list of mass-shootings. Some people called it a tragedy and some people called it Karma, because it was a strip club. It wasn't Karma. If it had been Karma, most of the victims wouldn't have been young women who were already being victimized, or a bunch of college kids too drunk to save themselves. If it had been Karma, people like Alex Gainey and that car salesman from Ohio with his bucket-list would not have been among the lucky ones that escaped.

I didn't escape, but thanks to the Gypsy, I survived.

Chapter Three

Any Ranger from the 75th Regiment would recognize the sound of a Kalashnikov rifle immediately. More commonly known as the AK47, they're the most popular assault rifle in the world. They're cheap, practically indestructible, and almost never jam. They aren't as accurate as some of the American models, but when you're inside a building shooting unarmed innocents that aren't shooting back at you, that doesn't matter. Most of the people inside the Exotic weren't armed. I always carried and Mickey had a gun behind the bar. One of the bouncers had a gun, but he was dead before he knew he needed it.

The Gypsy and I had our backs to the big room, and the first indication we had that we were in trouble was the look in Mickey's eyes as he lunged in our direction. He kept his gun under the bar, sitting on top of the antique safe that was left over from the thirties and still served as a decoy for would be thieves. He took three big steps, groping frantically. I knew he was reaching for his Glock. His eyes found mine as he pulled the gun from its hiding place, and he barked out a quick warning. "Shooters! Three...maybe four!"

I heard the loud pop of several individual shots. The first man was being careful with his ammo. Using the rifle on semi-automatic was the more accurate choice. The second shooter unloaded a barrage of automatic fire. Not as deadly, but far more intimidating. In the time it took to draw a breath, the Exotic was turned into a nightmare scene of terrified screaming strippers and equally panic-stricken customers.

The bar-hatch was still up and my bar-mate slid around just ahead of me as I yanked my gun from the holster under my arm. The service door wasn't latched, and I put a foot against it, then turned to the room. It was total chaos. Half-naked girls and wide-eyed college boys pushed and shoved and fought one another in their desperation, ducking and flailing uselessly at the air as they were cut down by automatic rifle fire. I glanced down for a second and pointed toward the open doorway. "Gabriel, run! Get the hell out of here."

She shook her head and leaned against the old safe. "No. Get behind me. They can't shoot through this thing."

There were four of them. It was a mistake covering their faces because it made them easier to pick out of the crowd. Mickey moved to the far end of the bar and we both leveled our Glocks at the same time. Handguns have their place, but when you're up against automatic rifles across a big, poorly lit room filled with people screaming and running for their lives, they're not a good option. One of the shooters spotted us and ripped off a burst in our general direction. The mirror behind the bar exploded and liquor flew everywhere, but the shots were high and we both returned fire.

Luck was with us, or more probably the fact that Mickey was very good with his handgun. The first man with the automatic went down. If I had hit the shooter it was dumb luck. The room was already filled with acrid smoke, adding another layer of sensory deprivation to the noise of gun fire and the surreal scene unfolding in front of us.

Screaming, crying, blood splattered girls scattered like gazelle ahead of a pride of hungry lions as the remaining three men moved into the room with their guns. I held off, afraid of hitting one of the strippers or the hapless patrons scrambling over chairs, upending tables, and each other as they tried to get to the front exit. One of the shooters met them there, firing coldly into the mob until they turned away as a group and rushed back toward the bar. The sharp-eyed among them spotted the open service door behind me and they all sprinted in our direction.

Three shooters were still standing. The two not guarding the front door had started moving along the far wall, taking the time to shoot anyone that wasn't quick enough to scramble out of the way or hide behind one of the giant oak tables that had recently served as platforms for the dancers. The pair on the far wall were working together with a goal in mind and moving toward the VIP room. Mickey realized it at the same time I did and we both turned in their direction.

I glanced down at the woman I'd just met. She didn't look frightened. I pointed at the open service door again as Alex Gainey stumbled from his office, fell to the floor, and crawled out through the opening. He was soon trampled by a dozen hysterical patrons climbing over each other as they tried to get outside, but I saw him fight his way to his feet and continue his escape. The Gypsy looked up at me, oddly calm, and shook her head again.

When I looked back, Mickey had leveled his gun at the two men on the far wall. They had stopped killing indiscriminately and were definitely looking for someone. The lead shooter crouched and rolled a body over, then shook his head and stood. The second man pointed in the direction of the VIP room and they started moving forward. I knew there was another exit back there, but the odds were good that it was bolted shut and that Alex Gainey had the only key. Anyone still back there would be trapped.

There was another burst from an automatic, this time from the man at the front door. This was a more accurate and deadly barrage. Mickey had his gun leveled, taking dead aim at one of the two men along the wall. Both our guns were standard issue and we didn't have the luxury of wasting shots. Mickey never got to fire his remaining loads. I don't know what kind of ammo the gunmen were using, but it didn't matter to Mickey. The impact of several shots tossed him against the backwall like a ragdoll, and he tumbled to the floor in my direction. His still form was surrounded immediately by a growing pool of blood.

I felt the Gypsy pull at my leg as she tried to stop me, but I lunged across Mickey's body and leveled my gun at the man with the automatic. I fired half a dozen ineffectual shots just as he returned fire. From my left, I heard one of the other shooters open up. I don't know which one of them hit me, but I knew I'd been hit. I careened off the bar and fought to stay on my feet as I tried to lift my gun again, but the Glock had become inexplicably heavy. It tumbled from my grasp as I went down, flailing at the bar, desperately trying to stay on my feet.

The next thing I knew the woman who called herself the Gypsy was dragging me back to the relative safety of the corner behind the old safe. Vaguely I heard the roar of another barrage from one of the AK47s and the remnants of the mirror disintegrated. Two of the plastic bowls sitting on the bar flipped into the air, throwing popcorn in every direction.

Reality faded as I watched each kernel spin through the air like a gentle snowfall. I imagined the giant bits of wet snow I had tried to catch on my tongue when I was five years old, never dreaming at that age that I'd be here now, fighting for my life. The popcorn tumbled down around me, mixing with bits of shattered mirror and pieces of broken bottles that were flying everywhere. The white puffs landed on me softly and on the floor, turning crimson quickly as each kernel absorbed the stain that was growing beneath me.

"Cain!" The Gypsy was kneeling in front of me suddenly and she held up my gun. "How many?"

I tried to respond, to concentrate on what it was she wanted me to say, but an enormous weight had settled on my chest and I couldn't get any words out. I felt detached and numb. The room was slipping away, turning dark. She jerked me up and propped me against the corner of the safe.

"I'm going to presume it's a standard clip. You didn't give me a lot of leeway."

I tried to shout at her to run, to get out the service door and save herself. As it was, I couldn't form the words. A dark veil was descending on my vision. My whole body refused to respond, and no words would come out of my mouth.

The Gypsy stood suddenly, and I blinked up at her through the red haze that was clouding my vision. All I could think of in that moment was how incredibly tall she was. Standing, and straddling my broken body with a well-muscled leg on either side of me, she looked like an ethereal giant: a beautiful Amazon, impossibly tall and equally invincible.

It was obvious that she knew her way around a handgun. She fired immediately, spun quickly and fired again, then dropped down and crowded me against the antique safe that had become our sanctuary. Improbably, she grinned at me. "Two down and one to go."

The remaining shooter knew our location and released a barrage from his automatic that rapped harmlessly against the plated steel of the old safe.

She put a finger to her lips. "Quiet now. He'll try to come at us from the other end of the bar." She tucked her coat around me and pushed it against the hole in my chest that was still oozing blood. "Hold this, tight as you can. I'll be back in a minute."

I made another attempt to stop her, as if I knew better than she did how to keep us safe. Long seconds ticked by as I fought to stay conscious, surprised by the growing silence. The only noises were made by the remaining survivors scrambling through the open doorway and the sobs of the wounded and dying. Then my gun roared again, twice.

The next thing I knew she was in front of me, pulling at a corner of her coat and using it to wipe blood from my gun. In hindsight, she was also wiping away her fingerprints. She smiled down at me like I was a petulant child and put the Glock on the floor beside me.

"I wanted to leave that one alive to tell his story, but he wouldn't give up his gun. Hang in there, Cain. You're going to be alright. I promise. But I can't stay here. In a couple of minutes, every ambulance and cop in Las Vegas will be here, and I have no interest in talking to the police. I'm sorry about your friend."

Her casual smile seemed out of place given all the death and destruction around us. Mitigate, she's said. Is that what she'd just done? A hundred questions flew through my mind, but I only had the strength to ask one. "Who the hell are you?"

She passed a hand across my cheek and smiled again. "I told you. I'm the Gypsy."

Chapter Four

Detective Jordan Murdock wasn't a happy man. He seldom was, but his mood today was worse than most. Twenty-eight people were dead including the shooters, and he had another mess to explain to the press. Granted, it wasn't as bad as the Mandalay Bay incident, but the reporters were all over his ass and he couldn't blame them. This wasn't an unhinged single shooter gone rogue because he was hearing voices or suffering from PTSD. This had been well organized. To even the most naïve, it had to look like a mob-hit gone wrong.

There had been four gunmen, all equipped with unregistered assault rifles. That alone would be enough to send the news crews into a frenzy and would have every anti-gun group in the country breathing down his neck within the week. What the press didn't know was the level of sophistication and planning it must have taken, and the fact that the shooters had a particular target in mind.

The witnesses he had interviewed were mostly useless, too terrorized to remember the moments just before and during the assault. But a couple of relatively clear-minded individuals, pinned down behind a table until they could make a break for it, had volunteered that at least one of the gunmen took the time to look at faces. That suggested they had been sent to kill someone. If that was true, it was possible that all the strippers and dollar-toting college kids that died that night had just been collateral damage. A ruse to cover the shooter's true intentions. That would be another particularly troubling bit of information should the press find out.

What bothered Detective Murdock most was the fact that the best pieces of evidence he had sat on the table in front of him, untouched. He had two cellphones, undoubtedly dropped by potential victims in the mad dash for safety. More crucially, he had the video player that had recorded the whole event. The club's security system was antiquated, but Murdock knew that the four cameras inside the club had been operational, and that a good portion of what had transpired had been recorded on the machine that now sat on the table in front of him. Twice he had attached the monitor and twice he had unhooked the cables.

The chief had been clear. Painfully so. The FBI had been on the phone with the mayor. An agent was due in his office by ten o'clock, and his orders were to wait for them. Don't watch the tape and don't touch the phones. It amounted to a crock of shit. Murdock glanced at the clock on the wall, then back at the machine. If they didn't show by ten-thirty, he was going to have a look.

Agent Blake Collins glanced at his watch, then risked a peek at his supervisor in the seat next to him. "We're just fifteen minutes behind schedule, Sir. We'll have wheels on the ground by nine forty-five."

The older man looked up from his laptop. "For the fourteenth time, Collins, stop calling me Sir. It's Agent Randolph. And Teddy is fine when we're alone." He paused and slid his glasses down on his sharp nose. "Seriously, fourteen times. I've been keeping track, and I have a damn good memory."

"Oddly so, Sir...Agent Randolph. It's called hypermnesia, or eidetic memory," Collins volunteered.

Randolph peered over his glasses again. "Speak English, and tell me something useful. Sometimes you surprise me and think of something I haven't. We're late to the party, again. By now the object of my affections is on the east coast, or half-way around the world. We could have passed her in mid-air. She probably thumbed her nose at us when our planes met. That's usually what happens."

"What makes you so sure she was there?"

"One of the eye-witness accounts I got from the detective at the scene mentioned a beautiful dark-haired woman sitting at the bar next to our hero, talking to him and the bartender that was killed."

"Our hero? That would be the ex-Army Ranger that Jennifer Mercer is involved with?"

"The same. He was right in the middle of it. He's in the hospital, but they think he's going to make it. Hell of a coincidence, don't you think?"

"That would be quite a coincidence if it's all connected. Jennifer Mercer has no way of knowing what her father is mixed up in, or even that he's alive. He's been dead for two years, allegedly."

"Unless she's involved. And from her file she doesn't strike me as someone who's capable of that kind of duplicity. Still, there's the other thing." Randolph tapped a key on his laptop and the crossword he'd been working on disappeared. In a moment it was replaced by a list of names. "The local cops identified everyone they could as they left the bar, those that didn't just keep running. Look at the fourth name down in the second column. And the third column, first name. I'm guessing that won't make it into the newspapers. Another coincidence?"

Agent Collins drew a sharp breath. "So, what was the intent? Who were they targeting? And why was your elusive femme-fatale there?"

"Spare me the hyperbole, Collins. But those are all good questions. The papers are already saying it was a turf war over drugs and hookers, but I don't believe that for a second. Why was Jack Mercer there? Did he come down to visit his sister? And if so, why wasn't he out front with her boyfriend when the shooting started?"

Collins studied the weathered face of his boss, then volunteered his thoughts. "It's odd that the woman was there too, of all nights. How could she know, unless she was involved? Are we going to follow up on this, or are we going to chase after her again?"

Agent Randolph flipped his laptop shut and scowled at his junior partner. "We might as well chase a ghost. We'll work the case because that's our job. Sooner or later, she'll reappear. She always does."

"If it was her," Collins cautioned.

Randolph looked down at the city as the airplane shuddered and the landing gear bumped into place. "I'd bet my pension on it."

"I trust you haven't watched that footage yet, Detective Murdock," Agent Randolph said as he settled into the chair across from the homicide detective. He nodded toward the video screen. "That would not be a good way to start our working relationship."

Collins flipped open his briefcase and tossed out a notepad and pen, followed by a handful of evidence bags. He pulled on a pair of plastic gloves, then eyed the cellphones sitting beside the security machine. He glanced furtively at Murdock, then spoke up. "We were promised full cooperation by your chief and told you would not screen the footage until we arrived."

"It's nice to meet you too," Detective Murdock growled.

Agent Randolph spoke up again. "Sorry. I don't like to make assumptions, but this looks like a nasty business with federal security implications. I'm Teddy Randolph, and this is Agent Collins." Handshakes were exchanged and the tension fell a bit.

"No, I didn't watch it," Murdock said, "or dig into the cellphones. But I did a quick check to find the timestamp we need to look at. There were four cameras: one at the entry, one in the main room, one in the VIP room, and one at the bar. They all seemed to be working, but the clarity isn't great. Odds are the lenses hadn't been cleaned in years. Hopefully the footage is good enough to identify people with facial recognition once we review all the angles."

Randolph nodded. "We'll send you a list, just as soon as we get through the footage. Any thoughts on motive, Detective? You would have to piss off another club owner pretty badly for him to send four hired killers to murder half your staff and a bunch of patrons."

Murdock had stopped listening. He was watching Collins drop the cellphones into his evidence bags. "What do you mean, you'll send me a list? I can put together my own God-damn list, and I already gave you most of what I know.

This is still my investigation, no matter what the Chief and the Mayor say."

Collins piped up. "We've been guaranteed your full cooperation."

"On what basis?" Murdock shouted. "I get that the feds need to be involved in something like this, but you're supposed to share information and help with the investigation, not run off with all my evidence."

Collins spoke again. "You'll get everything back once we've reviewed it. Remember, full cooperation."

"I heard you the first time, you pompous little prick," Murdock roared. "But I need answers right now. There's no way the chief agreed to this."

Randolph slid his phone across the table, his voice level. "Last call I made. Use my phone if you want to check in with him." Collins started to talk again but stopped when Randolph lifted a hand.

"I'm sorry if we've blind-sided you, Detective. But, as I said, we have good reason to believe there are national security concerns involved here. There was unregistered weaponry used, so our investigation takes priority. I'd prefer to do this the easy way, but I can have a court-order from a federal judge in about ten minutes and turn the ATF loose on the crime scene. That will just make both our jobs harder. You'll get the video back as soon as it's been studied and properly redacted, should that prove necessary."

"This is bullshit," Murdock said stubbornly. "Why did you even bother coming out here? I could have loaded everything on an e-file for you."

"As I said, some of what's on that machine could be highly sensitive, and we all know how unreliable e-mail is. The fewer people who have access to this the better. We don't want every detail splattered all over the newspapers. Not that you would do that. Agent Collins will return to the Bureau with the machine. A video copy, redacted as necessary, and a detailed report will be delivered to you personally."

"A redacted copy? That's just great," Murdock sputtered. "How long before I get that? The newspapers are all over my ass. And the Chief. And the Mayor. But then you already talked to those two worthless pricks. A fat lot of help they are."

"Agent Collins will get back to you by Thursday afternoon and deliver our findings. Also, he has the witness list you gave me. He will be conducting his own interviews when he gets back here. Not that you haven't done a thorough job, but another set of questions by an FBI agent might shake out some new information," Randolph said calmly, then stood as Collins finished pushing the machine into his briefcase. "I'll be in town for a few days,

Detective. I'll check in with you, and as is always the case, the Bureau's resources are at your disposal."

Murdock nodded and doubled down on his sarcasm. "Wonderful. Will those be getting redacted too? You FBI guys are all kinds of help."

Teddy Randolph grinned and extended a hand. "I'm glad to see you still have your sense of humor. Here's my card, and I'll call you tomorrow."

Detective Murdock slouched back in his chair and studied the card. Lying to the FBI wasn't a good idea, but neither was admitting that he'd watched the footage. He would have to dig deeper into the list of names he had. National security? He hadn't seen anything on the recording that would endanger national security, unless the woman was a Russian assassin. She could shoot like one. Maybe she was the security risk.

Murdock looked at the card again, then slipped it into his front pocket. Screw the FBI. He would find a way to do his job, with or without their help. He stood slowly and scrolled through the grainy pictures he'd saved on his cellphone. The cameras didn't show the far end of the bar, and that was where the woman must have been sitting. It was hard to say who did most of the shooting, but it looked like both of the men behind the bar were already down before the last three assassins were killed. Two shots, two men dead. A pause, then two more shots. Three dead hitmen with four shots. Impressive.

The woman had been out of view for the most part, but when she came around to go after the last shooter, she was partially visible from the entry camera. Very tall and dark, but most definitely a woman. Undoubtedly the same woman his witness had mentioned. A little digital magic at the FBI lab and they might know who she was. Question was, would they share that information?

Chapter Five

"What's the largest cash crop of Afghanistan?"

The answer was obvious. I'd seen mile upon mile of poppies in the province of Kandahar. Waves of pink, red, and purple disappearing over the horizon like buffalo-grass on a windy Kansas hillside. But why ask that question? Had the Taliban returned? They were the only ones that had ever managed to stop the locals from tending their fields, and as far as I knew, business was booming.

"Think," the irritating voice demanded again. "The largest cash crop. Six down, five letters. I need it to make my whole left side work."

Left side? My left side felt alright, but the right side of my chest felt like someone had parked a truck on it. Where was I, and why did that annoying voice keep asking the same inane question?

"Largest cash crop, Afghanistan, five letters. Wheat? That seems wrong. Barley? Nope, that's six letters."

I struggled to pull some air into my lungs. "Opium," I said. "Everyone knows that. It's opium."

"Adam! Oh, thank God. Can you hear me?" Blond hair and blue eyes swam into view as I opened my eyes, sorting out the fact that I was in a hospital bed and that Jenny was leaning over me. A tear dropped from the end of her nose and tumbled onto my forehead. I blinked and managed a smile. Jenny smiled back and brushed my cheek with her lips. "I was afraid you were never going to wake up."

Things were coming back to me. "She told me I'd be okay. She promised."

"Who?" Jenny asked. "The nurse?"

"No," I explained. "Gabriel. The woman at the bar."

"I don't know anything about that woman, I'm just glad you're awake. They put you under, like a coma, and they weren't certain you were ever going to come out of it."

"Not a coma," the voice offered, "just some serious drugs. They told me you'd probably come around this morning." It was a man's voice. The same one that woke me. "That's why I'm here. Nice catch, by the way. Opium fits right in there."

I turned my head as far as I could. The man was well dressed and in his mid-forties. He was sitting in one of the visitor's chairs with a newspaper sprawled across his lap. His suitcoat hung from the back of the chair, and his tie was undone. He clicked his pen, folded the paper carefully with the crossword on the outside, then stood slowly. He was rail thin, broad, and easily six-six. Nearly my height.

"I'm going down for coffee and a bite while you two catch up. How do you feel, Mister Cain? Do you feel up to talking about it?"

Jenny responded quickly and she sounded angry. "For Christ's sake, Teddy, he just woke up. He nearly died and he needs to rest. Your questions can wait."

The tall man smiled patiently. "I'll see that the doctor comes in and checks on him, and I'll get his approval before we chat. I'm sorry, Jennifer, but it really can't wait."

Jenny glared at his back as he left. "He been here doing his stupid crosswords and bugging me for two days. And he was here again at seven o'clock this morning. He has someone guarding the door night and day. He claims he's from the FBI."

Despite Jenny's objections, I touched a button and raised the head of my bed.

"Mickey didn't make it, did he?" I closed my eyes. I knew the answer. All the memories were coming back, flooding my head with the sound of gunfire and images of Mickey's body covered with bloody popcorn. "How is Justine holding up?"

"Not great. He was everything to her. She thought they'd grow old together."

"Tell her how sorry I am. There were just too many of them and they were too well armed. We were both shooting, but he was at the far end of the bar, more in the open. We were spread out to be less of a target. I'm sorry."

"She knows you did everything you could, obviously."

"And I'm sorry about the fight we had. I'm an asshole. Mickey even said that right before it happened."

"All that matters now is that you get better," Jenny said. Optimistic and generous. Mickey had been right.

I looked over at the second hospital bed. "Have you been staying here?"

"I had to, until I knew you'd be alright. I couldn't just not see you after everything that happened. The hospital has been great, and I think they made some exceptions because of the circumstances." Her voice grew husky. "I know what I said, Adam, but I'm not ready to give up on us."

I managed a smile as I drifted off. "Mickey said you wouldn't."

I woke up an hour later when a doctor unceremoniously pulled my eyelid open and pointed a flashlight at my pupil. He looked pissed off. I could hear loud voices in the hallway and Jenny was nowhere to be seen. The doctor turned to his nurse and nodded toward the door.

"Tell those two idiots to keep it down or I'll have security remove them. I don't give a shit if it is the FBI, this is an ICU."

A stocky nurse with spiked blond hair and a grim expression grunted her agreement. "I'm on it." There was more shouting, mostly by the nurse, then silence.

The doctor smiled and continued his exam. "I knew Gretchen could handle them. You're in high demand, Mister Cain. I know Detective Murdock, and he usually gets his way. But not this time. The feds have had a guy on the door ever since you came in. Miss Mercer is the only one they allowed in here, save for medical staff."

"How long have I been out?"

"It's Saturday. Usually, the attending does rounds on Saturday, but I wanted to see how you were doing. You're kind of a special case."

"I've been out for five days?"

He chuckled as he gently probed my right shoulder. "And you're probably going to be here for a few more. You lost an incredible amount of blood, which was the worst of it. But on a positive note, those two bullets sailed right through and never touched bone. They missed your heart and the subclavian branch by half an inch each. A couple centimeters either way, and we wouldn't be having this conversation. All in all, you were incredibly lucky."

"I feel lucky." It was all the sarcasm I could muster. Mickey had needed some luck. "How long before I can get up and move around?"

"You'll bounce back pretty quickly, I would guess. You're young and strong as an ox. But, like I said, you lost so much blood it was touch and go there for a while. You're past any real danger now, but you'll need to take it very easy for the next few days. I'd say, given two or three weeks, you'll be nearly good as new. We'll get you up walking this afternoon. Normally we'd boot you out of the ICU today, but I got word that you need to stay up here. I think Agent Randolph had a talk with the hospital administrator. You must be important."

I managed a smile. "I have no idea why."

"At least up here we can keep the television crews away." I didn't ask, and his explanation confused me even further. "We'll try to get you fixed up and protect your privacy, Mister Cain. But the press can be relentless, and people love a feel-good story like yours. You're quite a hero."

"You're quite a hero, Mister Cain," Agent Randolph said as he eased back into the chair he had vacated earlier. He held up his newspaper.

I didn't like Agent Randolph. No reason other than Jenny didn't. "That's a stretch," I said. "I thought everyone knew they grew opium in Afghanistan."

He rolled his eyes. "I knew that. Would you believe me if I said I was just trying to get your girlfriend to talk to me?" He lifted the newspaper again and pointed to a picture of me on the front page. "This is what I was talking about, not your grasp of the trivial. Very few people could've taken out those shooters the way you did."

"Mickey was there too. What makes you think it was me that killed them?" The Gypsy had made it clear she didn't want to talk to the cops. I didn't plan to volunteer any information.

"Ballistics. Three of the four gunmen were shot with your gun, two of them right between the eyes. Pretty impressive, Soldier. Somebody leaked that information to the press. They want to throw a parade in your honor."

"Those men were at the far end of the building, seventy or eighty feet away," I pointed out. "That would be impressive, but I don't remember firing those shots."

"What do you remember about that night?" Randolph had his pen out. He started drumming it against his newspaper and studying his crossword.

"I remember there were security cameras."

He folded the newspaper again and dropped it into his lap. "Poorly placed security cameras. The side door and the south end of the bar weren't even covered. From one angle, I could see you were talking to someone, but I never got a good look at his face. Or was it a woman?"

My chest hurt and I wasn't in the mood. "You know damn well it was a woman. I'm sure I'm not the first witness you've talked to. What is it you want to know?"

"There was a lot happening in that bar, Mister Cain. There were people screaming and running for their lives, finding Jesus and shitting themselves. Not many reliable witnesses. And there really isn't any decent camera footage. Like I said, we have no view of the far end of the bar. Whoever killed the last of those assholes, they stayed low and hid behind the tables and chairs that were thrown all over. We studied the footage from the entry camera and the person is impossible to identify. It might have been you. Who's to say it wasn't?"

"I'm to say. I didn't shoot those three men, and you know it. I was on the floor, trying not to bleed to death. What are you trying to pull? I'm ready to call my lawyer, so you better tell me what this is about. Do you even work for the FBI?"

He palmed his billfold casually and showed me his badge. It looked real, but then I'd never seen one before.

"Stop trying to con me, Randolph. Smart guy like you, you know there's more to this than a random shooting, or someone that had a hard-on for Gainey."

"Smart guy like me?" He liked that. He smiled.

"Most of you bureaucrats are smart enough, or at least smart enough to con the people around you. I don't think you'd be a bigshot at the FBI if you weren't reasonably sharp, despite the fact that you're terrible at crosswords."

This time his smile was genuine. "In a few years I'll retire from chasing down mass-murders, then I'll have all the time in the world to get good at my hobby. The two things aren't that different, you know. You sort out each little item, put them in the right spots, and pretty soon you've figured out the whole puzzle."

I yawned. "Wake me up when you get to the point."

"Okay, Cain. Let's talk about you and Afghanistan. I checked you out. You were the best sniper in your outfit, and one of the top shooters in the whole 75th."

"With a rifle. Mickey was ranked expert with a handgun, but I was lucky to qualify. Plus, I'd had a lot of beer. I didn't kill anyone that night, and I was trying."

"And over there?"

"What does Afghanistan have to do with any of this?"

Randolph was staring down at his newspaper again and fidgeting with his pen.

"You had quite a bit of trouble that last year. You put two of your own in the hospital."

"They were asking stupid questions."

He chuckled. "Trouble over a local woman is what the report said. Mind explaining?"

I relented. "There are a lot of beautiful women over there. Two of my guys cornered one and pulled her burqa off to have a look at her face. You don't do that to a woman over there, or anywhere. Not in my squad."

"And the other thing?"

"What other thing?" I knew what he was talking about, just not how he could know. The record of my court-martial had been sealed as part of the release agreement.

"I'd say it speaks to your character, killing that son-of-a-bitch the way you did. You did what needed doing, even though you had to know it would end your military career. I admire that."

"Sometimes you go with your gut," I muttered. I didn't care for the turn in the conversation. FBI or not, Randolph shouldn't have been able to access my trial records. "I did what the Army told me to do for the most part. Then one night I didn't. It was stupid, but I never claimed to be the smartest guy in the outfit."

"I'd say you're a smart guy, Cain. The papers are saying this was a turf war, over drugs and hookers. What do you think?"

"They were looking for someone."

"Gainey?"

"They could've killed Gainey any time they wanted, coming or going from the club. Why slaughter all those people just to get to him? They wanted to make a statement, and they were looking for a particular customer. Someone a hell of a lot more important than Gainey."

Randolph's pen moved. He filled in a few letters in his crossword, then looked up again. "How about the woman at the bar, who was she looking for?"

"She didn't say. I thought maybe it was going to be my lucky night, until the shit hit the fan. Good thing she was there the way it turned out."

"Then you're admitting the woman killed those three men?" When I didn't respond, he kept talking. "You called her Gabriel. How long have you two been friends, and how well do you know her?"

"You're putting words in my mouth, Agent. Some woman wandered into the bar and swiped my stool. Gabriel? Who's that?"

"You said her name when you first spoke to Jennifer. You weren't completely coherent, but you definitely said Gabriel."

"I'm highly medicated, practically delirious."

"Talented woman, this Gypsy," he said quietly. He was watching me, waiting for a reaction. "She put herself in danger by being there and exposing herself."

I nodded. "Apparently. Now the FBI is after her."

"Why would we be after her? If there's a parade, it should be for her."

"I agree. Throw a parade. Maybe she'll show up."

Agent Randolph took a deep breath, then blew it out through pursed lips. It was for effect. I was pretty sure everything Randolph did was for effect. Calculated. "Here's the thing, Cain. We need your cooperation."

"And I thought you were just looking for a quiet place to do the crosswords." I was tired and hurting. Taunting him seemed fair.

"Here's the thing," he repeated, leaning in a little. "We're at odds with the local authorities. I don't know if you heard the argument with Detective Murdock a bit ago, but he wasn't happy with the security footage we gave him. Now he's demanding an interview with you, and I can't keep you in this room forever. I'd like it if we were on the same page before you have that conversation."

"You want me to lie to him?"

"You were shot, and you went through a traumatic experience. It could be you did kill those three men and you just don't remember doing it."

The light bulb finally came on. "This isn't about me at all. You want to leave her out of it for some reason. Does she work for the FBI too?"

He leaned closer. "Can I be perfectly honest with you, Adam?"

I choked on a laugh. "Are we best buddies now? Don't act like you didn't have this conversation all planned out in your head. You were just waiting for me to wake up to see how much of this bullshit I'd be willing to swallow. Tell me what you know about her, then I'll tell you if I'm willing to lie to the cops for you."

He shrugged. "She isn't one of ours, and she doesn't work for any government agency as far as I can tell. On the surface, she is what she appears to be, a stock analyst. I think that's just a cover. She travels a lot, which gives her an excuse to show up at opportune times, sometimes half-way around the world. She has a talent for being in the right place at the right time, always when there's trouble. It happens too often to be a coincidence."

"You're the FBI. Pull her in and beat a confession out of her."

"You're a funny guy, Cain," he said, but he didn't look amused. "Honestly, the Bureau knows very little about this woman. She's more of a personal project of mine, a pet peeve."

"Still, you could bring her in and question her," I reasoned.

"For what? Showing up and preventing God knows how many people from dying at that strip club? I'm sure it was her, but I don't know if I can prove it without a lot of digging. And you're right, I'd prefer she wasn't pulled into this. Granted she killed three people, but considering who they were, I'm okay with it."

"Enlighten me, Randolph," I said. "This Gypsy woman shows up out of the blue, so you think she might have had an idea that it was going to happen. But you're trying to keep that information to yourself. Let's turn this around. How well do you know her?"

"Unlike you, I've never had the pleasure of buying her a drink." He didn't like me asking the questions and he deflected. "I have to wonder why she picked you to spend time with on that particular night."

"My boyish good looks? You know very little about this woman, but you're protecting her. What's that all about?"

He grinned. "Sometimes you go with your gut."

"That detective is your problem," I countered, "because he wants all the details, and you don't want him finding out about her. Because she's your pet peeve."

Randolph beamed at me. "See, you are a smart guy. The video we gave Detective Murdock had some redactions. Really, there wasn't enough on there to prove anything. We pulled a few frames when she went around the front of the bar, but that was it. Other than that, the footage showed you getting knocked down, then someone firing from the area of the service door. Who's to say it wasn't you?"

"Why would I take credit for what she did?"

"To protect her. The last thing this woman wants is to be identified. Being identified would make her a target."

"And you'd prefer I was the target?"

He grinned again. "Honestly, yes. I'll keep someone on the door as long as you're here. By then we should have a better idea who those guys were after and who's behind this. Those four men were second rate professionals. Nobody is going to come after you looking to even a score. They didn't accomplish what they were supposed to do, so you probably just saved someone a lot of money."

"You mean Gabriel did."

"Fine. But that's not what I want you to tell Detective Murdock. It happens all the time. Shooting victims have poor memories. Just say you don't remember anything, that it's all mixed up in your head. Lie. She needs you to lie for her, Cain, and you need to keep her safe. The good news is that you still get to be the hero and we won't have to cancel the parade."

"You know where you can put that parade, Randolph. If there's a parade, it better be for Mickey."

"Of course. And I am sorry about your friend. You both got caught up in something. Hopefully we can figure out who's responsible and make them pay for it. Mickey shouldn't have died, but implicating this Gypsy woman isn't going to help anyone."

"Fine. My memory just got bad. But if this comes back to bite me in the ass, Randolph, I'm going to throw you under the first bus I see. And if Detective Murdock starts figuring things out, you'd better back me up."

"Absolutely." Agent Randolph came up out of his chair and stretched to his full height. He dropped a card on the table next to the bed, then held out his hand. "You can always trust the FBI, and you can always trust me."

I ignored the hand and closed my eyes. "I don't know about the FBI, but I sure as hell don't trust you."

Chapter Six

Agent Collins pulled away from the curb and stopped in front of the hospital entrance. Randolph climbed in and buckled his seat belt. He picked up the small booklet that lay on the seat between them and grinned. "A hundred and one crosswords. You're quite the brown-noser, Collins."

"Sorry, Sir. I was waiting for my luggage at the airport yesterday and I thought you might enjoy it."

"Again, it's Teddy. But thanks for the book. I might find the time tonight, if I don't decide to go out and get drunk."

"I believe you said you don't drink...Teddy."

"I might start. Cain is too good a guy for what I've got in mind. I've talked to the Assistant Director and the funds will be allocated. It's a sketchy idea, but it just might work."

"Do you think Mister Cain will go along with it?"

"The bartender was his best friend so that'll motivate him. He tends to react violently when stressed and he strikes me as the kind of guy who would want to even that score. A lot depends on how things go with the girl. She's the key. She and I talked quite a bit while we were waiting for Cain to wake up, and she volunteered the fact that she's homesick. She said she really misses the snow and that she has family back in New York. Given the opportunity, I think she'll encourage him to go."

"Family. Jack?"

"Her mother passed away a couple of years ago. As far as she knows Jack's the only immediate family she has left. There could be some extended family, but she never said. I didn't want to dig too much."

"Unless you're reading her wrong and she knows that her father is alive."

Randolph gave his partner a dark look. "And I'm not. I spent two days with her. She's not that good a liar."

"What about your mystery woman and her sudden interest in Cain? She could get in the middle of those two and screw things up."

"I doubt her interest is sudden. She probably already knows better than we do what's going on with Adam Cain. All we have are a few snippets from an unknown mole and the fact that the Gypsy, or whatever she's calling herself this week, is involved. That woman is always three steps ahead of us. Of me. Of the Bureau."

By Sunday I was feeling better, and I told Jenny to go home. Hospital beds suck and I couldn't see her sleeping on one if she didn't have to. Home for her was Mickey and Justine's spare bedroom. Mickey wasn't there anymore, so just Justine's. Jenny had talked about helping me convalesce once I left the hospital. She didn't talk about moving back in, just coming over on a daily basis to take care of my every need. She was a generous woman. How could I say no to that?

Anyone with a working brain would want Jenny, and it had probably been a mistake to push her away. I wasn't sure if that kind of damage could be undone and I wasn't sure I wanted to undo it. I doubted I would ever be the guy she deserved, and I didn't want to hurt her any more than I already had. But I could still see the hope in her eyes. And, as Mickey had said, women like Jenny didn't come along very often.

The problem I had, and I blame my hypothalamus and eons of evolutionary adaptation, was that each time I closed my eyes it wasn't Jenny's face I saw. It was the Gypsy's. It's a common male flaw that served human evolution well before the advent of fire and the internet. We all want the woman we don't have.

It was a quiet night on the fifth floor. I had no business still being in the ICU, but Randolph had insisted. So far no reporters had tracked me down, but I did see myself on the six o'clock news. It was a younger version of me in a picture that had been cropped from an old Facebook post by a girl I dated briefly. The caption said I had single-handedly taken on a contingent of violent mobsters and managed to kill four of them before the others fled, happy to escape with their lives. A lot of horse-hockey, but it was the feel-good story of the week, and the anchor smiled a lot when he told it.

I struggled to the bathroom by myself around one in the morning without ringing for the nurse, then fell asleep again. I don't know what time it was when I woke up, but a new nurse was leaning over me. Her long hair brushed against my face. She was very tall and looked familiar. She put a finger to my lips.

"I brought the guard some coffee, but not the kind that keeps you awake. He's pretty much out, but we can't make a lot of noise."

I managed a grin. "I like the nurse's get-up. What do you have in mind?"

The Gypsy scowled. "Quit. You have a girlfriend."

"I have a friend and she's a girl. Am I allowed to call her a girl? She's twenty-nine."

"Semantics. I thought maybe you two had patched things up."

"The consensus is that she's way too good for me. I agree, but she keeps showing up."

"You need to give it another shot or you'll always wonder."

"Did you come here in the middle of the night to give me relationship advice?"

"Jenny has a part to play. So do you."

"Oh, right. Gypsy, the soothsayer." I'd been thinking and getting angry.

"I deduce things, like I do in the market."

"How do you explain what happened at the Exotic? You shoot a handgun better than anyone I've ever known, and you show up out of the blue in a strip club on the one night when four assholes with assault rifles need shooting."

"I'm not a fan of guns, but I know how to use them."

"You mitigate. That's what you told me. Why couldn't you have mitigated a little earlier? Maybe Mickey would still be alive." There was no way to make that sound anything but what it was, bitter.

She picked up my hand. "I wish that had been possible."

"I've thought a lot about it. If you had inside information, you should have stopped it somehow. You could have called in a bomb-threat or warned the guards. How did you know to be there?"

"I came there to find you, that's all it was. The rest was just luck."

"Find me. Why?" I got a blank stare. "I'm told you have a knack for showing up when things go to hell. There's an FBI agent by the name of Randolph that seems to know a lot about you, but he wants to know a lot more. I didn't tell him anything, because I don't know anything. All I know is that you shoot good, and you smell nice."

She smiled. "Are you done being mad at me?"

"I'm sure you would have saved Mickey if you could have," I begrudged. "Can you really see the future?"

"I deduce."

"Okay, deduce. What about us? Why did you come looking for me?"

"You need to heal up and try to make Jenny happy, at least for a while. You can do that."

"You didn't answer my question. Everyone thinks I shot those three guys because you used my gun. Have you seen the news? I'm the flavor of the month."

"You need to tell Jenny what really happened. She has to be able to trust you. Honesty is important in a relationship."

I feigned surprise. "Was that irony?"

She ignored the jab. "Who else knows I was the one using your gun?"

"Randolph knows, but I'm pretty sure the local detective isn't in on it. He grilled me for two hours and never said a word about you."

"Be careful of Agent Randolph. He's a good man, but he'd sell his grandmother's soul if he thought it would help him solve a case. He'll sell yours in a heartbeat."

I glanced down at my hand, the one resting in hers. "Are you reading my palm, or is that another deduction?"

"Secrets have a way of coming out, that's all." She stood suddenly and dropped my hand. "I have to go away for a while, on business. It might be a couple of weeks. Try not to get shot again while I'm gone."

"You're crushing my dreams right now, Gabriel. You haven't answered even one of my questions. At least give me your phone number."

"I knew I'd regret telling you my real name, and you can't call me." She leaned down and brushed her lips against my forehead. "Just relax and heal up. I'll come find you when the time is right, wherever it is that you end up."

It took me a second and by then she had breezed out of the room. I called after her. "What do you mean, you'll come find me? I'll be right here. In Las Vegas. Won't I? Gabriel? Gypsy?"

Chapter Seven

Detective Murdock glared across his desk at the bespectacled young man with the unruly shock of hair that lounged in the only extra chair in the sparse office. It was an oak chair, high-backed and extremely uncomfortable. Murdock had kept the slight man with the white shirt and haphazard bow tie waiting for fifteen minutes, hoping to inflict some measure of discomfort on his patient guest. Patient and smug. Murdock hated reporters, especially young ones with an axe to grind. This one had been sitting in front of him quietly with a silly smile on his face the whole time. Too patient, too smug.

Finally, Detective Murdock tossed his pen down, pushed the paperwork he'd been pretending to fill out to the side, and addressed his visitor. "Okay, Fella, you have ten minutes. I'm a busy guy."

"Thanks for your time, Detective. Just a few questions concerning the bloodbath at the Exotic last Monday."

"That's a piss-poor start, Scoop. Save those lines for that rag you call a newspaper."

Unfazed, the reporter smiled ruefully. "I apologize. That was a poor choice of words. And it isn't Scoop, it's James."

Murdock slid the reporter's card closer and peered at it. His scowl disappeared and a smile tugged at the corners of his mouth. "James Olson? You're a reporter for that lousy scandal sheet and your name is Jimmy Olson?"

The young man smiled again while Murdock lost the battle to control his laughter. "You are not the first person to point that out, Detective, but can we put that aside for now? I'm sure it'll be a good story to tell your drinking buddies, but twenty-eight people are dead. That's important. It's true my paper isn't known for hard-hitting journalism, but that doesn't mean I shouldn't try to do my job. And my job right now is to find out the truth about what happened at the Exotic that night."

"Sorry, Jimmy, but you have to admit, it's pretty funny." Murdock sniffled and rubbed at his eyes. "The truth is, four whack jobs started shooting people, then a couple other people started shooting back. Too bad those strippers didn't have a place to hide a gun, maybe the body count wouldn't have been so high."

Jimmy frowned. "I hope that wasn't a tasteless joke, Detective."

Murdock stopped laughing. "Tasteless is all the innuendo you and your newspaper have been tossing around about me and my department. I agreed to talk to you, but I don't have to put up with your shit. Yeah, a lot of people are dead. It's a tragedy, and I get that. But don't act like I'm the bad guy. I didn't shoot anybody, and there wasn't any way I could have prevented it."

"Have you made any progress in figuring out who hired those four men? They had no known connection to the club's owner, and they weren't associated with any cult or religious fundamentalist group with an axe to grind. They were thugs. That's public record. Two of them were recently released from prison."

"Funny, a liberal member of the press jumping to a conclusion like that. Apparently that prison time didn't help them see the error of their ways."

"Don't even get me started on our penal system, Detective. Okay, let's talk about politics. My sources tell me that a junior US Senator was tucked away in the VIP room of the Exotic that night. And that his presence has been expunged from the official account. Is it possible it was an assassination attempt, because of his politics?"

Murdock didn't blink. "I have no idea what you're talking about."

"It would certainly hurt his career if it came out that the Senator was there that night."

Murdock nodded. "So would getting shot full of holes."

"When will you be releasing the remaining names of the victims? And when will I get a list of all of the people who were there that night?"

"Most of the victims have been identified. We're sitting on a couple of names because we're having trouble finding their next of kin. Turns out some of those girls came from unstable homes. Shocker, right?"

"And the other list? I'd like to talk to more of the survivors."

"That's not going to happen, Jimmy. Strip clubs aren't illegal, and people have a right to their privacy. Why are you dogging this so hard? It's been a week, and your paper isn't even local. Go back to Los Angeles and bother the cops there."

"This is a big story, Detective Murdock, and there are things going on that nobody is talking about. I've talked to a few of the witnesses and I have leads on a few more. Mister Cain finally agreed to an interview. He says he doesn't remember shooting those three men, but everyone is telling him he did. It makes him look like even more of a hero, the way he's denying it. They started a GoFundMe page, but he wants all the money to go to the bartender's wife. I understand the man who was killed was in the military with Mister Cain."

"Cain sounds like a stand-up guy. How is that a problem?"

"It isn't, if he's telling the truth."

Murdock sighed. "You're a cynical little bastard, Jimmy. I talked to him too. It's obvious he shot those assholes and just doesn't remember doing it. It was his gun and it was lying right next to him when the paramedics scraped him off the floor."

"Is that what you really think? He was critically wounded, probably in shock from blood loss, but he still managed to shoot those three men? I've been in that club, Detective, and it's a pretty big space. I'm no expert, but I'm told that shooting a man between the eyes from the far end of that room with a handgun would be remarkable under the best of circumstances. And he did it twice, then dispatched the last shooter with two shots to the chest, all while critically injured and losing enough blood to kill most people."

Murdock shrugged. "He's a big guy, and people do unbelievable things when they're hopped up on adrenalin."

"Is that what the FBI thinks? I'm told there was a squabble at the hospital between you and one of their agents."

Murdock's face darkened. "Look, Jimmy, I get that you think it's your job to make mine a living hell. It's freedom of the press and all that crap. But aren't you going a little overboard? Yeah, Randolph and I butted heads. And yes, I did tell that nurse to kiss my ass. I might have even questioned her sexual orientation, which would explain why she was so eager to talk to you."

"That's a generous euphemism, considering the slur she said you used."

Murdock shrugged. "I can be an asshole. I'm old school, Jimmy. But I'm not admitting to anything, so that part of the story better not end up in your newspaper."

Olson grimaced. "I suppose it is possible Adam Cain did shoot all those men. He was an Army Ranger, and they're good at killing people."

Murdock reached out a long arm and waved a meaty finger under the reporter's nose. "You are starting to piss me off, Olson, so watch your damn mouth."

Jimmy leaned away from the threatening appendage and demurred quickly. "Sorry. That was another poor choice of words. I meant no disrespect to the military. I just want all the details I can get. This could be my big break, and the readers have a right to know."

Murdock snorted and laced his voice with sarcasm. "But just the facts, right, Jimmy? Because the people have a right to know. Not because the idea of a dozen naked young girls all shot to shit would make for a sensational story and get you a byline on the front page."

Olson slid forward to edge of the wooden chair, then stood slowly. His butt-cheeks had gone numb, and from the detective's tone he knew the interview was nearly over.

"Anything else you want to tell me, Detective?" he tried.

"Yeah. You're a blood sucking little parasite, and you make me want to puke. How's that for a byline, Jimmy? Put that in your God-damn newspaper. Now get the hell out of my office," Murdock snarled and waved his hand dismissively. Before Olson had moved, a small smile came to the detective's face. He pulled a business card from the top drawer of his desk and handed it to Olson. "Try this guy. He knows a lot more about this mess than I do."

The detective's smile seemed out of place and it didn't last long. Murdock ignored the hand the young man held out and pointed at the door again. "I said leave, and don't ever come back."

Olson waited until he had closed the detective's door to glance at the card. Theodore Randolph, FBI.

"Do we know if Jack Mercer ever made contact with his sister while he was in town?"

Agent Randolph looked up from the corner of the conference table. He and his junior partner had appropriated a space from the local agent's office. In the last week, Randolph had spent more time on an airplane than in his home office in New York, and a trip to Washington had pulled him away from the case.

"I don't recall," Randolph muttered, looking over the top of his glasses.

Agent Collins eyed his boss. "You don't recall? That's uncharacteristic of you, Sir. It would be odd if Jack was in town and didn't go to see her, wouldn't it? Maybe they aren't close, but maybe he told her why he was in that club. You said she misses him. That would imply they're on good terms."

"She said she misses the snow. I never said she misses him."

"Perhaps you don't recall that conversation either, Sir. Teddy."

"I do remember that conversation, clearly," Randolph grated out. "She said she has family in New York, and she also said that she misses the snow. You might assume from those two statements that she misses her brother, but you know what they say about assuming things."

Collins frowned. "That you're not following the path of established evidence?"

Randolph shook his head and favored Collins with a smile. "No. When you assume, it makes an ass out of you and me. Think about it."

Collins smiled when he put it together. "That's an interesting colloquialism. I studied law at Harvard and that never came up."

"Which is why you're working with me, Collins, to learn people skills." Randolph softened his tone. "Look, Blake, you're a really smart kid, but you can't get everything out of a book. It takes a while to learn to read people and figure the best way to get information out of them. Sometimes people volunteer more information when you just listen and don't ask too many questions. You catch more flies with honey than vinegar."

Collins nodded. "That one I've heard, Sir. My grandmother used to say that."

"Good. You'll need to remember that when you meet with Detective Murdock. I have to fly back to New York tonight."

"Shit! Sorry, Sir. I mean, I don't know if that's a good idea. I don't think Murdock likes me."

Randolph chuckled. "I don't think Murdock likes anyone, especially us. He wasn't happy that we redacted that video. And he wants those cellphones back, which he is not going to get. Tell him we're still trying to unlock them or that our program accidentally wiped them. Tell him anything you want, but he's not getting his hands on those phones, especially the one that incriminates the Gypsy."

"I assume..." Collins fought a smile and started again. "I don't know, but it seems reasonable that whoever had the presence of mind to record the incident must have seen that woman shoot the gunmen. And we know that Detective Murdock has interviewed that gentleman. What should I say if Murdoch asks about her?"

"That camera was all over the place, like the guy was hiding somewhere and holding it at arm's length. Maybe he never saw her. Obviously, he didn't have time to watch the video. I'm guessing there were more cellphones lost that night while people were scrambling to get out of the line of fire, so who's to say the one we have with the video is the one that belonged to the guy Murdock talked to. We know that, but Murdock doesn't."

"He'll be furious."

Randolph shrugged again. "Get used to it, Collins. It won't be the last time you piss off local law enforcement."

Collins spoke carefully. "Tell me this, Sir. Who is it we're protecting? Adam Cain, or this Gypsy woman?"

Randolph gave him a sharp look. "Think, Collins. Was that the right question to ask me?"

Collins returned the frown. "Probably not. But someday, if this whole business blows up in our faces, I'd like to have an idea of why you're protecting her. It might keep me out of prison."

Randolph laughed. "There's hope for you yet, Collins. When I get back, I'm going to sit down with Adam Cain again and see if he's willing to help us. Maybe I'll get to see Jennifer too. It could be that she knows more than I think she does. We still can't be absolutely sure that Jack was the target. You have good instincts, Collins, and you ask the right questions."

Collins hesitated, then threw caution to the wind. "Thank you, Sir. But you still didn't answer my last one."

Randolph opened his new crossword book and pulled out a pencil. "Let it go, Collins."

Chapter Eight

I was out of the hospital a week and a day after the shooting. The blond nurse with the spiked hair wheeled me out the front door with Jenny at my side, then tore into the television crew when one of them pushed a microphone in my face. They didn't leave, but they did back up far enough for me to climb into the passenger seat of Jenny's car. I thanked Gretchen for all her help and advised her against assaulting a member of the press. She nearly bulldozed a cameraman with the wheelchair, then went on another tirade. Most of it was in German and none of it polite in any language. Finally, she relented and went back into the hospital.

It surprised me that I was still in the news, but I didn't want them showing up at my apartment or harassing Jenny, so I decided the best thing was to get it over with. A pretty twenty-something woman had her face inches from my window and was shouting questions. I told Jenny to wait and lowered my window.

Some guy with a big camera and a bright light moved in and the young woman pushed her microphone forward. "Mister Cain, all of Las Vegas wants to thank you for what you did. How does it feel to be a hero?"

"I appreciate you saying that, but the truth is my friend Mickey was the hero. He was the one who lost his life, and a lot more people would be dead if he hadn't been there."

"The same could be said for you, Mister Cain. I understand you've asked that all of the contributions being made go to your friend's widow. That is unbelievably generous of you."

"It's only right. Mickey is dead, and they tell me I'll be good as new in a few weeks. I appreciate all the contributions, but nothing can bring Mickey back. He's the hero, not me."

"Spoken like a true hero," she gushed. I wanted to roll the window up right then, but she and her microphone were leaning in. "But it's my understanding that it was you who stopped the majority of the gunmen."

"I may have gotten lucky, but Mickey was a better shot with a handgun."

"Your employer has praised your marksmanship, Mister Cain, and I'm told he intends to promote you. Aren't you being unnecessarily modest? All the accounts of the shooting have you being the man who took down those killers." She moved on before I could confirm or deny anything. "What do you think their intent was? Do you plan to investigate and try to avenge your friend's death?"

"I have no idea why those men were there and I plan to let the police do their job."

"We're told you have a personal relationship with the FBI agent assigned to the shooting. Does he have any opinions concerning motive? Are they considering the incident domestic terrorism, or a random act of violence? What can you tell us about the investigation?"

"I'm sorry, but I don't know anything about the FBI, and I don't have any friends that work there. I'm tired and I need to heal up. Just to be clear, this is the only statement I plan to give concerning the shooting. Honesty, I don't remember much of what went on that night after I was shot."

She turned to face the cameraman, and apparently her anchor. "There you have it, John. Riddled with bullets from automatic gun fire, but still able to bring down his attackers and save an untold number of lives. Adam Cain, a modest man, and a true American hero."

I raised the window and motioned for Jenny to drive away. "Jesus," I muttered, "what a crock. It must be a slow news week."

"You might as well get used to it, Adam. Everyone I know has been calling me saying how proud they are of you. There are posters and pictures of you everywhere. The convenience store on the corner has your picture right next to a donation jar."

I slid down in the seat. "That's just great. This keeps getting worse and worse. Goddamn Randolph."

Jenny glanced over, perplexed. "You don't sound happy. What did Teddy do?"

"Teddy? You're on first a name basis with the FBI?"

She gave me a lopsided grin. "Jealous? We sat there for two days waiting for you to wake up, and he insisted I call him by his first name. He seems like a nice enough guy. He's just doing his job."

"There's a lot more to it than that. When we get home, I'll explain it to you."

"Home?"

I knew what she was asking. "My apartment, our place, whatever. I don't know what you want to do. I can get around by myself if you're going back to Justine's, and I get it if you'd rather. But I could use some help getting situated. I don't think I'm supposed to walk on my own or lift anything for a few days. We have to talk, and I don't mean about us. I have to tell you everything about the shooting. Randolph will be pissed, but the Gypsy said I should be honest with you. I trust her a hell of a lot more than I do Randolph."

"The Gypsy?" Jenny asked.

"Gabriel, the woman that was at the Exotic that night. It's a long story."

"So Gabriel and the Gypsy are the same person, but no one knows who she really is?" Jenny asked. She was helping me out of my clothes and into the recliner. Lying flat still hurt and I was trying to avoid taking more pain medication. We had stopped at Justine's and picked up some of Jenny's clothes. She planned to spend at least a couple nights and she had changed into her pajamas. Her pajamas amounted to an old shirt of mine and very little else. It was distracting.

"Randolph knows about her, but not a lot of details. He said she shows up when there's trouble, sometimes overseas, as if she knows somehow. He's been trying to track her down for quite a while."

"And you're sure it was her that killed the other three men?"

"It wasn't me. I was on the floor, propped up behind the bar. She shot two of them in the forehead from the length of the room, then snuck up on the last one and killed him too. Any idea how hard it is to hit a person at that distance with a handgun, much less a headshot?"

"No, and I really don't want the details. Why does Randolph want to protect her?"

"I have no idea. But now he's got me right in the middle of it. As soon as I can get around I'm going to go talk to Gainey. Maybe he knows something he isn't telling the cops. Four guys with AK-47s don't just decide to shoot up a strip club for the fun of it."

"Adam, you need to rest and heal up. I know how you are, but let the cops and Ted...the FBI handle it."

"They didn't know Mickey," I said. "We were like brothers over there. He always had my back, and if I find out who sent those bastards to that bar, I'm going to make them pay. The cops will give it a couple weeks and then sweep it under the rug. Randolph will go chasing after the Gypsy, and nothing will get done."

"It sounds like this woman is leading you both around by the nose. Or is it another part of your anatomy?"

I grinned. "Jealous?" She had moved behind me and was massaging my neck.

She snickered. "Okay, that's fair. But how did this woman know to show up when she did? Is she involved?"

"I don't know. Neither does Randolph, and that's making him crazy. He wants to talk to me again."

"About this Gypsy woman?"

"Maybe. I'm not sure. She came to see me again, but I'm not going to tell him that." I volunteered the rest. "She came to the hospital in the middle of the night. Sunday night."

"She's interested in you. And I'm not saying that because I'm jealous. Call it woman's intuition."

"I might have expressed some interest too." Jenny snorted loudly and I laughed. "You did just dump me. Besides, she said I should try to get you back. She said I could make you happy."

Jenny's grip on my neck softened. "Maybe she isn't as bad as I thought."

"She said I have a part to play in whatever this is, and so do you. She was all kinds of vague and mysterious."

"She is a gypsy. That's what they do."

"It's just a nickname. Or maybe she is part gypsy. Doesn't matter, it's not like she can see the future. But she did say I would see her again."

"So maybe I should be jealous?" Jenny came around and eased a leg over the arm of the recliner. She straddled my lap, facing me. "Let's forget about her. Explain that part about making me happy again."

Blame it on my hypothalamus, but I told Jenny I loved her that night. It was mostly true. I don't think she believed me, but she said it back and it did seem to make her happy. That was Jenny, warm and generous even when I didn't deserve it.

I didn't say it for the right reason. I said it for Mickey. I said it because he had wanted me to say it to her, and because I didn't get the chance to say it to him.

Chapter Nine

The raven-haired woman leaned forward in her seat and spoke to the cabby. "Could you take a right at the next red light?"

"If you wish, Madam, but that will take us out of our way."

"I'm aware. And if you could, wait until the cross traffic is getting close, then duck in. There'll be a generous tip in it for you."

The cabby glanced in his side mirror and inspected the car behind them, then looked at the woman in the rear-view above his dash. His English was impeccable. "If I may, Madam, this is not the first time I've been asked to lose a tail. Am I allowed to be creative?"

The Gypsy smiled at the brown face. "By all means, be as creative as you'd like."

The cabby eased up to the next intersection, slowed until the signal had turned from yellow to red, then accelerated into traffic. He took a hard right and created a space between two of the cars entering from the side street. The maneuver elicited a response from more than one angry driver. Horns blew and one man rolled down his window to offer a gesture.

Unrepentant, the cabby switched lanes quickly and swerved left, finding an alley before the oncoming traffic cut them off. He dodged a dumpster and twisted to the right at the next side street, then turned quickly left again into another alley. His next turn brought them out onto a wide street and into three lanes of traffic, half of which were also cabs. Another two blocks brought them to a one-way that paralleled the street that was their destination. The Gypsy leaned forward and glanced at the driver's information.

"Nice job, Rashid. This is why I don't take an Uber."

The slight man glanced in the mirror and offered a shy smile. "A woman as beautiful as you must have many suitors, Madam, but they should not be the kind who would force themselves upon you."

"It's not as simple as that, my friend, but I certainly appreciate the extra effort. The next time I fly in I'll try to request you as my driver. Perhaps we'll see each other again."

"If the Fates are kind, I would like that," he responded.

"Is it fate that has me going to this meeting today, Rashid, or is it Karma? If it's Karma, I must have been a real piece of work in my previous life." The Gypsy frowned and searched the face in the mirror. "I'm sorry, I didn't mean to make light of your beliefs."

The cabby laughed. "I am not the true believer my wife would have me be, and I am not that easily offended. I hope your meeting goes as you wish."

"That's about the best I can hope for," she replied. The traffic ground to a halt and the tall woman leaned forward again, reaching beyond the plexiglass that separated her from the driver with a pair of bills. "I can walk from here."

The driver took the money, then pointed at the meter. "This is much too much, Madam. And your bag?"

"All I have is my carry-on, remember? I pack light. Take your wife out for a meal. My treat."

The Gypsy slid out of the seat and threw the strap of her bag across her shoulder. The morning was cold and still. She exhaled slowly, relishing the sight of her breath in the frigid air. She smiled and watched the vapor rise slowly up and away. "You won't see that in Las Vegas," she mused aloud.

Each of the vehicles around her belched out their own trails of vapor that settled slowly to the street, swirling above the brown slop that pulled at her boots as she dodged between the cars. The city she loved smelled of diesel exhaust and the sea, and when she neared the far sidewalk, fresh pastries. She walked a block south, then ducked into her favorite shop.

Two attractive young women stood behind a glass case dispensing pastries and bagels to a small line of customers. An older woman, equally pretty and graying, sat on a small stool behind an old-style cash register, handing out change and quiet appreciation. It was the same every time, delivered in the same tone with the same small smile.

"Thank you, come again." When she saw the Gypsy, she tipped her head and eyed the opening behind the counter. Her smile widened. "He's in the back, and he wants to talk to you."

The Gypsy skirted the counter and helped herself before pushing through the curtained doorway into the back of the bakery. She slid onto a stool in front of a stainless-steel table and started picking at the apple turnover she had purloined. A tall, thick-set man with an apron worked nearby with his back to her, squeezing frosting onto four cakes, each one smaller than the first. The Gypsy coughed conspicuously.

Without turning, the man spoke. "Do you know what I am doing?"

It was a leading question, and the Gypsy knew where it was headed. "Contributing to America's obesity epidemic?"

Darius Luca turned and pointed a large finger in her direction. "I am making a wedding cake. The bride is twenty-two, soon to be twenty-three."

"And you think that's too young?" The Gypsy took another bite of her pastry. "I agree."

Darius sputtered. "You are in your thirties, woman."

"Early thirties. Why are you picking on me? You have two daughters who need husbands.

Not that any woman does, but it would keep you out of my hair."

"You travel too much, and you work too hard. And despite what you say, I know how dangerous it is. I remember those days all too well, and I hear things."

"Then you shouldn't listen. You made the choice to withdraw, and you're a baker now because you needed to be here for your family. I've heard the story a dozen times."

"I know about the trouble in Vegas," he grumbled. "I still have friends in the business, and I hear things."

"From friends, or from Gabby?"

Darius wiped frosting from his hands with a towel. "I said friends. My sister is no one's friend."

"Here's an idea, Uncle. Try to find her a husband." Darius was the Gypsy's mother's uncle, but it was an endearment she had appropriated.

"She has outlived three men already. Why would I put another one through such misery?"

"And what makes you think I wouldn't be the same if I was shackled to a man? People tell me I am just like her."

The man's eyes widened. "And those people still draw breath? You favor your mother, in temperament at least. I will admit, my sister was nearly as pretty as you when she was a younger woman, before the darkness took her."

"Stop," the Gypsy said, chuckling. "Granted, she's not always my favorite relative either, but she's driven, not evil."

"She came by this morning to ask if I had heard from you."

"I take care of business on my laptop and I don't carry a cellphone, as much to torture her as anything else. She wasn't happy that I got involved in Vegas. What else was I supposed to do? I was there, so I put an end to it."

"Lucky you were, from what I read in the newspapers." He lifted a brow. "Quite a coincidence, you being in that club when the shooting took place."

"Is that what your spies are telling you? You need to bake more and gossip less."

"Even the best of my spies cannot figure you out, Izzy." Darius had appropriated an endearment of his own.

"The organization has a lot of talented people that feed me information and make me look good. Vegas was a fluke. It was just luck that I was there when I was."

"Your mother had that kind of luck and it cost her her life."

"Don't," the Gypsy said quickly, then softened her tone. "There are always risks, Uncle, but what is the alternative? To watch and do nothing? We have an obligation."

"To whom much is given…that was what your mother always said. Just take care of yourself, that's all I ask. It was the worst day of my life when your parents were killed, and one of the worst for this country. Knowing there is going to be trouble isn't enough. You have to be prepared to deal with it."

"You sound like her," the Gypsy said. "Gabby, not my mother."

"I don't agree with her often, but I will admit, she has prepared you well. I'll give her credit for that."

"She's a true believer. In the cause, if not in me."

Darius shrugged. "She can be both, and she isn't quite the ogre I make her out to be." He glanced at the clock on the wall. "She's expecting you."

"I would rather face another shooting, but I guess it's unavoidable." The Gypsy stood and picked up her bag. "I'll stop later. Maybe we can do supper?"

"Joanna has already started cooking, so you'd better show up. Six o'clock."

The tall woman nodded. "I'm ducking out the back door."

"Of course you are," Darius said, turning back to his work. "And, Izzy…" She turned back to him, and he pointed at the cake. "Tick-tock, tick-tock."

The back door of the bakery opened into a small alley and the Gypsy followed it to a busy side street, then loped across through the traffic. Horns sounded, but it wasn't because she was blocking anyone's path. She was accustomed to that kind of attention, but she didn't encourage it, or men in general. She wasn't celibate, but sex was infrequent, something she occasionally had to do for work. Her real work, not her job as a stock analyst.

Marriage, despite what Darius said, was not part of the plan. But looking like she did distracted men who were usually more guarded. Sometimes it opened doors, and sometimes they were bedroom doors. She always did what was necessary and took what pleasure she could from it. But the job came first. Mitigation. It was a good word for what she did. The Gypsy walked another hundred feet to the back door of a brick building, peered to her left and right, then put her key in the lock.

The heavy steel door opened slowly, revealing a darkened storage area. The room smelled of cut metal and oil. Not the heavy odor of a mechanic's shop, but the redolent fragrance of gun oil and furniture polish. The gentle assault on the Gypsy's senses triggered a myriad of memories and brought a smile to her face. Her grandmother's shop specialized in custom-made clocks, rare and antique glass and lamps, and expensive jewelry. She found the light switch, then pushed the door shut. From the next room a man's voice called her name.

She responded. "Yes, Levi, it's me." She glanced around the room. Half a dozen grandfather clocks surrounded her like vigilant sentries, each patiently waiting its completion. Several smaller clocks lay partially assembled next to a vise, a tiny soldering iron, and an equally small grinder. Two swivel lamps sat perched on either side of the vise, with an assortment of magnifying glasses. Another lamp, this one an antique, awaited final repair. Near the back of the bench, beyond all the clutter, Gypsy found what she was looking for. She picked up the small object and hefted it. It looked like a cellphone, but it was thicker and half again as heavy.

"That's not done yet," Levi cautioned from the open archway that led into the retail shop. "I need to do more testing. I don't want it to blow your hand off the first time you use it." The gangly man stumbled forward awkwardly, tipping his head to see around the jeweler's glasses that were perched at the end of his nose. Despite the shine of a generous forehead, his sandy locks hung across one eye. He pushed the disheveled mess to the side with a careless gesture that left a smudge of grease on his cheek. He looked thirty-five, but the Gypsy knew he was much older.

"It's perfect. Tiny, and so thin. It'll be easy to hide practically anywhere."

"Not much thicker than the cartridges," Levi said proudly. "The ammunition still needs work to clear airport security." He gave the device a quick shake, exposing an aperture the size of a pencil, then flipped a small gun barrel into place. "All high tensile poly-carbons, like your knives. You said you might want to hide it in your private areas, so we don't want it to go off accidently."

His face colored slightly, but he plunged ahead. "I'm not sure which private areas you had in mind. Your breasts are certainly adequate, so you could drop it between them, or push it behind your brassiere. And it's thin enough to slide down the front of your pants, if that should be necessary. Even the crack..."

"Levi!" The Gypsy and the befuddled craftsman both turned to the opening behind them and looked at the tiny red-haired woman standing there. Three wide-eyed octogenarians peered over her shoulders.

"What, Gwyneth? Was that inappropriate? She's the one who suggested those hiding places."

"And now Mrs. Appelbaum and her friends have had to hear all about it. Keep your voice down," she whispered. "Hello, Izzy. My genius husband is brainless sometimes." The small woman spun quickly and returned to Mrs. Appelbaum and her traumatized friends.

97

The Gypsy grimaced. "Just let me know when it's ready. I'm sorry if I got you in trouble, Levi. I have to go upstairs. Have you seen her today?"

"No, and I don't know her mood, so don't ask. In fact, don't ask me any more questions. I'm in enough trouble as it is."

The Gypsy climbed the stairs to the apartment above the clock shop. Most days her grandmother left Levi and his wife to their own devices. She envied them that. She rapped lightly on the door twice, then three times quickly, then once more. It was a childish ritual, but one that her grandmother insisted on using. And the old woman always had a gun handy.

"Come," a muffled voice said. The eldest Luca had never bothered with pleasantries or most other societal norms. She hadn't taken any of her husbands' last names, even at a time when such things were considered necessary. The Gypsy found it gratifying that her mother had defied her grandmother in that regard. She and her grandmother shared too much as it was.

She slipped her boots off and crossed the hardwood floor, side-stepping the two hand-knotted silk rugs that adorned the shining oak. It seemed ridiculous that a woman who prided herself on being painfully practical would own rugs too valuable to walk on.

Her grandmother motioned to her impatiently but didn't look up when her granddaughter padded into the office and stood waiting. The room was bright, illuminated by a skylight and a small window behind the desk. The old woman's hair was still as dark as her granddaughter's, her skin bronzed, and her face smooth. Her long arms were toned and muscular despite her years. Only her eyes hinted of her age, eyes that finally lifted to access the Gypsy. She pointed at a chair and the younger woman sat.

"That was quite a mess you made in Las Vegas, Izzy." Isabelle was the Gypsy's middle name. It had been her mother's. Only people close to her used it.

"Nice to see you too, Grandmother. I'm fine, by the way."

The older woman's eyes narrowed. "Spare me. Why would I enquire about your well-being when you are here in front of me? If you weren't fine, I would expect you to be in the hospital or the morgue. You are neither."

"Your definition of fine isn't shared by polite society. It's not enough just to be above ground. Some people want to enjoy life."

"We don't have that luxury, Izzy. There are important things to be done."

"What happened in Vegas, that was important."

"Important to whom? It wasn't sanctioned."

"Sanctioned? I have plenty of support from the group, and I have free rein to use my discretion when the unexpected happens."

"But was it that? Unexpected? I think not. You killed three men, quite dramatically from what I've heard. That kind of thing will inevitably get you noticed. Being noticed puts you at greater risk of being identified, and that puts us all in danger."

"Your concern for my personal safety is overwhelming."

The old lady bit back a smile. "It isn't in me to become maudlin and weepy like some old dotard, Isabelle. But it doesn't mean I don't care about you. As you well know, there's more at stake here than you and I. There's a purpose."

"God knows how many more innocent lives those men would have snuffed out if I hadn't stopped them. That was purpose enough."

"Acknowledged. But you spent years training for this, and we, rather I, spent years training you. You are too valuable an asset to run off on a whim and endanger yourself without consensus from the group."

"It's called free will, Grandmother. It's one of the concepts we fight for." She had tempered her sarcasm and was rewarded by another brief smile.

"There are other people in the fight, Izzy, that's all I'm saying. You have an incredible set of skills, but you are still a member of a team.

100

Remember that. And I am one of the people in charge of that team. Remember that also. Your mother could never accept that fact."

"You manage to bring her into all of our conversations." The Gypsy took a deep breath and deflected. "Jack Mercer was there. Did you know that?"

The old lady leaned back in her chair. "I did. And a junior senator, as I understand. Who do you think was the target?"

"That was part of the reason I was there, to make that determination. Many more people would have died, but perhaps I should have let it play out. Then we'd know."

This time the old woman laughed out loud. "Well played, Izzy. What about the Mercer girl? Did you engage with her roommate?"

"That didn't go as planned, obviously. Coincidentally, Jennifer had packed her bags that morning and moved out. A lover's quarrel by the sound of it. I question our intelligence concerning Adam Cain. I doubt that he was a plant, or that he is capable of being an assassin."

The older woman tented her fingers and nodded. "Good looking?"

"He is, but I would not let that affect my opinion of him. I have no trouble finding a bedmate when the urge strikes, and I would never let sexual attraction interfere with my work."

"Unlike your mother."

"We've had this discussion," the Gypsy said, leaning toward the older woman. Her voice was quiet but grating. "That is the line you cannot cross. My mother's death was not my father's fault. He didn't deserve your hatred, or your pejudice. You wonder why I seldom come here, but when I do, you start up with that nonsense. Stop it, or one day I will not come at all."

"That is what I fear most, Izzy. That you will repeat her mistakes and pay the ultimate price."

"Don't bait me, old woman," the Gypsy snapped. Her grandmother didn't respond. She turned away and stared out the small window behind her. The younger woman calmed herself again. "I believe that Jennifer's relationship with Adam Cain hasn't completely soured, and I encouraged him to continue to pursue it. He will offer her some protection."

"And if he is what we fear?"

"He is not. He wouldn't have been there if he had known there was going to be an attack."

"Or he has you completely fooled."

"He was badly injured and his best friend was killed. I saw that pain in his eyes. My gut tells me that he has a part to play, I just don't know what it is yet."

"And my gut tells me that there is more to this than you are telling me. We will see who is right in the end." The older woman spun her chair back to the desk and picked up a folder. She tossed it onto the desk in the direction of her granddaughter. "For now, you have other fish to fry. The grandchild of an old friend has been kidnapped. He's an ambassador living in Brussels. You are to secure the child's release, should she still be alive, then eradicate the men responsible."

"And if they can be apprehended?"

"The girl is seven years old. If they would do harm to a child, they are unredeemable and don't deserve our mercy. Do what you were trained to do. Your flight leaves in four hours. You can dine with Darius when you return."

Chapter Ten

Detective Murdock didn't like the fact that it was he, not the smart-mouthed rookie from the FBI who had to drive the ten blocks to a meeting that he was pretty sure was pointless. Adam Cain hadn't told him much he didn't already know. He hadn't told him anything about the woman, and it wasn't something Murdock wanted to admit knowing. That made the interview difficult. He had hinted around the subject, but Cain wouldn't budge.

Cain said that he couldn't remember the details and that he wasn't sure how many gunmen were down before he was shot, or how the remaining shooters managed to end up dead. He couldn't remember getting up and shooting again, but admitted it was a possibility. Convenient memory lapses, but something that could have happened given the severity of his wounds. And plausible deniability if he ever got brought up on perjury charges.

It didn't matter to Murdock if Cain was lying, intentionally or not. Granted, maybe he wasn't the hero the whole city thought he was, but the bartender's widow was getting all the money that was being raised. What mattered to Murdock was the woman. She had to be a pro, and she probably knew why those shooters were there. And by now the FBI had to know who she was. So why wasn't Randolph sharing that information? It was possible the woman was an asset of some sort or a protected witness. The best Murdock could hope for was to get some information out of the junior officer he was meeting with. He had a couple of ideas about how to do that.

He climbed the three flights of steps and walked into the sparse office labeled FBI. There were two offices beyond the reception area and he knew both the local agents, but he wasn't sure where to find agent Collins. The intern behind the desk was on the phone. He held up a finger, then used it to point in the direction of a pair of hardbacked chairs against the wall. Murdock reached across the desk and pushed one of the unlit buttons on the machine.

"I'm here to see Collins. Tell your girlfriend you'll call her back, because I'm not waiting."

"Detective Murdock, nice to see you again," the young man said. "He's in Jefferson's office and the agent is out. Feel free."

Murdock pushed through the furthest door. Jefferson's office was the bigger of the two and Collins was seated in the back, using the small conference table for a desk. The younger man stood and extended a hand. Murdock took it, begrudgingly.

"Thanks for coming in, Detective," the agent said.

Murdock didn't return the smile Collins gave him. "I hope you have some good news for me, and some straight answers."

"Straight answers? Didn't you receive the recording of the shooting? I thought it was self-explanatory. And you have my notes."

"Self-explanatory? It was long on noise and short on details. And there was a full minute that was redacted. It isn't hard to guess what was cut out."

"The redactions were done by Agent Randolph and the higher ups at the Bureau. I'm afraid those decisions are above my paygrade."

"But you're the one that has to take the heat."

Collins offered a weak smile. "I wouldn't expect you to blame me for my superior's misdeeds. I will admit, I don't always understand the nuances of Agent Randolph's actions. Or his motives."

"So, what do you have for me? By now you've seen what was on those phones."

"That's not the case. There is a process, privacy issues. A judge needs to issue a subpoena."

"Don't lecture me about first amendment rights, Junior. Two of my witnesses have phones missing and they both said they're willing to share everything that's on them with us." Murdock leaned in. "Notice I said us? That's the way it's supposed to work. Normally the FBI works with me; they don't go out of their way to hide evidence. But I'm not blaming you. I know it's Randolph that's dragging this out and I know why. It's about the woman."

Murdock was reaching across the table, thumping it with his fat index finger while Collins leaned away and did his best to look confused. "What woman are you talking about?" he asked.

"The woman that shot those bastards with Cain's gun. One of my witnesses saw her come up from behind the bar and drill two of those pricks. One shot each. Then she went around the bar and took care of the last one. He thought he had some of it on his phone, but of course he lost that on the way out."

"Of course," Collins nodded. "Eyewitness accounts are suspect under the best of circumstances, more so when there's drinking involved."

"I'm not interested in busting Cain for lying. He says he doesn't remember anything after getting shot, and I'm willing to believe him. I just don't believe you."

"Then it would seem we're at an impasse." Collins pushed a file folder in the direction of the detective. "This is everything we have to date: updates from the lab, profiles on the shooters, possible connections to known terrorist groups. We will continue to provide more information as we get it."

"Great. That's just great." Murdock had a file folder of his own. He opened it and held up a single piece of paper. "I do have this."

Collins squinted at the page from across the table. "A DNA profile?"

"Our mystery girl left an article of clothing behind. It doesn't tell me who she is, but it does tell me that she has relatives on the east coast. I'm going to find her, sooner or later."

Collins watched the detective return the page to its folder and frowned. "You're withholding evidence from the FBI, Detective Murdock."

Murdock smiled. "Yeah? How's that feel, Junior? Get me those phones, then we'll talk."

"Agent Randolph has a federal judge on speed dial and he won't be coerced into a trade. He'll get a subpoena and impound your evidence."

Murdock's smile disappeared. "Randolph better watch himself, and you too, Collins. This woman is a material witness and you're hiding what you know about her."

"Based on what your unreliable witness told you?"

Murdock shrugged and switched gears. "There's been a reporter sniffing around. Have you heard from him?"

"Yes. He asked to talk with Agent Randolph, but I had to deal with him. Thanks for that."

Murdock grinned at the smaller man. "Just a little payback." Then he settled back into his chair and softened his tone. "You need to tell me what's going on here, Agent Collins. That reporter is a bulldog. There would be hell to pay if this all came out in the newspapers."

"That sounds like a threat, Detective."

"There could be a leak is all I'm saying. If I have to, I'll get on an airplane and start tracking down this woman's relatives myself. Sooner or later, I'll turn over the right rock. When I do, you and Randolph are going to look like idiots, or worse."

"Or you could share what's in that file."

"When I have those damn phones!" Murdock snapped, then took a breath and controlled his voice again. "Randolph and Adam Cain are covering for this woman. My question is why? There were too many eyewitnesses to keep it quiet forever. Sooner or later the truth is going to come out that this woman was the one who stopped that massacre and that the FBI didn't even bother to bring her in for questioning. I wouldn't want to be you then, Junior, because Randolph is going to plead stupidity and point his finger at you. There goes your career. Who the hell is this woman, and what does she know?"

Collins fidgeted. This was unexpected, and there wasn't time for a phone call. If being an agent meant reading people, then reading

Detective Murdock was part of the job. It didn't appear like Murdock was bluffing. "There is some indication there might have been a third shooter. By which I mean, someone other than Cain and the bartender."

"Actually, I've known that all along," Murdock admitted. "I watched the tape that first morning. Did you really think I was going to just hand it over without looking at it?"

"Lying to the FBI is a federal crime," Collins pointed out.

"So is covering for someone that killed three people. Granted, they had it coming, and it would be considered self-defense by any court in the country. But at the very least, we should hear her story. She had to know it was coming."

"If she knew, wouldn't she have brought her own gun?" Collins asked.

Murdock raised a brow. "Maybe you're not as stupid as I thought, Collins. How about you and I declare a truce?"

Collins took the hand Detective Murdock offered him. "Thanks, I guess. And maybe it would be prudent to keep the details of this conversation between the two of us. Perhaps we can compromise, if Randolph won't, and share some evidence."

"Maybe. Randolph wouldn't be happy with either one of us if he found out, and I really don't want to be on the wrong side of that guy.

But tell me, Collins, who is this woman and why is Randolph so hell bent on protecting her?"

Collins shrugged. "I hope you'll believe me, Detective Murdock, when I say I don't know. I would like to know the answer to both those questions as much as you would."

"Can I get in trouble for this?" The stocky, unshaven frat-boy pulled the envelope across the table and glanced inside. "I already told the cops everything I know."

Jimmy Olson studied the younger man as they waited for the waitress to unload their drinks. He tried not to form an opinion. It was a reporter's job to stay objective, but Jimmy had seen Kyle's type too often. Kyle looked like just another young stoner, a spoiled twenty-something who was living in his parent's basement because he spent all his money on drugs and girls, then made fun of the people who worked hard for a living. People like Jimmy. People who were going to win a Pulitzer someday.

"We're just reimbursing you for your time away from work, in cash. We do it all the time. Kyle, is it?"

"Yeah, Kyle." Kyle peered into the envelope again and thumbed through the bills. His smile grew. "I deliver pizzas, Dude. I don't make this much in a week."

"I'm sure your time is valuable, and my paper has committed funds to this story." Actually, it was Jimmy's money, but it would be worth it if he broke a big story.

"The television coverage was woefully inadequate, and I think it was inaccurate. They implied that it was a gang war, drugs or prostitution. I think there was more to it. I don't think we know the truth of what really happened that night. That's what I do, Kyle, I uncover the truth."

"Like Dateline or something? Cool, Dude. I'm all about the truth, and I was there for the whole show."

"Call me, Jimmy. Please. You said you were at the club with a group of people?"

"Yeah. A bunch of us. Eight or nine guys. It was a bachelor's party. Are you going to pay them to talk to you too? I should get a piece of that for coming up with their names, shouldn't I?"

"It depends. I need to hear your story first, then I can tell you if I want to talk to the others. I'm not paying eight or nine people to tell me the same story over and over. Is it okay if I record our conversation?" Jimmy put his cellphone on the table and tapped the screen. "Just tell me what you remember, exactly as you remember it."

"Okay. My buddy Derek, he's marrying this girl he met from Oregon..."

Jimmy raised a hand. "Kyle, I don't care about the wedding or why you were there. Just tell me what you remember about the shooting itself, and things that might pertain to that. If Derek got shot, that would be pertinent."

"Okay. So yeah, he did get shot. So that's pertinent, right, Dude?" Jimmy clenched his teeth and nodded. "He didn't get killed or anything, just a flesh wound. He made a run for the front door and one of the guys was there. He started cutting loose with his AR, or whatever, and Derek got hit in the side. He was lucky, I guess, 'cause it missed all the important stuff. He went down and just covered up and played possum. We thought he was dead for sure, but by then we were all shitting bricks and trying to save our own asses, you know?"

Jimmy nodded. "I can imagine. Every man for himself."

"Look, Dude, don't put it like that in your article, okay? You can't imagine what it was like. We figured they were just going to walk around and shoot us, one at a time."

"No, of course. But it is part of the story. People would expect you to be terrified. No one is going to think less of you."

"We were lucky, really. We were on the opposite side of the club from where most of the shooting was. There were four of them starting out, but one of them went down right away. The bartender had a gun and he started shooting at them. The other guy started shooting too, the one that was on the news."

"The bartender was killed, but Mister Cain survived. I know that he was shot as well. Where were you when this was happening?"

"Hiding under a table, Dude, what'dya think?" Kyle had started rocking back and forth slightly in his chair and was kneading his hands together nervously. He dropped his eyes from Jimmy's face and stared at his latte, then bounced the fists he had knotted together repeatedly against the table. He continued that for a full minute, bouncing his knuckles softly and staring down at the checkered tablecloth, oblivious to Jimmy's further conversation.

Olson tapped his phone to stop the recording. "Are you okay, Kyle? You have to have been traumatized by this experience. If this is too difficult, we can continue the interview later."

Kyle settled back in his chair and finally looked up. "I'm okay. I guess. I mean, it messed me up, no doubt. One of the guys with us, his dad's a lawyer, he said we can sue for emotional distress and stuff. I thought it would just be an easy way to make some coin off the deal, but...I have to admit, I can't stop thinking about it. And I shake sometimes for no reason at all." He picked up his latte and attempted a sip, as if to demonstrate, spilling more than he drank.

"Take it easy," Jimmy said. Kyle put his elbows on the table and dropped his head into his hands, shaking visibly. Jimmy tried again. "Just relax, Kyle, okay?"

Kyle pushed his hands through his hair and looked straight at Olson. "It's just that I keep thinking about all those girls, Jimmy. Pretty girls. Really beautiful girls, you know? They were all shot to shit. They were screaming and crying and scared out of their fucking minds. And there was blood, Jimmy....there was blood everywhere. They were bleeding all over the place, and they were still trying to run. And some of them couldn't even try, because they couldn't get off the floor. Because they were dead, Jimmy. They were all dead, or they were dying. And they never hurt anybody, Jimmy. I mean, why? Why'd that have to happen to them?"

Olson reached across the table, hoping contact would pull the younger man back to the moment and away from the memory, but Kyle pushed away from the table and gripped its edge while he continued.

"And...and we just had to hide there like a bunch of pussies, because there wasn't anything else to do. That was the worst of it, just having to watch it happen. That was the worst part of the whole deal, Jimmy. And it still is! We couldn't help them. Do you know how bad it is to remember that? We couldn't help them.

115

There wasn't a thing any of us could do but hide like rats and watch them die. It keeps me up at night. You know what I mean, Jimmy?"

Kyle reached out with a trembling hand and took a drink of water, then gathered himself and slid his chair back to the table while Olson fought to stay objective.

Jimmy sat quietly for a moment, not trusting his own voice. "Okay, Kyle," he said finally. "Let's take a break and eat something, then you can tell me the rest. If you're able."

Olson stared across the table, contemplating the young stoner as the waitress took their order. Jimmy knew he wasn't the person Detective Murdock had accused him of being. It had turned out that Kyle wasn't who Jimmy thought he was either.

Somewhere between his second latte and a piece of apple pie, Kyle dropped a bombshell. A game changer for a reporter looking for a front-page story.

"So you don't think it was either of the men behind the bar who killed the three remaining gunmen?"

"I know it wasn't. We had two tables tipped over and we were waiting for a chance to run for it. There was a door open up by the bar and we could feel the cold air blowing in, so some of the guys ran right away. Lenny and I and my buddy Mark, we were the furthest away and hiding behind the second table. The one guy by the front door could almost see me, so I was watching him really close, getting ready to make a run for it if he started coming our way. Anyway, I heard a couple of shots, different than the machine guns, and the guy goes down like a sack of rocks.

"I told myself, that asshole ain't gettin' up. And I told Lenny I was pretty sure he was dead. So we waited a few more seconds, then we all got up and ran for the back door as fast as we could. That's when I saw her."

"Another stripper?"

"I don't think she was a stripper, Dude. I got a good look because she came around the bar just before I got to the door. She almost ran me over."

Olson flipped a page in his notes. "There was a woman working there doing cleaning and maintenance. Delores Martinez. Thirty-nine, five-two, dark hair?"

"Not her, Jimmy. This woman was big. Way taller'n me."

"You could tell that? It had to be chaotic with everyone trying to get out of that one service door."

"She was from me to you, Jimmy, and I saw her plain as day. She was six feet and then some, with long black hair. And crazy good-looking. Besides, she wasn't running out the door, she was going in the opposite direction."

117

"She was coming back inside?"

"She was never outside, Jimmy. She was hiding behind the bar. But the door was right there, and she didn't even try to get away. And she didn't look scared. Not at all."

"What was she was doing?"

"She had a gun in her hand, Jimmy, and she looked pissed. I'm pretty sure she shot the last one of those assholes, because a minute later she ducks out that same door and runs off along the side of the building. When we all got out of there, we ran across the parking lot and everyone was hiding over by the dumpsters. People were calling 911 and losing their shit, but I kept watching the door in case one of those bastards came out with a gun. I saw her sneaking away."

"Dammit," Jimmy said loudly. "That means Adam Cain isn't the hero everyone thinks he is."

"Is he the guy on the news?" Kyle asked.

"Yeah. Everyone is saying he's a hero, and I was starting to think so too. But it sounds like this woman might have been the real hero."

Kyle frowned and took another bite of his pie. He had finally stopped shaking. "I don't know, Jimmy. He was kind of a hero if you ask me. He was shooting back while the rest of us were all trying to run away."

"I doubt if people will see it that way if this gets out. Are you sure about this, Kyle? Did

Lenny or Mark see her? Did any of the other guys mention her?"

"Lenny and Mark saw her, and at least one of the other guys. But don't take my word for it. Mark told me he got some video before we got out of there. He says it's pretty rough and kind of all over the place because he was using his phone like a periscope. He didn't want to stick his face up and get it shot off."

"A video? Who has the presence of mind to record a mass shooting?"

"Dude, that's what cellphones are for. Mark was going to put it up on YouTube, but he was afraid someone might come after him. Like, shoot him, because he was a witness. One of the other guys was recording it too, but he lost his phone."

"Mark. Is that his real name?" Olson asked cautiously.

Kyle shrugged and slid his phone across the table. "I'm not going to shake you down for his number. I'm done with the whole deal. You'd figure it out anyway, and I just want to forget that night ever happened."

"What about the police? Did you tell them about all of this?"

"Twice. And the one guy was from the FBI. But I didn't rat Mark out, so I don't know if he ever gave them his phone. But he said he saw that woman pop up from behind the bar and shoot the asshole at the front door and one of the other guys. Boom, boom, that quick. Two shots and they both went down. I guess he managed to get a little of that on his phone too. He said the camera angle was terrible, but you could definitely tell it was a woman doing the shooting." Kyle's smile came back. "Call him up, Jimmy. A video like that would be worth a lot, wouldn't it?"

Olson entered Mark's number into his phone, then slid Kyle's back to him. "Probably, but Mark should turn that video over to the cops, Kyle. It's evidence, not something people need to see. I think we need to let those poor girls rest in peace."

"Yeah, Jimmy, that sounds right." The young stoner rubbed at his eyes. "I just want to sleep at night."

Olson glanced down at his phone, contemplating the number he had just entered and the story he was going to write. "Yeah, Kyle, I want to sleep at night too."

Chapter Eleven

It had been three weeks since the shooting at the Exotic. I was moving again and could manage a shower and dressing myself. Jenny was at my place most of the time. She hadn't officially moved back in, but most of her clothes were in my closet. She had continued fussing over me, but all of her vacation time was used up and we both agreed it was time for her to go back to work. The casino I worked at had given me a month's wages and time to heal. Generous, and good publicity for them.

Mickey's funeral had come and gone while I was still unconscious and in the hospital. Justine came to visit shortly after I was released and we spent a teary-eyed afternoon telling stories about Mickey and mending whatever fences we needed to mend. We were never close, but we shared the bond you have when you both lose someone.

Today was the day the Exotic was going to reopen their doors and it was time to talk to Alex Gainey. My doctor had assured me that internal bleeding was unlikely, and Jenny had been redressing both wounds every day. I was a long way from full strength, but I could stand up without my vision going black, and I was anxious to get out of the apartment and into my own vehicle. I had fibbed and told Jenny I would take a cab to the club, but getting behind the wheel of my pickup felt good, and normal. I needed normal.

Nothing had been normal after I got out of the hospital. The television crews finally lost interest when I refused any more live interviews, but one of the newspaper reporters kept after me until I gave in. It was hard to lie. It felt like a betrayal, even though I knew the Gypsy would prefer I did and Mickey was beyond caring. People at the grocery store stopped and thanked me for my service, and my picture was on a jar on the counter stuffed with bills. All the money was going to Justine, but when an old woman asked for a selfie, I decided to let Jenny do the shopping without me for a while.

Gainey knew I was coming but he was late. There was a service truck outside the building and three cars. It was a gloomy gray day, and the Exotic looked drab and dirty without the spotlights and neon replicas of dancing girls illuminating the front of the building. The front door was propped open and I stopped at the entrance, sucking in a few deep breaths to prepare myself.

I'd seen my share of death in the war, but the memories weren't as immediate or as intimate as that night three weeks ago. In the heat of battle, or in the moments just before I joined Mickey on the floor behind the bar, there wasn't time to process the details of what I was seeing. Those details, including the sights and sounds of young women, dead and dying, had come back to me while I was in the hospital. I wanted to be ready when I walked into the club.

I stepped in and gave my eyes a moment to get accustomed to the dimmer light. Two electricians were on stepladders working on the new security cameras. They had been busy. It looked like every square inch of the Exotic would be under surveillance when they reopened in a few hours. New cameras, new lights, and a fresh batch of Gainey's Girls.

I spotted someone I knew. Deloris Martinez saw me and walked over, her eyes big and shiny. I nodded and when I said her name she rushed forward and threw her arms around me. When I flinched, she realized her mistake and backed away.

"God, I'm sorry. I should've known better. I knew you were in the hospital, but you look good. Did I hurt you?"

"No, I'm fine. But how are you? I was happy to hear you made it out."

"I was coming up to the bar when it happened and the side door was open. I just ran as fast I could and called the police from my cellphone. I could hear all the shooting." Her eyes filled and the tears came. "Poor Mickey. He was such a great guy. And all those poor girls."

She leaned in again and I wrapped her in a careful hug. "Are you sure you should be back here?" I asked.

"A person has to eat. I guess the insurance company is going to offer a settlement for anyone willing to take it." She pushed away again and looked up at me. "Why are you here? It has to be hard for you too."

"I can't sit at home knowing that whoever sent those shooters is still walking around breathing our air, Deloris. Mickey isn't. Those four lunatics didn't just show up. Someone sent them."

"And you think Gainey knows something?" Her eyes dropped and her voice grew guarded. Gainey had managed to salvage some of her loyalty.

"Probably not, not knowingly. But maybe he knows something he's not telling the cops. I know you think he's a good guy, but he doesn't always do things by the book."

She leaned toward me and lowered her voice. "Not all of the people that come in here are college kids and tourists. We get all kinds. Bad men sometimes, really dangerous men. Gainey talks to them and makes deals with them. It makes me wonder about him. Did you know there was a US senator in here the night of the shooting?"

That was a revelation to me. "They sure as hell didn't mention that on the news. I presume the police know, and the FBI agent?"

"They must. I think the local cops snuck him out the back door, and as far as I know, Gainey has the only key. I tried to ask him about it but he clammed up right away. Those four men must have been after that senator. I can't imagine who else."

"Did you see anything more that might help? I'm no detective and I'm grasping at straws, for Mickey."

"I saw the mug shots of the guys that shot up the place online, and I think I'd seen one of them in here before." Her voice dropped even further and she leaned toward me again. "But you can't tell Gainey that I told you this. Really. I need my job."

"I won't say anything to him. One of them was in here? Was he a customer?"

"Maybe, but that's not why I remembered him. I was cleaning behind the bar one morning a few days before the shooting, early in the day. Gainey and this guy came out of his office. I'm not a hundred percent sure it was the same man, because Gainey always has people in there, booking parties and special deals. I normally don't pay much attention, but he went out through the service door, and that was unusual."

"And according to Randolph, that area wasn't covered by security cameras. Did you tell the cops about it?"

"No." Deloris dropped her eyes again and looked at the floor. "I'm sorry. I was afraid Gainey would know I told them and I would lose my job."

"But that's important, Deloris. Maybe Gainey tipped them off that the senator was going to be here."

Her eyes narrowed and she came to her boss's defense. "Alex is a bad man in many ways, Mister Cain, but he loved those girls, and he loved Mickey."

"I didn't mean he thought they'd come back and kill half his staff. But maybe this guy was doing re-con and Gainey didn't realize it. He could have played it off like he wanted to book a party and the business about the senator just came out accidentally. Regardless, the cops need to know that one of those shooters was in here before that night."

"I'll bet Mister Gainey told them. I know he was griping about the detective being a real prick, and he said the FBI really raked him over the coals too. They had him take a lie detector test. He said he volunteered."

"Okay, probably he did then. He probably told them." I wasn't convinced.

Deloris nodded her head toward the bar. Alex Gainey had walked in and was watching the electricians work on the security system. "He's here," Deloris said, picking up her cleaning supplies. "Remember, you promised."

"You need to tell the police what you know, Deloris. I said I wouldn't say anything to Gainey, but we have to tell the cops or the FBI that one of those shooters had been in here before. Gainey probably already told them, but I need to be sure of that. Mickey and all those dead girls deserve that much." She shrugged and shuffled away. Gainey waved his hand and pointed toward his office.

"Adam, my God, it's good to see you. Have a seat. You're looking good for a man that took two bullets."

I sat down in the chair he indicated and let him pump my hand. "Lucky to be here from what the doctors said."

"The club owes you a huge debt, that's for sure. As terrible as it was, it would have been a lot worse if you hadn't been here. I made a contribution to the fund you set up for Justine. An hour doesn't go by I don't think of Mickey. Heroes, both of you."

"Thanks. Justine is having a tough go of it and she needs all the help she can get. I'll have a couple scars, but not the kind that she'll have to live with. She told me the hardest part was the fact that he spent all that time in the war and never got hurt. Then he comes home, gets out of the Army, and gets killed right here in his hometown. Behind a bar."

"I don't know what to say, Adam. It was a horrible thing. A tragedy. All those girls, all those college kids, Mickey." To his credit, it looked like he might tear up. "The cops are still trying to figure out why those bastards did it."

"That's about all we can do now," I agreed, "move on and make sure whoever was responsible pays for it."

"I hired more security, and I'm putting an armed guard at the entrance. I can't bring people back to life, but I'm going to make damn sure my employees are safe from now on. I know you have a job, but if there's anything I can do for you, money, work, consider it done. I'll help you any way I can."

"The truth, Gainey." We locked eyes. "I want the truth."

He looked away, squirming in his chair. "I'm not sure what you mean."

"I don't know if the cops or the FBI are ever going to get the people who sent those four men here. It doesn't seem like they're getting anywhere, and that's not okay. I want whoever's responsible for Mickey's death to pay for it, preferably by being dead themselves. I'd consider it a bonus if I got to pull the trigger."

Gainey glanced nervously at the camera in the corner of his office. "Look, Mickey said you're a great guy and everything, but he told me about the times you flipped out over in the war. That shit won't fly in this country. I don't think those cameras are working yet, but you have to be careful what you say. I get that you're upset, but you can't just start shooting people and accusing people of things."

I stood and leaned toward Gainey, planting my hands on the middle of his desk. I was still bandaged up and about as dangerous as a ten-year-old girl, but I was angry. I didn't trust that Gainey didn't know more than he was saying and my intention was to make an impression.

"More times than I can count, Mickey had my back when we were in Afghanistan. He kept me alive, and he kept me out of Leavenworth when the Army wanted to lock me up. A couple of days ago I got to hold his widow and listen to her sob for an hour because her husband is gone. I'll kill the son-of-a-bitches that are responsible if I get the chance, and you better not be covering for them. Do you understand me?"

He pushed away from the desk, leaning away from my reach. He was sweating, and nervous. "Jesus, Cain, calm down. I told the cops everything I know. You can't really think I had anything to do with what happened. Mickey was like a son to me."

I'm not a small guy. I'm a pretty big guy in most company, short of professional linebackers and Lebron James. Gainey was not. Despite the fact that he had to know I couldn't do much, he wanted no part of a fight. He slid a desk drawer open and I expected him to pull a gun from it. Instead, he pulled out two glasses and a bottle.

I sat back down and he slid a glass in my direction. "Look, I get that you're worked up, but I'm not the enemy here. I liked Mickey, and I cared a lot about those girls. A lot of people think I'm a terrible guy, and I get that. But I've always looked out for my girls and the people that work for me."

"You're a pimp, don't sugar-coat it," I said. I tipped the glass up and let the brown liquor burn some of the anger from my voice.

He shrugged. "If not me, then the next guy. But I had nothing to do with what happened that night. You have to believe me."

"Any idea why they were here? I know you talked to the cops, but I want to hear it for myself."

"No idea. We had a guest that night that might have been the target, but he had his own security. One guy, so if you hadn't stopped them, he would have been in trouble." He shrugged when I didn't say anything, then continued. "It was a US senator, and he slipped out the back before the press got in here. I'm guessing the FBI is all over that, but they're not about to tell me anything."

"A guy like that, he didn't just show up," I said.

130

"No, he had a small party with him. One of his aides was getting married, is what he told me. I have a couple of dividers back there, so they more or less had their own private room."

"And no one else knew he was coming?" I studied his expression.

"No one. An important guy like him gets caught in a club like this, it looks bad. Bad for him and bad for the club. He was happy as hell when I got them out the back door."

"I saw you run out that night. You snuck back in?"

"As soon as the shooting stopped. They were loading you on a stretcher when I came back in and told them who I was. I'm not proud of running. I panicked."

"It happens," I acknowledged. I looked him in the eye again. "Had you ever seen any of those shooters before?"

He shook his head. "No. And I didn't see them that night, just their mugshots when the cops questioned me. I didn't recognize any of them. A lot of people come in here, and they could have checked the place out without me knowing about it. The FBI said they must have, because they knew about the VIP room."

I emptied my glass. I couldn't swear he was lying. Deloris might have been wrong, or maybe the mugshots were out of date. Maybe he was as innocent as he wanted me to believe. Innocent was the wrong word, because he wasn't that. I stood up and ignored the hand he extended.

He overlooked the slight and smiled. "Remember what I said. If you ever need a job, you have one here."

I tried to keep my mouth shut, because there was a chance I'd need to talk to him again. I just couldn't do it. Instead, I told him what I really thought.

"It's funny to me that Mickey liked you, Alex. I know you think you're an okay guy, but you're not. Running a strip club is one thing, but making these kids sell themselves is something else entirely. You're a low-life pimp and Mickey was worth ten of you. One of these days I might get it in my head to come back and give you the beating you deserve, so you'd better be telling me the truth."

He took that about as well as I would have expected. "Sorry you feel that way, Adam. I have extra security these days, so it would be better if we just don't see each other again."

The way things turned out, he got his wish.

Chapter Twelve

I went straight to the FBI. The truth was I already had an appointment, but now I was anxious to know what Gainey had told them. Randolph had called and asked if he could come to the apartment, but I didn't like the idea of meeting him there. Jenny had a way of popping in if she managed a long lunchbreak. He'd said we needed a quiet place to talk and that it had to be alone.

I wondered if he wanted to talk about the Gypsy again. It had been two weeks since I'd seen her in the hospital, but she drifted through my dreams every night. Dreams that were filled with gunshots and bloodied young girls.

The office was on the third floor and there was no elevator. I was winded and a little dizzy by the time I walked through the door labeled FBI. The guy behind the desk looked like a college kid, but when he saw me, he jumped out of his chair and led me into one of the offices. Agent Randolph nodded to the kid, then pushed the door shut. There was a single desk but he pointed to a small table in the back.

"It's quiet back here and we'll be left alone. Jefferson is on vacation and I sent Collins out to get us lunch. You don't look so good, Cain. Are you okay?"

"Too many steps," I replied, settling into the chair he offered. "They tell me it'll take a couple more weeks to get my bloodwork back to where it should be. Any news?"

He peered over the top of the cheaters he was wearing, then tossed them on the desk and rubbed at the marks they'd left on his long nose. "I was going to ask you the same thing."

"You're the investigator. Are you any closer to figuring out who was behind the shooting?"

"Oh," he muttered. "I thought you were talking about the Gypsy."

I chuckled. "Obsessed much?" Jenny was right, the Gypsy had gotten into Randolph's head too.

"I am, I'll admit it. But for good reason. I'll bet she could tell us who the target was or confirm what I already suspect."

"I talked to Gainey today," I offered.

"Just catching up, or are you sticking your nose in where you shouldn't? Murdock's bad enough without you playing detective."

"Gainey's no friend of mine, but I thought he might tell me some things he wouldn't tell you." I lowered my voice. "I don't know if you've heard this, Agent Randolph, but some people don't trust the FBI."

He scowled. "Good one. You're a funny guy. What's the point?"

"I spoke to a witness who said she saw Gainey talking to one of the shooters a few days before it happened. The guy came and went through the service door, so he wouldn't have been on camera. I wasn't specific, but I jumped Gainey about it. He claimed he'd never seen any of them before."

"She? Deloris Martinez?"

"Good memory," I said.

He nodded. "So I'm told. I haven't talked to her, but her name is in the file."

"She wasn't sure. She's going by a mug shot she saw on the internet, and she's worried about losing her job."

"Tough luck. It's a rotten job and twenty-eight people are dead. I'm bringing Gainey in for questioning again, and her too. She can find another job." He made a note, then slid a file out of his briefcase. "You're pretty good at this, Cain. You're a smart guy."

"The last time you told me that you talked me into something I already regret." It wasn't meant as a joke, but he laughed.

"How badly do you want to get the people that are responsible for Mickey's death?"

"You're a smart guy too, but that's a stupid question. I'll do whatever it takes. Do you know who it is or are you speculating?"

He opened the file and slid a picture across the table. "Do you recognize this man?"

Before our fight, Jenny had a picture on our dresser from when she was a teenager. The young man with his arm around her had the same blond hair and blue eyes. I didn't see anything to gain by lying.

"That's Jack, Jenny's brother. I've never met him, but I've seen plenty of pictures. She did say he was coming into town for a visit one of these days. He's involved?"

"Maybe he was going to surprise her while he was in town. He was at the Exotic the night of the shooting, and we think he might have been the target." Randolph slid the picture back and closed the file.

"Not the senator?" I asked.

"What senator?" He sat stone-faced for a moment, then acknowledged the truth with a shrug. "No, not the senator. We're reasonably sure Jack was the target."

"That's why she was looking for me," I mumbled. "She wouldn't say."

Randolph cocked his head. "Jenny?"

"No, the Gypsy. She said she came to the bar that night to find me. But maybe it was about Jenny's brother. I still don't understand how she would have known I was there."

"Maybe she didn't. Maybe she knew Jack Mercer was there, and maybe she knew they were coming after him. But it gets worse. Has Jenny ever said anything about her father?"

"Just that he died a couple of years ago working overseas, and that her mother passed away shortly after that. Jack's her only family."

"It gets worse," Randolph repeated. "And again, what are you willing to do to get the people that killed Mickey?"

"I already told you, anything. But how the hell is Jenny's brother involved in this?"

Randolph got quiet and sat staring at me for too long a time. Finally, he spoke, "You can't tell anyone what I'm about to tell you, no matter what the circumstances. Not your best friend, not the Gypsy, and not Jenny. Especially not Jenny."

He stared coldly until I nodded, then continued. "Jenny's father, Frank Mercer, was involved in some nasty goings-on in Europe, and here in the States. A para-military group. And not just involved, he and his partners started it."

"You mean like the Proud Boys or Antifa?"

"No, not like those. Much worse. When Frank left the Army, he and a couple of his friends started a security company. Three guys, three cities. Boston, New York, and Philadelphia. Jack Mercer still runs the New York branch."

"Jenny told me about that. She said Jack's doing really well."

Randolph nodded, bouncing his pen on his desk. It was a nervous habit. Nervous and annoying. "This all started years ago, before they split up the company, if they ever really did. On paper, it looks that way. Things were going well until they started contracting overseas. That's when it got dicey. Pretty soon, every time there was a shooting or a bombing over there, Frank Mercer or one of his partners' names came up. It was rumored that they were involved in a coup in a small eastern European country, a very violent one. The president of a fledgling democracy was assassinated."

"Kind of over-reach for a security company," I acknowledged.

"Yeah. It got them noticed, and not in a good way. Their security details started looking more like a militia or a small army. They turned into wholesale mercenaries. Mercenaries without a conscience. Kids kidnapped, wives murdered, and whole families extinguished if that's what the client wanted. And it wasn't necessarily political. They worked for whoever could afford them."

"Knowing Jenny, it's hard to believe her father could have been that kind of guy."

"I'm not sure he is," Randolph stated. "The company needed capital and contacts in Europe. They took on a fourth partner, a Belgian with ties to organized crime. One of Frank's original partners disappeared shortly before the Belgian bought in. By then, Interpol and our intelligence guys over there had turned up the heat, so they started moving most of the organization back to this country. Their operation in Europe is still active, but several of the original employees came back to this country and took positions in the three security companies. We think."

"People willing to kidnap and kill?"

"A variety of nasty bastards. Already mercenaries, some of them, willing to do anything for the right price. Disgruntled soldiers of fortune, some of them, looking for a big payday. Idealogues, some of them, getting ready for the war to end all wars. Just plain bat-shit, some of them. Altogether, not a good bunch of guys."

"This Belgian," I asked, "and Frank Mercer?"

"Frank came home for a while to set Jack up with the New York branch. We think the Belgian came with him at that time, but no one is sure. It seems unlikely they decided to clean up their act, but so far there've been no complaints tied to the New York operation, or the other two. It was three years ago when they reduced their footprint in the UK and moved most of their people back here. Frank's accident happened a year after that."

"Accident?" I was starting to have a bad feeling.

"There was an oil rig fire off the coast of Algiers, sabotage, and five men were killed. Their bodies were never recovered. Frank Mercer was declared legally dead."

"You just said you're not sure if he is that kind of guy," I said. "Is. Present tense. That's what you meant by it gets worse. The bastard's still alive."

"We're nearly certain he is. Money came and went from his bank account for months after the accident, and there were international calls made to the New York and Boston branches of the company using one of his phones. He was being investigated in the UK and Germany, and they were getting close to an arrest. Being dead took the heat off."

"Not much of a family man," I commented. "According to Jenny, her mother started drinking full-time after Frank died in that rig fire. She fell in the pool one night and drowned. This'll tear Jenny to pieces."

"She can't know, Adam. And considering the kind of guy Frank is, maybe she's better off not knowing. You agreed not to say anything. You can't tell her."

I didn't have to think for too long. He was right. Better she didn't know. "Okay, for the time being, I won't say anything. What does this have to do with Mickey and the shooting?"

"We're fairly sure Jack Mercer was the target, but we're operating on a lot of assumptions. That's not something I like to do. We had a mole in the operation, but he died when that oil rig went up. Back then, there was a lot of infighting, and we're guessing there still is. Our informant thought that Frank and Tyrel Davis, the other founder of the company, wanted to keep things legitimate in this country, but that the Belgian had different ideas."

"So he went after Jenny's brother? Why not just kill Frank?"

"We don't know. Our intelligence is old, but we've always suspected that the security businesses are a front. It's possible Jack and his people aren't involved in anything dirty, but we know some of the men from the pseudo-militia are working for him. Also, Jack, and some of his employees are involved in a gun club. It's at an old farm and meat processing plant a couple hours north of the city. It's the kind of gun club where they have military drills."

"How is that not like the Proud Boys?"

"There are plenty of people who like to play at being soldier, without wanting to overthrow the government or kill people. It could be perfectly innocent, like civil war re-enactments or that kind of thing. But it resembled what was going on in Europe enough to draw our attention." He reached into the file again and slid another picture in front of me. It was a long-range drone shot. A couple of dozen men in uniforms were lined up in a military formation and it looked like they were marching. The quality was poor, but it looked like they had rifles.

"Not my thing, but that isn't illegal." I turned up the sarcasm. "But it's a good use of our tax dollars, taking pictures of people who haven't done anything wrong."

"Yet. But you're right. These pictures would be worthless if it came to getting a warrant. One thing. They have a private range and permits to shoot the big stuff. The range is over half a mile long."

"Still not illegal," I pointed out.

He shrugged. "Another odd thing is that this group doesn't have any online presence. Legitimate clubs are usually looking for new members. Socializing, advertising their bake sales, recruiting. These guys don't. And there are very few cellphones."

"You can tell that?" I didn't expect an answer, and I didn't get one.

"Suffice it to say, there are red flags. It looks like they're training for something."

"But if Jenny's brother is in on it, whatever it is, why kill him? And why do it in Vegas?"

"It's possible the group has fractured. Maybe it was a warning to keep Frank in line or pull him out of hiding. We killed your son. Your daughter could be next."

"That's a wild theory, considering how little you know."

"True. But the most obvious answer is usually the right one."

"Still, it's just a theory," I said.

"It's the only thing I have," Randolph replied. He started bouncing his pen on the desk again, then got to the point. "The thing is, Adam, we need someone on the inside. Someone with access to Jack Mercer, and someone who would have something to offer a militia. There's a stipend, if that helps."

At that point I wasn't surprised by what he was suggesting, but it felt wrong. "No way in hell, Randolph. I won't do it."

"You're our best shot, Adam. Our only shot. Somehow you ended up right in the middle of this, you and Mickey. Jenny said she and her brother had talked about you working for him if you moved back east someday, so it's the perfect cover story."

"When did she tell you that?"

"We had coffee recently. I told her I was concerned about your mental health." He chuckled at his own joke, then continued. "I may have suggested you have PTSD and that getting out of Las Vegas would be the best thing for you. She's the one that brought up New York."

"Why would Jack open up to me? I don't know the guy."

"He'll have to do a background check to get you bonded, and I can make sure he's able to access your military records. He'll know you had a beef with the Army, and that you're a marksman. Every militia needs one of those." He nodded and grinned, hoping his enthusiasm was contagious.

He continued. "Look, we don't know that Jack is doing anything illegal. Maybe he's like you and he's just caught in the middle of something. But if they came after him once, they might do it again. Or, they might target Jenny the next time. We need someone on the inside to get to the Belgian, and to find Frank. They were willing to kill a couple of dozen people, and Mickey, just to hide the fact that they were after Jack. How many people will they kill next time? It's your best chance to get the bastards responsible for Mickey's death."

That part was convincing. "You're doing a lot of guessing. I'll have to think about it."

"Sure, but you need to be careful what you say to Jenny. She may know more than she's letting on."

I shook my head. "There's no way Jenny knows any of this. What if it all comes back to Frank Mercer somehow?"

"Frank Mercer isn't going to try to kill his own son. It had to be the Belgian."

"Still, I don't like it. Things are okay with Jenny now, but I don't want to drag her across the country and have her get the idea we're going to settle down for the long haul."

He chuckled. "You could do a lot worse. And she was already planning to go back to New York after you moved on. Her words. She talked like she's expecting it."

"How much coffee did you two drink?"

He shrugged. "Granted, it's not my business, but she did say you weren't big on commitment. She said she had already made up her mind to move back to New York this spring, with or without you."

"And if her father and brother are murderers, then what? Then I'm in the middle of it. Regardless of what happens long-term, I care about her. I wouldn't want to be the guy who takes her family away from her."

"No," Randolph muttered, "that would be my job."

"Sorry, but I just don't know. I want to get whoever's responsible for getting Mickey killed, but there are too many holes in your story."

"Then consider this. If you do go to work for Jack Mercer, there's a good chance you'll see the Gypsy again. I have no idea what the connection is, but it's there. You, the Mercer's, the Belgian, you're all on her radar."

I couldn't hide my smile. "How long have you had this fixation with her?"

He chuckled and tipped back in his chair. "Shortly before Frank Mercer's accident, three members of his group were caught on camera in Lisbon. There were a lot of eyewitnesses too. Three men on foot were chasing a woman, a very tall, very attractive woman, right through the busiest part of the city. Shooting at her, right there in the middle of the street. Dozens of witnesses, but none of them could identify her. They all agreed she was tall and good-looking, but some said she was blond, some said brunette, some said her head was covered.

145

Eyewitnesses are notoriously unreliable and there wasn't a lot of camera footage. But Mercer's people all had a history and photos on file, so they were identified right away. That's why Interpol shared everything with me."

"Obviously they didn't catch her, presuming it was the Gypsy," I said.

"No, they didn't catch her. But before they could be rounded up, all three of those men turned up dead. No one ever tied it all together, but that's when I got interested. It's not an official investigation and I have very little hard evidence. But with facial recognition as good as it is now, it's harder for her to hide her movements, especially from the FBI. Like I said, there's a pattern. She shows up, the shit hits the fan, and someone turns up dead. Often as not, it's someone that has a connection to Frank Mercer."

"Almost like a vendetta," I said.

"Almost, but it isn't just Mercer's operations. Two years ago, she stopped a bank robbery in Boston. Two twenty-somethings. She disarmed the first one and used his gun to kneecap the other. That time she had to stick around and answer questions. The investment firm she works for owns the building, and she said she just happened to walk in on it."

"And managed to take out two young guys with guns?"

146

"Pilates and self-defense classes. That's what she said when they asked her how she managed to break the first kid's arm and put the second one down with one shot."

"And no one ever thought to ask her name?"

"Of course. Fake name, fake address, fake passport. And her employer covered for her, or is unaware."

"At least you finally got a good look at her."

"She's in the system, but I tagged her file so I'm the only one with access. I get a ping whenever she gets on an international flight. She's doing business in Europe this week, but I doubt it has anything to do with the price of the Euro."

"That's all very interesting, but I still don't know why she'd come looking for me."

"Because Jenny's a Mercer," he said confidently.

"How would the Gypsy know about our relationship? And why go to the trouble of finding out who Jenny was with? I think she was there looking for Jenny's brother. The question is, was she there to protect him, or to kill him?"

"I don't think she's an assassin. Not for hire, at least. I think she was as surprised as you were when those four guys walked into that club with AK47's, or she'd have been better prepared. And I don't think she's likely to kill someone in cold blood, vendetta or not. She could have easily killed those kids at the bank that day, but she chose not to."

"Well, that's good news. It seems to me she's the only person I can trust in this whole mess. And I'm including you in that."

Randolph chuckled. "There's Jenny. You can trust her."

"Until she finds out I might be the one to send her brother to jail, or her old man, who is already dead as far as she knows. That conversation couldn't possibly go well. Look, Randolph, this isn't my fight. I can keep Jenny safe if we just stay here."

"Can you? Jack would probably be dead right now if not for this Gypsy woman. We don't know for sure who was after Jack, but Jenny might still be a target. You can't watch her twenty-four seven, and let's not forget about Mickey."

"She said you were a good guy."

The smile returned to Randolph's face. "Jenny said that?"

"No. The Gypsy."

The smile grew. "Equally as good."

"She also said you'd trade your grandmother's soul to solve a case, and that I shouldn't trust you."

"Well, I know Jenny wouldn't say that. It's interesting that the Gypsy thinks she knows me well enough to have that opinion."

"Still, I need to think about it. I need a few more weeks to heal up before I do anything. I'll let you know when I figure it out."

He looked disappointed but shrugged and tossed his pen down. "Okay. Think about it. I'm guessing you'll do the right thing, one way or the other."

There was a rap on the office door and a man a few years younger than me pushed through it. He had a pizza box in his hand. "Sir?" he asked, glancing back and forth between us.

"Come in, Agent Collins." Randolph waved his hand and pushed a pile of paperwork to the side. "This is Adam Cain, our witness and shooting victim." Randolph glanced at me. "Collins is my junior associate. He's aware of most of the particulars of the case."

Collins dropped the pizza on the desk and started pumping my hand enthusiastically. Some grease had soaked through the box. Now it was on my hand.

Randolph noticed and chuckled. "Collins went to Harvard," he said. "We're working on his people skills."

Collins ignored the slight or missed it. "I am very glad to meet you, Mister Cain. Your efforts at the club the night of the shooting were exemplary."

"Not really, but thanks for saying so."

"Agent Collins will be your liaison when I'm unavailable, on a need-to-know basis, of course. And, depending on what you decide."

I nodded and stood. Collins stepped back and looked up at me. "I should have bought more pizza."

I passed on the pizza and left the office, considering Randolph's proposal as I negotiated the steps again. It wouldn't bother me to leave Las Vegas. Justine was moving back to Florida to live with her parents and she was the only reason Jenny would want to stay in Nevada. It would be an easy sell, and it did seem like my best chance to even the score for Mickey.

The Gypsy had said she'd find me wherever I ended up. Is this what she'd meant?

Chapter Thirteen

I brought it up that night. "Is your brother still coming out here, or did that get canceled when you decided to move out?"

Jenny eyed me cautiously. "He's been planning to call you. He came into town the same day that I moved out, so it was awkward. He talked about coming to the hospital, but I didn't want him to upset you. I told him to hold off until things settled down."

"Why would he upset me?"

"By talking about it. He was there that night."

I feigned confusion. "He was where?"

"He was at the Exotic when the shooting happened, and he wanted to thank you. He said they were trapped in a side room and just covered up and prayed. Unbelievable coincidence, right?"

"Yeah. Unbelievable," I agreed. "Do you miss him? You'll probably move back there someday, won't you?"

"Justine will be leaving in a month, so I'm not sure what I'm going to do." She bit her lip. "Do you not want me to live here? I thought we were doing better."

I still wasn't sure what I was going to do, but one lie was enough. "You know I care about you, Jenny, but chances are I won't always be around. I just don't believe in things lasting the way you do. Nothing ever does."

The smile never left her face. "I get that you feel that way, and it's okay. When the time comes that it isn't, I'll tell you."

"My loss," I said. "I'm just not good at making promises. Seriously though, do you ever think about going back to New York? I'm not trying to get rid of you, I'm just curious."

"I'd love to go back. I love the Catskills, the skiing, all the shows. Jack lives in the city now and he has all kinds of connections. He can get cheap tickets to the theater and the opera. And baseball games," she added quickly, then qualified her enthusiasm. "I mean, if we did end up going back there together. Do you even like baseball?"

"More than the opera," I said. I still wasn't convinced, but I didn't want her going off alone, not after my conversation with Randolph. "I've been thinking about moving, maybe getting out of Las Vegas."

"It might be good for you to get away from here," she said cautiously. "It's been a month since the shooting, and I know you miss Mickey. But maybe it would be better not to be reminded of him constantly." It was a thinly veiled attempt to manipulate me. Not for her benefit, but for mine. Because that was Jenny.

"I do miss him. Afghanistan would have been a dozen times worse if he hadn't been there. I'm not going to forget that."

"Leaving here doesn't mean you have to forget about him," Jenny said. "Just try to remember the good things. Forget about the shooting and that damn war."

Easier said than done, but I painted on a smile. She wanted me in New York and so did Randolph. Maybe leaving Las Vegas was a good idea.

"I'm not saying anything for sure, but I still own my dad's old duplex south of Poughkeepsie. Sooner or later I have to fix it up so I can put it on the market. Maybe, if you want, you could help me paint and remodel. It's not the city, but it's only an hour out. We could stay there for a while and see how it goes."

She beamed at me. "Really? That sounds wonderful." The hope was there again. I knew it would only make the lies hurt more when she learned the truth. "You won't get sick of me?" she asked.

"I'm sure it'll be the other way around," I said. Whose lies would hurt her more? Mine or her father's? I should have left it at that, but I'd just been reminded of Afghanistan, and I wasn't feeling particularly optimistic. "Just don't read too much into it."

Her smile dwindled for a moment, then came back. "We'll see how it goes, like you said. I'm fine with that."

I had joked with the Gypsy about Jenny being too good for me, and it had never felt more true than in that moment. "Sure," I said. "Maybe it is a bit of PTSD, but I worry about keeping you safe, Jenny. Bad things keep happening to the people I care about."

She misunderstood who and what I was talking about. "I'm sorry about what happened to Mickey, but I'm not leaving you anytime soon."

It wasn't Mickey that was on my mind right then, or all of the girls who died with him that night at the Exotic. I was thinking about a dusty street in the province of Kunar and a laughing grey-eyed girl playing hopscotch with her friends. She was ten years old and too much of a child to know how to hate. It didn't matter to her that I was an infidel or that there was a war going on. In her language, I was the Dark Giant, the tall American soldier that watched them play their games and always had a pocket full of candy.

One minute she was laughing and waving shyly from the far side of a dusty marketplace surrounded by a crowd of younger children that were her charges; the next, she was gone. Gone, in a cacophony of noise and calamity that shook the ground beneath us, stopped the laughter, and filled the air with acrid dust and the cries of the wounded.

It shouldn't have happened that way. There was a truce. There was going to be a treaty.

On that morning, the local Taliban chieftain that was hiding in the mountains nearby decided to violate the truce. That night, I did the same thing.

I put Randolph and Jenny off for a couple of weeks. I went to physical therapy and started walking and working out. Suggesting a move to Jenny hadn't been the best idea. It started to feel like the choice was being made for me. She didn't come right out and say so, but she couldn't hide the excitement in her voice when she told me her brother had a job waiting for me anytime I was ready. She talked about a new start and leaving the bad memories behind. That part sounded good, but I wasn't sure what I would be getting myself into.

Bundled up against the wind, I found myself searching the faces of the people who greeted me on my morning walks to the gym, looking for the dark eyes and razor jawline of the woman who might have the answers I needed. Given the opportunity and a phone number I would have called the Gypsy. She probably knew more about what was going on with the Mercer family than Randolph did, and it didn't matter to me if she had deduced that information or consulted a crystal ball. I trusted her. Truthfully, I just wanted to see her again.

The shooting was six weeks behind us, and as far as I knew, the local cops were no closer to knowing why it happened. At least Randolph and the FBI had come up with a plan, sketchy as it was. Going back to New York might be the only way to find out who had sent those four men to the Exotic and extract any kind of justice for my dead friend. But, after two weeks, I was still on the fence.

It was about eight blocks from my apartment to the gym. Often as not someone would recognize me on my morning walk from the pictures in the newspapers and on television. Usually they smiled, gave me a thumbs-up, or stopped to thank me for what I'd done at the Exotic. I tried to appreciate the gestures, misguided as they were, and get to the gym as fast as I could. This morning was different.

The small apartment building where I lived had a security door. If I'd been completely awake, I would have noticed the group waiting for me and avoided another conversation with the press. The same young woman who had pushed her head into the front seat of Jenny's car was waiting for me when I stepped out into the cold morning air. She pulled a stocking cap down around her ears and scurried forward when she saw me, pushing her microphone ahead of her. The sun must have been in the right spot, because the guy with the camera didn't have the light on.

There was a small crowd behind the reporter, and a middle-aged woman with a cellphone in one hand raised the other in a fist. "You're disgusting," she screamed. "I want my money back!" She was accompanied by another dozen people of varying ages and sizes that all started yelling at me and screaming obscenities. I hooked the door with my foot and kept it from closing all the way.

The little blonde with the microphone was undeterred. "Would you like to make a statement, Mister Cain?"

"Why would I make a statement?" I eased the door open with my foot and backed into the entry.

"Perhaps you would like to explain why you took credit for stopping the shooting at the Exotic last month, when we now know it was someone else. Thousands of dollars, tens of thousands of dollars in donations have been made in your name."

"I didn't take credit for stopping the shooting, and all those donations are going to Mickey's widow. What's this about?"

"You claimed to be the person who shot the last three terrorists at the Exotic. We now know that it was someone else. A woman, as it turns out."

"I said I couldn't remember what happened. I told you that."

"I beg to differ, Sir." She slid closer to be sure her face was in the shot, then shook her head dramatically. "As I remember you claimed to be the hero of that day, when indeed, you were not!"

"I said I didn't remember, and you kept insisting I must have shot those men. Maybe you should stick to reporting the news instead of trying to be the story. Get out of the way." I pushed her microphone out of my face and pulled the entry door shut. A half empty water bottle bounced off the glass and I double checked the latch.

Jenny was on the couch when I walked back into the apartment. She had the local news on. She gave me a wide-eyed look and picked up the remote, rewinding. The footage was dark and grainy, bouncing from the intended scene to the floor, then to the ceiling, then back to the woman that was winding her way through the chaos in front of the bar at the strip club. I knew it was the Gypsy, but no one watching that video could have identified her. In the few moments she was on camera, her long hair obscured most of her face, but there was no denying she was a woman and that she had a gun in her hand.

The anchor pointed out the fact that an eyewitness had said that the unidentified woman was also responsible for killing two more of the assassins before stopping the final one. Be advised, he said, graphic footage to follow. He went on. "In a related story, Alex Gainey, owner of the now infamous strip club where twenty-eight people died just six weeks ago, was found dead this morning. It's been reported that the cause of death was a gunshot wound."

I plucked the remote from Jenny's fingers, turned the television off, and asked the question she'd been waiting for. "Are you ready to move?"

Randolph called at noon. By that time, I'd gotten a half a dozen other phone calls. Two were from the press, three from concerned citizens suggesting that the world would be a better place without me in it, and one from the casino telling me that I was no longer employed. Jenny had gone in to work, planning to give her notice, so she wasn't there to hear me give Randolph an earful.

"We didn't leak that video, Adam," he said. "I have no idea where it came from."

"I was going to call you and tell you I was ready to go, but now I'm not so sure. This doesn't help me trust the FBI."

"There were just too many witnesses. You had to know it was going to come out sooner or later, but it didn't come from us. You'll have to play it off to Jenny's brother somehow. Tell him you and Mickey shot the first three, and the Gypsy shot the last one. There's no video evidence saying differently, and New York is a long way from here. If Jack Mercer is in the middle of this, he's not going to care that you're a liar."

"What about Gainey? Who shot him?"

"We're looking into it. Do you have an alibi for that one?"

I didn't think that was funny. I ended the call.

He called back half an hour later. He had already transferred money into my bank account for relocation and he sent me two phone numbers. "Agent Collins is a nerdy guy, but extremely sharp. You can tell him anything you'd tell me. If you absolutely need to talk to me, use that second number. But I wouldn't use your phone when you're in the Mercer building. They're likely to have people with cyber-security expertise and the technology to hack your phone. If the FBI can do it, they can too. And if they take you out to the farm, leave your cellphone at home or in your vehicle. Just make damn sure no one has access to it."

"I have a gun safe," I said.

"Is Jenny greasing the wheels with her brother?"

"We're going to Skype with him tonight, but it sounds like a done deal."

"Perfect. I know this isn't ideal, Cain, but it's our best bet for finding out who set up the shooting. If that gun club is up to no good, it'll take some doing to gain their trust. A lot of those guys are anti-government, so play up the trouble in Afghanistan. Act like you're still pissed-off at the Army for court-martialing you."

"I am still pissed-off that the Army court-martialed me. If Mickey and Peterson hadn't stood up and lied, I'd be in prison right now."

"That was a raw deal, and I'll make sure Jack Mercer has access to those records. That story will add to your credibility as a troublemaker."

"Yeah, that sums up my last year in the Army."

Chapter Fourteen

Everyone knew about the small camp ten kilometers east of the village, just a stone's throw across the border shared with Pakistan. Most of the Taliban had been pushed back to the north, into mountains so perilous that even the 75th had stopped trying to dig out the hordes of religious hardliners. We stuck to the trails and winding roads, depending on mine sweepers and heavily armored vehicles to keep control of one of the more remote posts in our jurisdiction.

The attack on the town shocked everyone. Dozens of women and children had been killed, and even the most intimidated and fearful of the inhabitants were quick to volunteer the name of the person responsible. Alizai Rahimi commanded a small group of Taliban fighters that spent most of their time deep in the mountains, content to fire at American convoys from afar or to steal sheep from the local farmers. Our platoon was aware of his camp, but the word was that the higher ups were leaving it to the Pakistan government to take action. Another round of impending peace-talks meant that we were only allowed defensive action.

As a rule, I was the guy that followed orders. But it was my third tour in Afghanistan and I had seen a lot of political maneuverings that never led to results. I didn't understand the nuances of a religion I didn't practice or the politics of a people that hated their own countrymen enough to kill a group of school children. I just knew it was wrong.

When the word came down from headquarters that we were to stand down and not retaliate, I knew that was wrong too. I spent the day thinking abought those grey eyes and the happy smile that had stopped existing because a fanatic had filled a car with explosives. Then I snapped.

I took my position while it was still very dark. By midnight a three-quarter moon climbed into the sky, illuminating the rock-strewn high desert where Rahimi's camp was crowded up to the base of a jagged rock wall. I had already spotted two sentries in the hills above the camp, undoubtedly armed with Russian Dragunov rifles. Those guns were nearly as accurate as the M24 that I had borrowed from the arsenal at our camp. Once the sun came up, that would be a problem.

We had one "light fifty" that had more range and firepower than the gun I carried, but it was more than I was prepared to drag over the mountain in the dark of night. The heavier rifle would shoot through almost any barrier a temporary camp was likely to have, but I didn't want to unintentionally kill women or children. Sooner or later Alizai would show himself, hopefully before daylight exposed my position, and hopefully before the platoon sergeant discovered my absence.

Mickey and the other ranger posted as perimeter guards had turned their backs when I left the camp and would probably face a disciplinary hearing because of it. They wouldn't tell what they knew, but anyone in the platoon would know where I had gone and why.

As the night wore on, I started to worry. Once the sun came up, any movement on my part would attract attention and one of the outlooks would spot me. If the first shot didn't kill me outright, it would alert the camp. Then my chance would be gone. I might be able to take a few of the militants with me, but picking out their leader would become impossible.

The camp had been there for a few weeks, long enough for a temporary outhouse to be erected. Age, and a swollen prostate were Rahimi's undoing. Throughout the night a few men made their way to the latrine, one by one. As dawn approached, three men walked across the twenty meters of open space that separated the small enclosure from the rest of the camp. I was sure one of them had to be Rahimi, and that the other two were his bodyguards.

I would have guessed Rahimi was the man in the middle, but when they reached the

164

latrine, the man on the far right and the one in the middle stopped, deferring to their commander. The man closest to me went in, reappearing after a full three minutes. The other two men took their turns but were much quicker about it. It surprised me that they didn't hurry back to their beds. Instead, they took a few steps toward the camp and stopped, smoking. Apparently, they weren't worried about standing in the open, silhouetted against the light-colored sand. But why would they be? There was a truce.

It wasn't a difficult shot. Four hundred meters downhill with no wind. The light wasn't great, but I could see all three men clearly when I laid the scope on them. I shot the closest one first because I was reasonably sure that was Rahimi, then took the other two before they could scramble to safety. I didn't bother firing at the group again. I was sure. Then I pulled the gun off the rock I was using as a rest, put it to my shoulder, and shot the closest sentry. By the time I swung toward the second man, I was under fire. I ignored the wail of a bullet that hit the rock I had just been kneeling on and squeezed off two quick shots, then ducked behind a large outcropping of rock.

Below me I could see people spilling into the night and hear their shouts. I knew it wouldn't take long for them to wipe the sleep from their eyes and figure out where the shots had come from. I threw the strap of the rifle over my shoulder and started running.

I made it across the steepest part of the trail and put eight kilometers behind me before the sun came up. By then I was starting to like my chances of getting back to the camp alive, and starting to worry about the consequences of my actions. I was being pursued, but I wasn't carrying any gear and I was moving fast. You couldn't be a Ranger if you weren't in damn good shape, and I was. It didn't hurt that I have very long legs, or that I was plenty scared. I came over a steep hill and could see the village sprawled out in the foothills. I had forgotten about the road.

The road east wasn't much, but it did offer a path of lesser resistance around the perpendicular boulder strew wasteland that I had just crossed. As I topped the last hill, I picked up the dust trail of two vehicles, both four wheel-drive Toyota pickups. One had a fifty-caliber machine gun mounted in the back. At the least, they would lay down enough fire to pin me down until the men behind me caught up. Snipers behind me, a heavy gun in front. I would be trapped.

It surprised me that they would be bold enough to come after me, basically within sight of the village and a sizable contingent of Army Rangers. At the same time, it brought a smile to my face. It was a good indication that one of the men I had killed was Rahimi, and that they were mad enough to risk retaliation. I knew I might end up dead, but it seemed like a reasonable price to pay for a courtyard full of children.

I pushed on because I didn't have a choice. Once the men behind me cleared the rise, they would take advantage of their elevated position and one of their sharpshooters would kill me. Far below, I could see that the trucks had stopped at a turn in the road. They all climbed out and started pointing at me as the man in charge of the big gun swung it in my direction. I could hear the chatter from below. They were excited. Eager to extract their revenge.

I'm prejudiced, but it's my opinion that the 75th Regiment is the best fighting force in the world, mostly because the people that sacrifice and serve are among the best trained. They're also the most well equipped. I heard the howl of the shell from our RCMG passing overhead before the heavy thump of the launch. I threw myself down behind a boulder just in case, but the impact was beyond the crest of the hill.

I was still quite a distance from the base and the Taliban pickups were further yet, but the next shell hit within fifty meters of their location. Another explosion raised the dust seconds later, closer still. The misses were intentional. I knew that and so did the Taliban. After a brief argument that I was close enough to hear, they scrambled back into their vehicles and sped off back in the direction of their camp. I kept moving down the hill as fast as I could. Another shell screamed overhead, presumably to dissuade more pursuit. It landed surprisingly close.

Twenty minutes later I walked into camp under my own power. I was exhausted. I was also under arrest and stripped of my duties as commander of my squad. Under different circumstances I would have been locked up and guarded, but manpower was limited and our unit commander was an understanding guy. The captain wasn't as generous, but he had to answer to the higher ups and explain why a prominent member of the people we were trying to make peace with had been shot.

I fully expected to spend ten or twenty years in Leavenworth, and I probably should have. I had broken my promise to follow orders and not behave in a way that would discredit my unit. And, I had killed five people. Surprisingly, the fact that they had crossed the border into Pakistan and were killed there was what saved me.

Because of the continuing talks, the trial became a political football. No one wanted to admit that the Taliban camp was across the Pakistani border. Peterson and Mickey both stood up at the tribunal and lied their asses off. They claimed that I couldn't have been the one who shot the Taliban chieftain because I'd been asleep in my bunk the whole night. Nobody in the unit could explain the unprovoked attack that morning, but the 75th had used minimal force to turn back the perpetrators. Because of the truce.

Nobody believed our story, but given the circumstances, no one in the chain of command had the appetite for throwing an Army Ranger with ten years of service into prison. When it came right down to it, killing Taliban was what we were there to do. My lawyer actually thought there was a chance I'd get off with time served, but when they offered me an honorable discharge for an immediate resignation, I took the deal. By then Mickey had completed his tour and gone back to civilian life and the wife he had waiting in Las Vegas. It sounded like a good place to be.

I left the Army with very little money and some very bad memories.

Chapter Fifteen

"Nice job, Kid. Adam Cain is no saint, but he didn't deserve what you did to him."

Jimmy Olson continued standing, just in case. "Thanks for seeing me, Detective. I think you know that I had nothing to do with the video that was released. May I sit?"

Detective Murdock grunted and pointed at the same chair Jimmy had used before. "I think you're full of shit, Jimmy. But I am confused."

Jimmy risked a smile as he sat down. "Perhaps, if you'll refrain from calling me a parasite again, I can help you with that."

Murdock ignored the remark. "Young guy name of Mark Jansen showed up here the other day. He said he didn't want to go to jail for not turning over evidence. One of his buddies had called him all worked up and talked him into bringing his phone in."

"Sometimes people do unexpected things," Jimmy said.

"Maybe he had a come to Jesus moment, or maybe you twisted his arm. He did mention your name."

Jimmy shrugged. "Either way, you weren't expecting it."

Murdock nodded. "Alright. I'll admit I was a little rough on you before. I don't know if you watched what that kid had on his phone, but it wasn't the same video I saw on the television."

"Still, I didn't want you to think I'd leaked it."

"You would have put those pictures on the front page of your newspaper, not given them to the local television station."

"I've only seen the one recording, Detective."

"Well, there's more than one, obviously."

"There were a lot of people there that night. Millennials. They all grew up with a cellphone in their hand and they're quick to use them. Are you going to subpoena the television station for their records?"

"What's the point? I have several eyewitness accounts, and that recording didn't show me anything new."

"And the woman with the gun? Any idea who she is?"

Murdock grinned. "Slow down, Jimmy. I like you better than I did, but I'm not sharing information about an active investigation. Besides, I don't know anything about her."

"And the FBI, are they being helpful?"

"No, but don't put that in your newspaper. Say the investigation is being hampered because of unnecessary red tape caused by the federal government. I don't want to let the bastards off scot-free, but I've already pissed Randolph off about as much as I want to. Not that I care, but they are the FBI and they carry a big stick. Someday I might need a favor."

"Agent Collins wasn't helpful at all when I talked to him. I'm going to keep after Randolph until he agrees to see me personally."

"Great. I hope you ruin his day."

Olson grinned. "I'm not done ruining yours. What's your best guess about this woman? Obviously, she has some extraordinary abilities."

"Because she shot three men?"

"From a considerable distance, with incredible accuracy, killing the first two instantly."

"It might be better if you left that detail out of your story, Jimmy, now that we've come to the understanding that you're not a carnivorous bug. You might consider the fact that this woman wants to stay anonymous. I'd hope you don't make her sound like a professional."

Jimmy shrugged. "I suspect she is."

"Maybe, but I'd like to play nice, considering how many lives she saved. Maybe people won't dig so hard if they think she just happened to be there and got lucky. Your story is the fact that Adam Cain lied."

"He strikes me as the least guilty of anyone involved," Olson observed. "He was shooting back, and he was nearly killed. What he did was heroic, even if he didn't stop those shooters. And I'm still not convinced he remembers what happened."

Murdock shook his head. "Or he was coached, to throw me off. I don't like being lied to, not by witnesses, and not by the FBI. I'm going to find out what the deal is with that woman, and Randolph too, but I'm going to do it quietly. It would help if you downplay her involvement."

"And let the local television crew have the story? I appreciate the sudden good will, but what's in it for me?"

"They'll spend two days on Cain, then give it up. There's a bigger story here, Jimmy. The FBI is covering for this woman, and Randolph knows a hell of a lot more than he's saying. Does he know her? Does she work for the FBI or some branch of the government?" Detective Murdock was talking fast, and he leaned forward eagerly. "That could be a big deal, Jimmy. It might be your big break, your cover story. Hell, you might want to write a book."

Jimmy shrugged. "I guess I can steer the story away from the woman for now. And if Agent Randolph is involved in a coverup, that would be a big story. He must have really pissed you off."

"We're all supposed to be on the same side, and Randolph keeps hiding evidence from me. Yeah, that pisses me off."

"I want a list of everyone who was at the club that night, and I want to talk to everyone myself. Granted, the senator might not admit to being there, but I'm not going to let that stop me."

"Senator?" Murdock asked.

"Yes, senator. Don't try to con me, Detective. You know who I'm talking about. This could work out for both of us. We could work together and share information."

"I appreciate you sending that kid in here, Jimmy, but that doesn't mean I'm going to share what I know with a journalist. I have a rule about that."

"You'd be surprised how much people are willing to say when you're not a cop," Jimmy said. "I got that cellphone footage for you, and you didn't even know it existed. Those kids would never have told you everything they knew. I'd say you could use some help, since you can't get any from the FBI."

"And what is it you think I can tell you if I were inclined to break my rule?"

"I want to know who that woman is. I want to know how she ended up being there and if Agent Randolph already knew her. I want to know why Alex Gainey ended up dead. I want to know every tiny little detail of this whole damn mess, because it's important. Did that woman know what was going to happen, and if so, why didn't she stop it before all those girls died? That's the tragedy here, Detective. Thirteen young women, all under the age of twenty-five are gone. For what reason? And five of those

174

girls had little kids. Children who've lost their mother and probably don't have anyone else."

Murdock leaned back in his chair, distancing himself from the reporter. "Alright, Jimmy, calm down. Nobody is happy about all those strippers getting shot."

"Really? Because all you hear on the television is that Adam Cain lied about what he did. That shouldn't be the story, but that's all they're talking about. The little blonde covering the shooting set him up as a hero, and now she's more than happy to stick a knife in his back. For ratings. She's more worried about getting her time in front of the camera than telling the truth."

Murdock nodded seriously. "Blood sucking little parasite, right, Jimmy?"

Olson snorted out a laugh. "Point taken, Detective. And I guess I owe you something for pointing that out to me. But I've heard too many horrific stories about that night to not take this seriously. It is a big story, but I don't want to sensationalize it. I want the facts. I want to know why it happened, who's responsible, who's covering up what, and why. No bullshit, no fake news, just the facts."

Murdock raised a brow. "Wow, Jimmy. Did I misjudge you?"

Jimmy studied the detective carefully. "Was that sarcasm? Because I really can't tell. And

175

don't get me wrong, I just might write that book."

"And I just might read it," Murdock said, tapping a few keys on his desktop. He retrieved two pages from the printer that sat in the corner of his office and handed them to Olson. "Let's start small. Here's a list of the victims, and everyone we know of that was there that night. Don't make me regret this. You didn't get this from me, and we never had this conversation."

"And you'll share what you learn about the mystery woman?"

"You scratch my back...then we'll see. I know very little about her, but it's obvious she's dangerous. Maybe she is someone's hired gun and she'll come after you if you start digging too much."

The reporter objected. "You said you don't think she's a hired gun!"

"But I'm not always right. I am pretty sure there's more going on here than just the one shooting, bad as it was."

"Not just one. Now there's Gainey."

"Adam Cain paid him a visit at the club and I'm told it got heated. And according to his military file, Cain's got a nasty temper. But he's not the kind of guy to shoot someone in cold blood. Plus, he had an alibi. I don't know for sure that Gainey's killing is connected to the shooting at the Exotic, but the timing is suspicious. I have one other person of interest, a father upset because his daughter was working as a stripper. A guy like Gainey probably upset a lot of people. It may be a long list before I'm done."

"In the interest of cooperation, were you informed that Gainey might have talked to one of the shooters a few days before the incident?"

Murdock nodded. "I got that memo from Randolph. Unfortunately, it was the day before Gainey was killed. I have other cases and I didn't get to him soon enough."

"More suspicious timing?"

"I doubt it was intentional. Another case of the FBI not doing their job."

"You really don't like Agent Randolph much, do you?"

Murdock sighed and looked at his watch. "I like my job, Jimmy, and I'm pretty good at it. But mostly I don't have time for people. And that's because when I do my job, I see the worst of them. I definitely don't like people that make my job harder, which Randolph is doing. So don't make my job harder, Jimmy, and we'll get along just fine. Now, go away. I'm a busy man."

Jimmy grinned and stood up. This time the detective took the handshake he offered.

Agent Randolph peered across the conference table at his understudy. "Did you file your report about that kidnapping in Yuma?"

"I did, Sir. Not a good ending to that story. Another naïve college kid thinking he could outsmart a drug smuggler and the cartel. He crossed the border, then ended up back in this country sometime early yesterday morning. Unfortunately, the missing person's report was moot by the time I got there. They found his body in a ditch on 95, just north of San Luis. His hands were zip-tied behind his back, and his throat had been slit."

"That sends a message."

"Indeed. I'm just wondering, because I haven't fully unpacked from my time at home yet, but will I be staying here for a while? Here, being Las Vegas?"

"Just a couple more days. I want you to sit down with Murdock again and see what you can get out of him about Alex Gainey's murder. It's his case, but it has to tie in with the shooting at the club." Randolph slid a folder across the table. "Have you read the report? According to the Martinez woman, Gainey met with one of the shooters a few days before the incident."

"And you'll be tied up?" Collins asked cautiously.

Randolph grinned. "I'll find something to do. You said your last meeting with Detective Murdock went well, and it'll give you another chance to work on your people skills."

"I doubt he'll want us involved since it appears to be a simple homicide."

"Nothing simple about that homicide, Collins, not considering all the circumstances. You can volunteer our help and smooth things over with him. He's still pissed about the cellphone thing, and I guess I can't blame him."

"Obviously, at this point, he knows about the woman's involvement."

"You saw the news this morning?"

"I did," Collins replied, closing the folder he'd been scanning, "and the interview with Mister Cain. He didn't seem happy."

"The good news is that he's ready to cooperate."

"You mean return to New York with Jennifer Mercer? She must be very persuasive."

Randolph glanced up and frowned. "He might have gone anyway. He owns property there, and he's not very popular in Vegas right now. I'd say Jenny is pretty damn loyal to stick with him, all things considered."

"Sorry. You did say she was the key."

"I did. We need them to stay together long enough to see this thing through, then I hope she kicks him to the curb. He doesn't deserve her."

"Their relationship is troubled?" Collins asked. He continued before his boss could respond. "I'm not gossiping, I'm just trying to understand the dynamic, should I be tasked with dealing with Mister Cain in the future. He's an imposing individual. I don't think I'd want to be on the receiving end of his ire."

"No, I don't think you would. He's been known to hurt people when he's upset. As far as the Mercer girl, she wants things he isn't capable of. Not our business, but I suspect she'll tough it out for a while if they go back to New York together. Hopefully they'll last long enough for Cain to establish a relationship with her brother and work his way into the organization. I took advantage of his friend's death to motivate him."

"Sounds more like vinegar than honey, Sir."

Randolph allowed himself a smile. "It's not a good example of how I'd like things done, Collins. Do as I say, not as I do. It's a lousy way to get him involved, but he's absolutely our best bet."

Collins smiled. "Our best bet of nailing Frank Mercer, or of seeing the Gypsy again?"

"Cain wants to see the Gypsy as much as I do. She has that effect on people. Men, at least." Randolph looked up again. "Are you making fun of me, Collins?"

"No, Sir," Collins said, then chuckled. "Maybe a little, Sir. You've said this Gypsy woman is quite beautiful. Jennifer Mercer is very attractive too, don't you think?"

Randolph's frown deepened. "Why are we having this conversation?"

"People skills, Sir. I'm trying to understand Mister Cain's motivation. And...yours."

"I'm not obsessed with the Gypsy, Collins. She's just another riddle. Like the crosswords."

"And Jennifer Mercer?"

"Another piece of the puzzle. Understood?"

Collins nodded, burying his grin. "Yes, Sir. If you say so."

Chapter Sixteen

"I quit my job at the newspaper," Olson said, trying his best to get comfortable on the wooden chair in the detective's spartan office. "Why don't you have decent furniture in here for people to sit on?"

Detective Murdock scratched his two-day-old stubble and tossed his pen down. "If I had a better chair, more people would come in here telling me things I don't care about. How does you quitting your minimum wage job have anything to do with me?"

"They insisted I drop the story about the shooting because it didn't happen in Los Angeles, and because no celebrities were involved." Murdock crossed his arms and scratched his chin again. Olson shrugged. "They didn't really say the part about the celebrities, but they did say I needed to stick to more positive and relevant stories. Fluff, in other words. This story is relevant, and you were right, that newspaper is trash."

"And what are you going to do for money?"

"As soon as we solve this case, the book will sell itself."

"We? There is no we, Jimmy. When you were a member of the press, I was somewhat obligated to talk to you. Now, not so much."

"I have an appointment to see Agent Collins this afternoon. Shall I give him your regards? Any questions I can ask the FBI for you?"

"Collins and I get along pretty well now, Jimmy. It's Randolph that chaps my ass. But, okay, you're really going to write a book? An expose about the corruption you found in the FBI, I hope."

"We'll have to see. I really should thank you, Detective. You mentioned the idea, and the more I thought about it, the more I liked it. I have a couple of interviews, but finding a job in my line of work will be challenging. I'll keep looking, but I have savings and I really think this is a story worth telling. I know a few people in the publishing industry, so who knows?"

"So far there isn't much to write about. A lot of dead ends."

"Come on, Detective. Give me something. Randolph went back to New York, so I have to deal with Collins. Any bets on whether or not Randolph knows the woman on that tape? I still can't believe he didn't share what he knew about her with you."

"Don't stir the pot, Jimmy. Any luck with the names I gave you?"

"Same story over and over. No more videos, but a couple more descriptions of the woman that were interesting. Beautiful, long black hair, probably mixed race. She was sitting at the bar for quite a while talking to Adam Cain before the shooting, and they were being pretty chummy. Did you ask him about her when you interviewed him?"

Murdock shook his head. "I didn't. Did you?"

"I wasn't aware of the woman when I interviewed Mister Cain, but I presume you were. I didn't have a complete witness list, but after some of my recent conversations, I know you were told of her existence. That, and the fact that she killed at least one of the shooters."

"Okay, Jimmy, you got me. But I didn't ask Cain about her. I was hoping he'd volunteer that information. He said he saw a woman sitting at the bar, but not that he talked to her."

"And he never said a word about her to me."

Murdock grinned. "He's probably one of those guys that doesn't trust reporters."

Jimmy didn't laugh. "That's everyone these days. Why wouldn't you bring him in if he lied to you?"

"He would have just said he was traumatized by the shooting and couldn't remember anything. I'm sure Randolph put him up to it. Besides, I already knew about the woman. I've been known to tell a fib or two in my day too."

"Now I'm intrigued. What are you talking about?"

"This is off the record, book or no book," Murdock said. Jimmy nodded and the detective continued. "I watched the security footage before the FBI got ahold of it. They redacted the part with the woman in it, but I knew about her from the start."

"It wouldn't be unusual for the FBI, or the police, to not reveal something like that to the public," Jimmy pointed out. "But it came out anyway. Partially because of my reporting, I might add."

Murdock snorted. "Bob Woodward you're not, kid. But here's what's interesting. The video that was on television wasn't from a random cellphone. And, it was the unedited version."

"It was the original footage from the security cameras?" Jimmy asked. "Holy shit."

"Yeah, Jimmy. Holy shit." Murdock grinned across his desk as the reporter connected the dots.

"Someone from the FBI leaked it to expose the woman? But why? Maybe she's stopped cooperating."

"I have Adam Cain's contact information in case I need to get ahold of him," Murdock said casually. "He's from New York originally, and he's moved back there. I guess he got tired of people yelling at him here in Vegas."

"You think they leaked that video to discredit Cain?" Jimmy asked.

"I don't know why that tape came out, but I know it's the same footage I saw from the security cameras. Collins supposedly took it back to the Bureau and Randolph and some higher-ups decided what to redact before they gave it back to me. When I got it back, all the shots of the woman were gone. But why use it to run Cain out of town? Granted, there may have been another reason to leak it, but that's certainly the most logical."

"Why are you telling me all this?" Jimmy asked. "Aren't you breaking your rule about reporters?"

"You said you quit, and I want a favorable mention in that book." Murdock chuckled and waved a hand. "Not really. But look, obviously the FBI isn't being straight with me. I don't know if it's Randolph, or Collins, or both. Did they just want Cain out of Vegas, or was the intent to get him to go to New York? Were they hoping he'd move back there, or did they send him? And why?"

Jimmy didn't know why the detective was being so cooperative, but he leaned into it. "Do you think Cain knew who that woman was before that night? Maybe they're friends."

"Exactly. She's the key to this whole mess, Jimmy. At the very least, I'm guessing she knows why those men were at the Exotic."

"And you want my help in finding her?"

Murdock nodded. "And I think I know where to start looking. Which makes it all the more interesting."

Jimmy's smile grew. "You're being serious? You want me to help you investigate?"

"I didn't say that. But you are writing that book and it's a free country. If you wanted to go to Boston and check out this woman's relatives, I couldn't stop you."

"You've identified relatives?"

"One for sure, probably more. Her DNA was all over the coat she wrapped Adam Cain in. Nothing came up on her, but she has a close relative that's in the FBI's database. He was a murder suspect, but he was released for lack of evidence. He's an older guy, so probably a cousin or an uncle. Two degrees of separation at least. And it took some digging to find him. He runs a bakery now, of all things."

"A murder suspect?" Jimmy's eyes widened. "And I'm supposed to go talk to him? This woman's relative is a murderer and she might be a professional assassin. All of a sudden writing about the Kardashians doesn't sound so bad."

Murdock frowned. "Then go back to Los Angeles and give up on your book, Jimmy. Continue being a loser."

"That's inspiring," Jimmy said dryly. "No, I'm committed to writing about this case, Detective Murdock, and it sounds like you want someone to do the leg work for you. But people are dead, and I think Alex Gainey was killed because he knew something. It's reasonable to be cautious."

The detective waved his hand dismissively. "As far as I can tell, the woman is clean. She did shoot three armed killers, but that was basically self-defense. And this relative of hers was accused of killing some drug-dealer that nobody's going to miss. Truth be told, I don't think the cops in Boston tried very hard to convict him. I doubt you'll be in any danger. Figuring out who this woman is and where to find her would be big. Worst case, you might get tossed out of the bakery and not find out anything. Either way, bring me back some fresh bagels."

"You don't think I'll be in danger?" Jimmy asked.

"No." Murdoc grinned at the young reporter. "But like I said, I'm not always right."

"And if the FBI finds out I'm investigating this? They have to know about this woman's relative, don't they? Won't they be watching him?"

"I have the woman's coat in my evidence locker. I told Collins I'd trade him for the cell phones they impounded, but he won't budge, or Randolph won't. No one has handed me a subpoena yet, so I think we know something they don't. Why are you meeting with Collins?"

"Just reviewing some of what I've already been told. Can you tell me anything about Alex Gainey's murder?"

"He put all kinds of new security equipment in his strip club, but he didn't bother with a camera at his house. And he was between girlfriends, or strippers, so he was alone. No sign of forced entry means he probably knew the shooter. It wasn't the pissed-off father, because he had an alibi, like Cain. If I knew who hired the first four shooters, I might have some luck figuring out who did it. But of course, if I knew who killed Alex Gainey, I might know who sent those idiots to his club."

"I'll see what Collins has to say about it," Jimmy said.

"You haven't talked to me if he asks. Got that?"

"I thought it was Randolph you don't like."

"Birds of a feather, Jimmy. I don't trust Collins either."

"I still don't understand why Agent Randolph is protecting this woman," Jimmy mused.

"Find out who she is, Jimmy. Then maybe we'll both know."

Chapter Seventeen

After my mother passed away, we moved downstate into a duplex that my father bought from my mother's long-lost uncle. It came with a tenant in residence, my equally long-lost grandmother who agreed to take me in when my father was deployed. And he was always deployed. Now they were both gone and the place belonged to me.

"I take it your father wasn't much of a carpenter," Jenny said after a brief tour. Always the optimist, she grinned at me. "We can fix it up. It'll be great."

"He really let the place go after my grandmother died. He always drank a lot, but the last time I was home it looked like that was all he did. I mentioned treatment and he threw me out. He died a month before I was discharged. I was tied up with the court-martial by then, so I didn't even make it home. There was nothing I could have done anyway."

"I'm sorry. My father was no prize either. And he was always gone too."

"Your brother seems like a good guy."

"Mostly, but he's a workaholic, same as my dad was. He asked me about the trouble you had in Afghanistan. You said to tell him if he asked, so I did. I thought those records were sealed."

"I thought so too. Luckily, he's an understanding guy." Jenny knew most of my history, some of what I'd told her and some of what Mickey had told Justine. Mickey had pointed out that honesty is important in a relationship. Whether he was talking about his relationship or mine wasn't clear.

Both Mickey and the Gypsy's advice aside, I didn't feel very good about all the lying I'd been doing to Jenny. If Jack had been the target of the shooting, maybe it was like I hoped, maybe he'd just got stuck in the middle of something. I sure had.

"My sister tells me you're going to be very busy for the next few days," Jack Mercer said, motioning toward the high-backed leather chair in front of his desk. Mercer Security was in a sizable building on the north end of the city. Bigger and far more pretentious than I had imagined. Jack's office was spacious and faced south, high enough to afford an admittedly breathtaking view of the brick and glass cluster of technology that was Manhattan.

"We're still trying to make my dad's old place livable," I said as I took a seat. "And I'm told we need to spend a couple of days seeing the sights before I start my new job."

He shrugged and laughed. "We have enough people, so there's no hurry. Jenny did say that you're off limits until next week. I'm just glad she's back here, so I'm not going to argue with her. I never win those arguments anyway. She's my baby sister, and I'd do anything for her. It's great that you two could move back here together."

"I didn't realize she missed New York as much as she did. It didn't take her long to pack once I suggested we get out of Vegas."

"Rotten deal the way that town turned on you. Jenny said you told them a dozen times you didn't think you shot those guys, but no one would believe you. I still think it was crazy that I happened to be there that night."

"Yeah, crazy," I said. "I was going to ask you about it during our video chat, but I didn't know if I should, what with Jenny sitting right there."

"That wasn't the first time I'd been to a strip club, and she knows that. Still, I don't imagine she'd want to hear the details of the shooting. I usually carry, but I didn't want to hassle with the airlines, so I left my gun at home. Maybe a good thing I did. I can shoot, but I probably would've gotten myself killed. Ironically, I was in town for a gun show."

"Jenny said you two talked while I was in the hospital."

"Thank you again for what you did. And I don't mean to be insensitive. I'm really sorry about your friend Mickey. We were all lucky that you were both there, and armed. I'm not the gun nut some of my friends are, but if somebody is shooting at me, I think I have the right to shoot back. It's lucky that woman was there, from the sound of it. Any idea who she was?"

"She was sitting down the bar from me, but that's about all I remember." I didn't know Jack Mercer, other than the hour we'd spent talking on Skype, but I already liked him. It didn't strike me as odd that he would ask about the Gypsy, because after the video came out, everyone had. I told him what everyone else already knew. "Whoever she is, she could shoot. I'm told it was my gun that killed three of those guys. I might have hit the first one, maybe one of the other three, but like I said, I don't remember anything after I got shot."

"Maybe the cops will figure it out and find her. I'd like to thank her personally," he said.

"Me too," I agreed. He lifted a single piece of paper from the top of a pile on the corner of his desk and looked down at it, suddenly more serious.

"I pulled your military records. No big surprises. Jenny already told me about the trouble you had over there and about the court-martial. Any thoughts or comments?"

"The men I killed were terrorists. They killed forty-six civilians, most of them women and children, with a car bomb. I disobeyed orders when I went after them, but they were rotten orders. I'd do it again in a heartbeat."

He looked down at the paper again. "And the other incident?"

"A couple of our guys were disgracing their uniforms. I stopped them."

He glanced up at me. "We have a training officer. He'll go over the concept of reasonable response and proportional force when a client is threatened. I don't want you tossing someone through a window because they pulled out a selfie-stick."

I grinned. "I wouldn't do that."

He was all business. "Just remember, contrary to what you might have heard, New York City is not a war zone. It isn't likely you'll ever have a reason to hospitalize or shoot anyone, so try to restrain yourself. Eventually I'd like to get you on one of the bank trucks. The bonding company never said a word about your military record, so there's no reason you won't be able to start right away, or as soon as my sister gets through with you."

"Given the choice, I'd start tomorrow. But she did take care of me after the shooting, so it's only fair I play tourist with her for a few days."

"And you two are good? I know it was touch and go there for a while. It's not my business exactly, but she is my sister."

I shrugged. "Someday she'll come to her senses and give me the boot."

The crooked smile came back. "I'm thirty-six, I have two ex-wives, and a girlfriend that hasn't spoken to me in weeks. I have no room to talk." He hesitated, then continued awkwardly. "I understand your friend Mickey was married?"

"Yeah. He said it would always be Justine, till death, and all the rest of the things you say when you marry someone. Turned out he was right."

"I wish I'd brought my gun with me," he said solemnly. "Maybe it would have distracted them enough to change things."

"Gainey told me something odd about that night," I said. Jack looked up, more curious than guarded. "Was there anyone in that VIP room that had a gun? Maybe a bodyguard?"

He shrugged. "I couldn't say for sure. It was two rooms really. They had a temporary divider up because there was a private party in the back half of the room. Who was back there?"

"I don't know," I lied. "I just know that Gainey said there was someone in there with a security detail. Just one guy, but he was armed. Did Gainey let you out the side door of the VIP room after it was all over?"

"No, we went out the front. By the time I walked outside they already had cops talking to everyone, getting names and phone numbers and taking statements. That side door was locked."

"I guess Gainey unlocked it so this person didn't have to face the music. If he had security, and they had a gun, they could have stepped up too. Like you said, one more gun might have made the difference. It's possible Mickey would still be alive."

He frowned in my direction. "You're not going to let this go, are you?"

"No. Would you?"

He didn't answer, just stood and extended his hand. "Monday. Give me until nine o'clock to get things rolling, then I'll give you the grand tour and introduce you to a couple of the guys you'll be working with. And I wasn't kidding about the training officer. You'll spend the first day with Captain Gregory learning the ropes."

"Captain?" I asked.

"Not a real Captain, but everyone calls him Cap or Captain, because he runs the meetings at the gun club. His real name is Matt." He waved his hand dismissively and chuckled as I backed toward the door. "He'll tell you all about it. He's always looking for new recruits."

It didn't sound sinister the way Jack said it.

I was ten years old when the Twin Towers fell. I remember it was a weekday and I was at home because I either had the flu or I was doing a good job of faking it. I do remember being on the couch, drenched in sweat and covered by a sizable pile of blankets, so probably not faking it. I also remember the dread in my mother's voice when she answered the telephone that morning and watching her rush into the living room to change the channel on the television.

As everyone in America knows, it was horrific. And more so in real time. My mother's shock overwhelmed her maternal instincts, and I watched as several people leapt to their death rather than be burned alive. I suspect someone at the network finally had the good sense to self-censor the graphic coverage, but the carnage went on and on. Everyone, including me, knew the fate of anyone trapped on those upper floors. Then the second plane hit and it all started again.

It was a defining few hours for the country, and for me. It defied the budding sense of machismo that pubescent boys generally have when watching someone else's tragedy. It was astounding and transformational, and when my mother wept, I wept with her. When the towers came down my mother sat beside me, holding my hand as we watched with gut-wrenching fascination and macabre wonder. Oddly, the memory of my mother's tears as we watched it happen are among the most vivid I have of her. It would take years for me to learn to compartmentalize the hate I felt on that day.

Inevitably, and because everyone over the age of twenty-five has some memory of it, the 911 memorial is on the must-see list of everyone who visits New York, and sooner or later, everyone who lives in the city. Shunning it is like turning your back on a page of American history. It's unpatriotic. You might as well go to Washington DC and not stand in front of the Lincoln Memorial. Jenny wasn't about to be one of the outliers who broke with tradition.

I did manage to convince her that we should visit the site during the week, when the crowds would be smaller. We decided on Thursday, and it was our first stop. She had tickets that covered the museum, the memorial, and several other touristy spots that the natives all took for granted and usually didn't bother with.

Or maybe that was just me. I'd spent eight years living within a hundred miles of the city and never bothered to cross the river for a Yankees game, much less go to a Broadway show. All that was about to change if Jenny had her way. She had spent a week sitting beside my hospital bed, so I'd made up my mind to go along and not complain.

We got to the site half an hour early and stood in a short line until they opened. By then, the line behind us was considerably longer than the dozen people that had arrived before us. Early March in New York can be mild, or not. It was definitely not. It was bitterly cold, and the wind howled down between the pillars of steel and glass that stretched above us, ushering the worst of the gusts to street-level and tossing bits of sand and grime against our faces until we were forced to turn our backs to the gale.

We spent an hour and a half in the museum, learning the particulars of a day that most people would like to forget. Then we slipped out and made our way up to the reflecting ponds. We walked the perimeter of the south pool, but the crowds were growing, and we couldn't get within a dozen feet of the railing. The second location, where the North Tower had stood, was less crowded and the wind less severe.

New York, even more than the nation as a whole, is a melting pot of humanity. The times of unequivocal welcome are no more in this country, if they ever truly existed, but big cities by their nature are overflowing with a variety of people and cultures. There was a time when that was considered a good thing by many, and at the very least, interesting by most. Considering the reason for the memorial, it was understandable to me that New Yorkers would perceive outsiders with a certain degree of skepticism. Like me, it had taken them a while to compartmentalize the fact that everyone who wore a headscarf wasn't the enemy.

Tribalism is ingrained in our DNA, and I'd seen my share of it, both in the Army and in Afghanistan. The crowd at the North Reflection Pool was diverse, but everyone there shared in the quiet respect that people have for the dead.

People were talking, but in hushed tones that were whisked away quickly by the wind. If you weren't standing right next to someone it was hard to hear them, and no one was willing to shout. We were all bundled up, wearing long coats and hats, some with winter parkas that included hoods. Some with scarves, some with hijabs. All with our backs to the wind.

She was there, standing just a few strides beyond Jenny with her head down and a scarf covering most of her face. She had on a short jacket that revealed the bottom half of a black dress and black leggings that were pulled over heeled boots, boosting her already considerable height. That alone should have triggered my memory, but she might as well have been someone from high school that I hadn't seen in twenty years. I thought I should know her, but without proper context, my memory failed me. Then the wind shifted slightly, sending her delicate scent in our direction. It was the same fragrance she had worn the night of the shooting.

There are physiological reasons why odor triggers such vivid memories, brain chemistry and the shared pathways of the olfactory senses, but it's much more satisfying to romanticize the connection. I was staring at her over the top of Jenny's head when it finally dawned on me who I was looking at. I'm sure my expression went from curiosity, to surprise, to excitement in a matter of moments. Jenny saw that on my face. She spun quickly and appraised the woman standing to her right.

The Gypsy continued staring down at the names etched in the black granite directly in front of her. Only the top half of her face was showing, but her eyes were full, and the wind hadn't dried her cheeks. Her left hand, gloveless and white-knuckled, rested on the granite plaque. It was shaking. Perhaps from the cold, perhaps not.

Jenny stepped away from me, closer to the monument and closer to the Gypsy. She reached out slowly and rested her mittened hand on the taller woman's bare fingers for a moment, then covered the Gypsy's whole hand with both of her own. The Gypsy rolled her hand over as Jenny slid closer. They stood like that for a few quiet minutes, bodies pressed together, hands clasped for warmth, both staring down at the names in front of them.

Finally, Jenny spoke. "Did you lose people that day? Someone close to you?"

"My mother and father," the Gypsy said quietly, nodding at the plaque. "They were above the impact zone. There was no coming down from there."

Jenny said the only thing you can at such a time. "I am so sorry."

I stayed where I was, three paces away, as we all mourned the loss of the Gypsy's parents and the nearly three thousand other people who had perished on that day. The wind picked up again, but we stood resolute and quiet, each wrapped in our own thoughts and winter wear. We stood there for twenty minutes. No one spoke, and Jenny's hands never moved. After a few minutes I moved to stand beside Jenny, but neither woman acknowledged my presence.

The fact that the Gypsy was there should have surprised me. In all of New York, on the coldest day in March, she had picked the exact place and time as we had to visit the Memorial. I thought I knew the reality. She must have arranged it somehow with Jenny. Certainly, there was no changing the names on that plaque, and I was pretty sure that she had been standing there when Jenny and I walked up. Coincidences that big don't just happen. Perhaps, as Randolph had suggested, Jenny knew more than she was saying.

The Gypsy kept her head down and never looked in my direction. I risked a couple of glances, but bundled up as she was, there was no eye contact. She offered no hint that she knew me or that she had arranged this impromptu meeting. I decided to follow her lead, if that's what it was.

After a particularly biting blast from the north, she extracted her hand from under Jenny's and stepped back. Her eyes never wavered from Jenny's face. "Thank you for your understanding. You're very kind."

"It was nothing," Jenny said. "Take care of yourself."

With a nod, the Gypsy turned and started to walk away.

I wanted to call out and ask her what this surprise encounter meant, or ask if I would ever see her again. But I wasn't completely sure that Jenny knew who she was so I held back. Jenny didn't.

"Gabriel," she called, above the breeze.

The tall woman turned, walking backwards for a couple of steps, then stopped.

"Thank you," Jenny said.

The Gypsy tipped her head. "Why are you thanking me?"

"My brother was there that terrible night at the Exotic." Jenny nodded in my direction, and a hint of a smile appeared. "And you managed to keep this one alive. That couldn't have been easy."

The Gypsy still didn't look in my direction. She held Jenny's gaze. "He's in over his head. Keep yourself safe, Jenny. You're in the middle of this too, so be careful who you trust."

Jenny's response only confused me more. "I trust you. And don't worry, I won't tell anyone I've met you."

"Thank you. That may be important before this is over. Goodbye for now. Cain." She nodded her head at each of us, then turned and walked away.

Without a word to me, Jenny tucked her hands in her pockets and started walking. My legs are considerably longer than hers, but I had to hurry to keep up with her. I chased after her for a couple of blocks, then risked a question.

"Where are we going? You already passed the train station."

"I'm hungry." Judging by her tone, she wasn't happy. I followed in silence. It seemed to me that if anyone deserved to be upset, it should be me.

The restaurant preferred reservations but the lunch rush was still an hour away. We sat down and the waiter gave us coffee and menus. I wrapped my cold hands around the hot cup and waited for an explanation. None came.

"Why are you angry?" I finally asked.

"Why didn't you say something?"

"It wasn't the time or the place. And you two were having a moment."

"Were you ever going to tell me who she was?"

"Like you didn't know," I scoffed. She started to respond, then dropped her head and studied the menu. I gave it a minute, then asked. "Did she call you?"

"Me? I've never talked to her before. I presumed you set it up, since she's involved somehow."

"She knows a lot about the shooting," I said. "Things that the cops don't know. But she didn't call me, and I have no idea how to call her. Would you like to look at my phone?"

"Do you want to see mine?" she asked, then brought her eyes up. They were red and misty. "That's what it's come to? We can't trust each other? Did she follow us to New York? And how could she possibly have been there this morning if you didn't talk to her?"

"I haven't talked to her since that night at the hospital, in Las Vegas."

"We ended up standing within a dozen feet of her parents' names. How did that happen?" Jenny asked. "Unless she was lying, and those weren't her parents. But she'd been crying."

"She did seem upset," I agreed. "I don't know her last name, do you?"

"Of course not," she snapped, then lowered her voice. "I really think those were her parents' names. She was standing there when we walked up."

"I didn't notice," I said, then dug in. "But, Jenny, you knew who she was."

"Are you calling me a liar?" Several heads turned and she lowered her voice. "Look, it doesn't matter. It happened. I saw you looking at her and I put it together. She has to be six-four, for Christ's sake. Not many women are that tall, and I remembered you talking about how impressively long her legs were. Or maybe that was Teddy. You're both so fucking obsessed with the woman."

I wasn't going to let that pass. "Oh right, Agent Randolph. I keep forgetting you two are such great friends. How much did he tell you?"

She stared down at the table, suddenly cautious. "Nothing. Just that he knew about her before the shooting and that she's God's gift to the human race. Men in particular."

"That's all he said? And you two had coffee again?"

"He had more questions. About Jack, mostly. But he said the same thing that Gabriel did just now, that I need to be careful about who I trust. Why do I need to be careful, Adam?"

It was a fair question. I asked my own. "Why was your brother at the Exotic that night?"

She shrugged. "Why does any guy go to a strip club? He was in town with a bunch of his friends and he'd just gotten divorced."

It was dangerous ground. I didn't want her asking Jack too many questions and I didn't know how much of it would get back to Randolph. Jenny knew more than she was saying, I was sure of that. But then the Gypsy knew more than she was saying, and so did

Randolph. I only knew one thing. I was in over my head.

"That's why you're here, isn't it?" Jenny asked, half a breath from an epiphany. "You didn't come here because of your dad's house, or because you wanted to be with me, or to get away from Las Vegas. You came to New York to figure out who's responsible for Mickey's death, and to see Gabriel again."

"All of the above, Jenny." I admitted. "And to keep you safe. And maybe to keep Jack safe too."

"Or to put him in jail," she hissed.

"That would be Randolph's job," I quoted the agent. "Look, none of us knows why those guys walked into the Exotic and started shooting that night, but Randolph is trying to figure it out and I'm trying to help him. I don't know about the Gypsy, but she's involved somehow. Right now, you seem to know more about what she's doing here than I do, or was all that at the Memorial just woman's intuition?"

"I told you, Adam. I've never talked to her before and I had no idea she would be there today."

I couldn't let it go. "But you led us right up to that spot, Jenny, and we ended up standing right next to her."

"There were people everywhere else, and it was the only place left to stand. I don't know how that happened or how she knew to be there. I only knew who she was because of the way you looked at her."

"How did I look at her?" I asked, exasperated.

"Like you've never looked at me," she said levelly, then picked up her napkin and wiped at her eyes.

The maître d was giving us sour looks. I studied my menu. "I'm sorry, but it's not like I have it all figured out. I came back here for a lot of reasons, but a big part of it was because I care about you. I knew you wanted to move back here, and I thought fixing up my dad's house would give us some time to be together."

"Until you moved on," she said bitterly.

"Until we figure out who's behind this."

"And then what?"

"Then we'll figure out us. First things first, Jenny. I want you to be safe. Somehow, you and your brother are tied to what happened at the Exotic. I don't think it was an accident that it happened the night Jack was there."

Her voice cracked. "And my father? Was his death an accident?"

"How would I know that?" I asked. Not lying to her was becoming more and more difficult. She was starting to piece things together, and Randolph wasn't likely to thank me for that.

"Teddy knows, doesn't he?" she asked.

I was tired of hearing her call him Teddy, and my response was loud. "Ask him yourself, the next time you two have coffee!"

She sat quietly for a full minute, then closed her menu. "I'm done," she said. "You don't get to act jealous of Agent Randolph. We both know it isn't real. You have to feel something for someone to be jealous, and you're not capable of it. Not for me at least."

She read the look on my face more accurately than I would have hoped for. "Don't worry, I won't screw up the investigation, or whatever you and Gabriel have cooked up. I trust my brother, but if he's in danger then I trust you to help him. Do it for Mickey if not for me."

This time it hurt, and I said as much. "I want us to try, Jenny. I really do care about you."

She sat with her head down, pulling nervously at the corners of the discarded menu. She hadn't expected even this much resistance.

"It's too late. You said it yourself, Adam. You don't believe that things can last. Maybe they can't, but I want someone who's at least willing to believe that they might. I need at least that. Jack has an extra bedroom. I'll tell him we're just taking some time apart and that he still needs to hire you. Whatever you think you can find out from him, I won't interfere. And I won't tell him what you're up to."

"Are you sure about this?" I asked.

"I said I'd tell you when I couldn't do this anymore and that time is now."

This time I knew there would be no changing it. I threw some money on the table, nodded to the waiter who had finally appeared, then followed her out of the restaurant.

Chapter Eighteen

The woman known as the Gypsy walked quickly across the small opening on the south end of the park, then ducked to her left and followed a bike trail. She always had the cab drop her off near the greenspace. It was a poor place to be after midnight, but it was close to the quiet neighborhood that she had called home for the last eighteen months. It was a short walk, and she had eluded more than one tail by slipping into the small clusters of trees that were scattered throughout the large greenspace. Not that the park wasn't usually safe, and not that she had much to fear, but she had been followed on more than one occasion. They were watching her movements, closing their perimeter.

It was a good neighborhood. Peaceful. Full of two car garages and mini-vans, swing-sets, and laughing children. Her house had shutters on the windows and a picket fence, a pool in the back yard that she never used and a Jeep Wrangler in the garage with fifteen hundred miles on it. She was seldom home, but she knew she would miss it when she had to move again.

She followed the bike trail until she neared the street, then walked a hundred feet to the north and pushed into the shadows of a short, bushy tree. Her hair and clothing matched her surroundings, dark. She stood there quietly for ten minutes, resisting the temptation to bounce her legs or hurry because of the chill in the air as she watched the trail behind her and the rest of the park for any signs of movement. She never varied her vigilance; it was a part of her.

Satisfied, she continued down the bike path and crossed the quiet street, then followed an alley to the next block. This was her street, her neighborhood, her safe place. She was only a hundred yards from her door when she heard the crush of landscape rock behind her. The sound was close.

She bolted instantly, stretching to a full run before the man reaching for her could close the distance. Men. There were two sets of shoes hitting the sidewalk a dozen paces behind her. She ran for a full block, twisting and dodging, expecting the impact of a bullet at any minute. When it didn't come, she stretched her legs and adjusted her pace. There was only one set of shoes softly scuffing the street behind her now. Tennis shoes, she guessed. She risked a glance over her shoulder, then redoubled her efforts.

"Of all the nights for this to happen," she muttered to herself. The fleeter of her would-be assailants had lost a little ground, and the shorter, stockier of the two was at least a dozen yards behind them. They weren't the professionals she was expecting. "Kids," she muttered.

Not kids really, but young men. Not professionals, but up to no good. Dangerous in their own way for most women alone at night. At the very least they wanted money, and considering the length of the chase, probably more. Money might not satisfy them, and it was possible that had never been the intent. Maybe it had been about rape from the start.

On any other night she would have slowed her breathing, stretched out, and left her pursers behind. But not tonight. Tonight, she was angry and hurting. Sharing that seemed fair.

They crossed a side street fully three blocks from where they'd started, and she recognized the empty house for sale on the corner. It was a suitable place to make her stand. There was a short chain fence across the front yard, and the back yard faced the alley. She surged forward, then turned into the yard and easily cleared the fence before running into the shadow of the two-story building.

The first man came over the fence behind her as the slower of the two rounded the house and ran toward the alley, intent on cutting off her escape. The lankier man cleared the fence without missing a beat collided with the Gypsy's forearm as she clotheslined him in the throat. He went down hard, slamming the back of his head on the stone pavers the realtor had suggested to speed the sale of the house. When the second man rounded the corner and plunged into the shadows, the Gypsy was already in the air. He was coming straight at her and she planted a solid kick in the center of his face, breaking his nose and sending him to the ground beside his unconscious partner.

Bleeding and groggy, the shorter of the two watched as the Gypsy plucked a wallet from his partner's back pocket, then retrieved a knife from his jacket. The taller man moaned, then rolled over on his back, dazed. "Stay down," she said. She motioned to the second man. "I need your wallet."

His response was a string of expletives and the first man rocked forward, trying to get to his feet. The Gypsy planted her boot on his neck and slammed him to the ground again.

"I'm going to kill you, bitch," the bleeder said, trying to get to his feet.

"Not likely," she declared, shifting from the shadow. A long arm came up and there was a gun in her hand. She brandished the weapon and repeated her demand. "I said, wallet."

"Go to hell," he shouted, flailing as he fell back to the ground.

"Wallet," she said again. When he didn't respond she pulled the trigger. Fortunately, the pavers didn't extend to that part of the yard. The bullet buried itself in the dirt between his legs, perilously close to their intersection.

"Jesus, Lady," he moaned, "a silencer?"

"It comes in handy in my line of work," she said. The implication wasn't lost on him. When he hesitated again, she pointed the gun at his face. The taller man stirred, and she shifted her weight, then motioned with the gun. Her voice was cold. "You two aren't worth my time. It's going to be easier to kill you."

"Jesus! Here." The bleeder was still holding his nose with one hand, but he tossed his wallet with the other. The young man with the Gypsy's foot on his neck looked up, eyes wide.

"Thank you," she said dryly. "What kind of idiot muggers carry their ID's?" She slid both wallets into her jacket pocket and stepped away. Then she lifted the gun again and aimed it at the talker. "You first?"

"You're going to kill us for trying to take your purse?" The stockier man was near tears. The taller of the two still couldn't speak, but his eyes grew wider.

"Do you see a purse?" she snarled. "Or was it going to be rape? And maybe this one would stick that knife in me when you were done." Neither man could see her face clearly, but there was no mistaking her grim tone.

"No, please, " the second man pleaded. "We just wanted money. We don't do this, ever, but we were desperate. Don't, please."

"It must be your lucky night," the Gypsy said as she stepped to the short fence and opened the gate. "I'm feeling generous. I'm taking your

215

stuff to the cops tomorrow, so they'll know who you are. And I'll be filing a complaint, so you might want to lay low for a while."

"It's us that should file the complaint," the shorter man dared, crawling toward his partner. "You almost killed Randy."

The Gypsy pointed her gun at him again. "If you talk to the cops about me, I'll hunt you down. Then I will kill you. Stay away from here. It's a quiet neighborhood, and the people are nice."

She walked away, feeling unclean and ashamed of herself. There had been no reason to engage with them. Punishing them was a risk she didn't need to take and an exposure the group and her grandmother wouldn't approve of. But there was some satisfaction in it, and a lesson for two young men who would think twice before accosting someone again. They would stay away from her neighborhood in the future. They had better.

He was a small man with a pencil mustache and a straw Fedora. He settled into the chair offered him and placed his hat on the table. It was a large table, but only two of the men had place-settings. Each had another man standing behind them. Their supper would wait. Bodyguards seldom ate on time. There were two glasses of wine already sitting on the table, and a bottle reclining close at hand. The man already seated motioned to the glasses. "I took the liberty."

"Thank you," the short man said. "And thank you for this invitation. I don't get out very often. I considered it worth the trip to clear the air."

"I appreciate that," his host said. "Is the FBI watching you too?"

"I'm sure this meeting will raise some interest, but I don't think they realize who I am. They seem convinced that Rafael Mertens is a much larger man, one with blond hair and an Irish nose. Perhaps they have me confused with you, or Frank."

"Perhaps that's what you want them to think. I haven't done anything they can prove, so they can watch me all they want. It's your friend Frank they really want."

"Our friend, you mean."

Tyrel Davis shrugged. "Of course. The beef is good here. Shall we order?"

One of the bodyguards stepped to the opening and came back with a dark-haired woman who took their orders.

"How is our friend Frank? Have you talked to him recently?" the bigger man asked.

"No. He communicates by text from an encrypted phone. He is still being very cautious. Being dead is a difficult ruse to continue on a long-term basis. I'm sure he wishes he could come and drink a glass of wine with us."

Tyrel snorted. "Or shoot us both. It wasn't my fault he took the heat for that job in London. He was the one that was careless. And if he hadn't faked his own death, maybe his wife would still be alive and there wouldn't be all this bitterness."

"Maybe," the Belgian admitted. "But he doesn't trust either of us."

"He made that clear to me before he disappeared. At least he still communicates with you. That's what I wanted to talk to you about. Trust. You and I need to be able to trust each other, even if Frank isn't capable of it. This deal is too big for me to handle alone."

The shorter man shook his head. "How much money is enough, Tyrel? I came to this country to hide from my government and live out my years in peace."

"We both know it won't be that easy."

"And we both know it was you and Frank, not me, that was responsible for the disaster that still haunts us. And now Vegas. Why? How can you think Frank would trust you after that?"

"Vegas?" Tyrel raised a brow. "I thought that was you. Perhaps it was what they're saying, a feud over drugs and hookers."

"Very unlikely, but it wasn't me. I have nothing against Jack Mercer, and I don't need his father knocking on my door. It was a bloodbath, and a lot of innocent kids ended up dead. That has been your specialty in the past, Tyrel."

The big man's smile disappeared. "Easy, old friend. There is no reason for us to be unpleasant to each other."

"I am not your friend, Tyrel. I am your goat. Your scapegoat, I think the Americans call it. I trusted you and Frank, and it's led me to this."

"I wondered if he would think it was me who sent those shooters after his son, but he hasn't retaliated. It's not like him to let something like that go."

"If Jack were to be killed, Frank wouldn't need to come after us. We both have men working for us that are still loyal to him, and they would turn a blade on either of us if he said the word. You and I will never have that kind of loyalty. It can't be bought."

Tyrel ignored the slight. "But what about Vegas? If neither of us, then who? Were those four men just lunatics? The woman that was at that club that night, they're saying she killed all but one of those gunmen. A professional, certainly. From the description, it sounds like the same woman that gave us all that trouble in Portugal a while back, and plenty more since. I'm not sure what her connection is, or why she keeps getting in my way, but I'm getting close. One day soon I will find her. When I do, I'll enjoy asking her those questions myself, before I put an end to the bitch."

"I want no part of that," the Belgian said. "There is no honor in killing women and children, and if pointing that out to you is unpleasant, so be it. There are some in my organization who will join you, and I won't stop them. But when it's done, I'll be done with them and done with you."

Tyrel chuckled. "Then I'll be free to spend your share?"

"I don't want a share of what you have in mind. Not that I'd expect to live to see it. This is not a third world country, Tyrel, and I won't be involved. I am making an honest living now. But I will say this, whatever happens, whomever you target, stay out of my city."

Tyrel laughed again. "Is that a threat? You've been in Boston just a couple of years, now it's your city? It was Codona's city before it was yours and look what happened to him."

"I paid dearly to have you and Frank as partners after his death. I considered Frank a friend, which turned out to be a mistake. I don't plan to suffer the same fate as Patrick."

Tyrel leaned forward and put his hands on the table. Behind the Belgian, his aide reached inside his jacket. Tyrel glanced at him and sneered. "I am trying to keep the peace between us, Rafael. Neither of us can afford to draw attention to ourselves. Why must we disagree?"

220

"For the same reason that Frank is not joining us. Trust, you say, but only when it works in your favor. Frank still thinks it was you who sabotaged that oil rig. He has not become a ghost only to hide from the authorities, but from you as well."

"And what about Jack? He seems content to open doors for rich people and pilfer quarters from the banks he pretends to protect. What money is there in that?"

"He's doing well from what I hear, without breaking any laws. But because of what we did before I came to this country, I can't walk into my own shop without being arrested, much less have a personal conversation with Jack Mercer. I'm not sure if Jack realizes that some of the people he has working for him were willing to commit murder for his father, or that they're still capable of it."

"Jack doesn't have the balls or the brains for an operation like I'm planning. And you know Frank is still running things. They have to be talking to each other. I...we, need people in that location for this to work. Frank's people. If Frank would just listen to reason and come in and talk to me, I know we could hash it out."

"He's a man with a target on his back, and he thinks you put it there. He's not likely to talk to you, much less risk everything on your word. Frankly, I'm surprised you're still alive."

"I'm not easy to kill, Rafael, even if your name is Frank Mercer. Having my people in New York is important, and Jack better not get in my way. You either. Don't get in my way, Rafael. Talk to Frank. I know you can reach him. Tell him he needs to come talk to me, to keep the peace and get his kid on the right track. One last big score, then we can all disappear and go our separate ways."

The Belgian shrugged. "I'll reach out to Jack. Maybe he can convince Frank to at least talk to us, but I wouldn't bet on it."

Tyrel Davis leaned forward. "Listen closely, Rafael. I intend to talk to Frank Mercer, and it needs to be soon. I will do whatever I have to do to make that happen. If Frank doesn't want more bloodshed, his family's blood, he needs to show himself."

The Belgian smiled grimly. "That reminds me of another expression unique to this country, Tyrel. Be careful what you wish for."

The hotel was a good one, undoubtedly with a good bed. The Belgian was looking forward to climbing into it. The meeting had been stressful and exhausting. After a good night's sleep, he would return to Boston and figure a way out of the predicament he found himself in. His hired man slid the door card into the slot and opened the door. After a quick search he returned to the opening and nodded.

"Good night, Kasey." He touched the bigger man's arm. "I'll call around seven and order room service, presuming you'd like to eat with me."

"Seven sounds good, Mister Mertens, and so does breakfast. Have a good night and call me if you need anything."

The Belgian watched him walk toward the elevator and sighed. Hard to know who to trust in a business like his, but Kasey had been with him since the relocation. He pushed the door shut and dropped the chain into its place, then slid a chair under the handle. He turned the television on but left the volume muted, then went to the bathroom and turned the shower to scalding. He emptied his pockets, put his Glock on the counter, then undressed. As an afterthought he locked the bathroom door.

His shower was long and luxurious. The hot water eased the knots in his shoulders and washed away the day's worries. Cleared his head to think.

Dealing with Tyrel Davis wouldn't be easy, but it would have to be done. The man's greed and ego knew no boundaries, and what he was planning was insane. If Tyrel went to prison, he would roll over on everyone he knew, including his most recently acquired partner. The FBI had played nice so far, mostly because they had no proof of his activities in the UK, but if Tyrel Davis was faced with life in prison or rolling on his partners, Rafael knew he and Frank would be the first people given up.

Compared to Tyrel and Frank Mercer, his transgressions seemed minor. But that wouldn't keep him out of prison. Tyrel had to be dealt with. Unfortunately, the man was constantly surrounded by his own security team, and the only person who might convince them to turn on their boss was in hiding. He had to talk to Frank Mercer. Everyone in the organization respected Frank, or feared him. Together they would be able to deal with Tyrel Davis, one way or the other. He had to get Frank to show himself, not because Tyrel said so, but to save his own skin.

Happy with his resolution, the Belgian yawned as he toweled himself dry, then stretched. Funny, he mused, he didn't remember leaving the volume up on the television. When the realization that he hadn't dawn on him, he pulled the towel tighter around his waist and picked up the Glock, then quietly unlocked the door. Peeking through a crack to spy on an assassin would be both dangerous and unseemly. He decided to meet his fate like a man. He yanked the door open quickly and raised his gun.

A woman was sitting on the edge of his bed. A very attractive woman with dark hair that tumbled down her back. She had the remote in her hand and was watching NCIS. She turned to him and smiled. "No, I'm not from room service. And I'm not a hooker sent as a bribe. Put some clothes on, Rafael. We have a lot to talk about."

Chapter Nineteen

I looked at my phone and read the text for the third time. *Can you fly an airplane?* I didn't recognize the number, so I ignored it until another message came through. *It's not required, but your presence is. Details to follow.*

It was Friday afternoon, and I was painting. Alone. It had taken Jenny considerably less time to load her car and drive away than it had to pack when we were leaving Las Vegas. I'd suggested we stay friends and she suggested I go to hell. I knew that anger wouldn't last, but the breakup would. Jack had called and I was still scheduled to start work the following Monday. He said once Jenny had time to cool down the whole thing would blow over. I knew better, but it was good that he believed that. I needed time to infiltrate the gun club, and I needed a job.

She's safer at her brother's place, Cane, the next text said.

The misspelling confirmed what I already suspected. But how did she know about my recent breakup? And why did she want to go flying? I sent a reply. *Not a fan of airplanes.*

Her response was a Google-maps link to a small airport, roughly halfway between my father's house and Boston. *9 am, Sunday.* I responded with a thumbs-up emoji. I didn't like to be required to do anything, but the Gypsy and I had a lot to talk about.

Connecticut isn't nearly the size of New York state, but there is a surprising amount of countryside west of the river that cuts the state in half. North and west of Hartford the roads get narrower, and the houses crowd the asphalt. Most of those roads and many of the houses were built when horsepower had a different meaning and flying was something only birds did.

It wasn't much of an airport. There was a small building with a windsock and a dozen cars parked off to one side. A few private hangars lined one side of the runway, and several light planes were tethered to the ground on the opposite side. A weathered sign offered daily flights to Hartford, Bridgeport, and Boston. Another proclaimed that it was the home of Jerry's Jumpers, and that lessons were available. Jumping out of perfectly good airplanes was part of my training, but it was never something I enjoyed.

I was early, but so was she. The big door of the furthest metal building was open and a late model Jeep was parked beside the entrance. She waved a hand and I drove out there. March had taken a turn, as it often does in New York. Still jacket weather, but sunny, and the wind had blown itself out.

The Gypsy was climbing out of the airplane when I pulled up. Her long hair was pulled back and tied with a scarf. She'd replaced the dress I'd last seen her in with jeans and a sweatshirt, but she had on the same heeled boots. She smiled at me and nodded toward the airplane. "Glad you could make it. We're clear to take off. Two commercial planes a day and they've both left already."

"What is it we're doing?" I asked. "And what was that at the Memorial the other day? Did you follow us?"

"Get in, we'll talk on the way." She motioned me toward the pilot's side of the airplane. "Dual controls, but I want you to have the full instrument panel."

I objected. "I can't fly. I told you that."

"Calm down. I'll show you everything you need to know. This thing flies itself."

She ignored my questions for the next few minutes while she warmed up the airplane and did what I presumed was the required preflight check. The cockpit wasn't built for someone my height and I struggled to find room for my legs while we taxied out to the end of the runway. I have no doubt I looked nervous. The Gypsy gave me a wry smile and handed me a headset, then added power.

We climbed easily for several minutes until the fields and ponds became a patchwork of green and blue, then she eased forward on her

228

yoke and slowed the roar of the prop. Her headset had been turned off, but suddenly she was in my ear.

"Want to take the controls?"

"Is that why I'm here, for a flying lesson?"

"You looked a little queasy when we took off. Being the pilot will take your mind off it. Didn't you have to go to jump school to be a Ranger?"

"Those were bigger airplanes, and the last jump scared me just as much as the first one. Is this your airplane?"

"No, it belongs to a friend."

"A banker friend?" I asked.

"This has nothing to do with my job as an investment counselor."

"I have a lot of questions," I replied, "and none of them have anything to do with the stock market."

"I'm sure you do. But for now, fly this thing."

She pointed out the altimeter and airspeed dials, then the attitude indicator and the turn coordinator. And she explained skidding. Skidding was bad. Skidding caused crashes. Great to know if you're a budding pilot, but I was losing interest in a hurry. Still, she insisted on showing me how to make a gradual turn without diving, climbing, or losing airspeed. All things I didn't plan on ever needing. Then she turned a knob and pointed to another gauge.

"Just keep that little airplane pointed straight up and you'll take us right where we want to go."

"How far is that?"

"You'll see."

"Why am I learning to fly this thing? You're not going to jump out, are you?" I glanced over my shoulder. Someone had removed the back seats, leaving a bigger storage area. There was a large black bag lying behind the Gypsy's seat. Happily, it wasn't a parachute.

"What did Jenny have to say after I saw you two?" she asked.

I grimaced. "She said goodbye. But you knew that already. I accused her of knowing you would be there and she didn't take it well. We fought, and she left."

"Isn't that what you wanted, no commitments?"

"No. Maybe," I admitted. "But I was starting to consider the alternatives. You're the one that said I should try to make her happy."

"You brought her back to New York. That'll make her happy."

"Nothing ever lasts," I grumbled.

She frowned in my direction. "She'll be happy again, but I'm not so sure about you. You might always be this grumpy."

I fought back. "So, Gabriel, predicting the future again?"

"We've had this conversation, Cain. I prefer *The* Gypsy to Gabriel."

230

"Okay, the Gypsy, how am I doing?"

"You're gaining a little altitude. Ease forward on the yoke."

I made the correction, then started asking my questions. "How did you know to be there?"

"Which time?" I looked at her and she chuckled. "Would you believe me if I told you the thing at the Memorial was a complete accident?"

"Not for a minute. And I don't believe you're a stock analyst either."

"I am a stock analyst, and I'm good at it. But I'm more than that. I'm sure your buddy Randolph filled you in."

"He's got you somewhere between Mata Hari and Jason Bourne. Why am I here? Why me? And why did you come looking for me that night at the Exotic?"

"I can't tell you all my secrets, Cain. But I will tell you that I went there because of Jenny, in case you weren't what you appeared to be."

"And what would that be? I was a barely employed security guard that got tossed out of the Army ten years too early."

"To us, you looked like a man who might have a chip on his shoulder. A man known to be dangerous when provoked, and a man who might have taken money to get close to a young woman caught in the middle of things. Someone who might be willing to hurt her. I knew you weren't that guy ten minutes after I sat down next to you. You're too empathetic to be a murder."

"Us?" I pondered that for a moment, then looked over at her. "Who's us?"

"I have a support team. People who let me borrow their airplanes and give me expensive toys to play with. Together, we deduce things. No fortune telling involved."

"Randolph said you probably know more about what's going on with Frank Mercer is up to than he does."

She turned toward me quickly, her eyes open wide. "Are you telling me Frank Mercer is alive?" I swore under my breath, then her laughter filled my ears. "I'm kidding, Cain. I knew that. But if you're going to play detective, you have to learn what not to say to the people you're pumping for information. There are things I'm not ready to tell you. You're just going to have to trust me."

"Where are we going today? We have to be close to the New York border by now."

"Another forty-five minutes. North of the Catskills."

"Why are we flying? It can't be more than an hour's drive from my old man's duplex."

"It's not a place we can go without an invitation. There's only one road nearby, and I don't want to have to explain why we're parked on it."

"Is this about the gun club?"

"Every other weekend they sight in their rifles, knock back a few, then go back to their real jobs. But some of them go there more often and their training looks more serious. They're getting ready for something, and there's more than just this one group."

"Randolph knows about them. He can't dig too much because most of them are from this country, but he claims they're not political."

"Depends on what you mean by political," she mused. "I need to grab something."

She tipped her seat back and clambered through the opening between us, then started digging through the bag behind her seat. I continued watching the instruments, secretly proud of the fact that I managed to keep us headed west, and airborne. After a moment she slid back over the seatback, then reached around and pulled a large brown object after her. It had wings, eyes, and feathers. The feathers were painted on.

"A drone?" I asked. "We can't just fly over and just have a look?"

"Once maybe, but more than that and we'd attract attention. A friend of mine designed this. Very fast in this configuration, but with the wings extended it can ride the thermals like a bird. It's painted to look like an eagle or a turkey vulture. Turkey vultures fly so high you barely notice them. This little wonder of technology has a high-definition long-range camera with infrared and heat sensing capabilities."

"One of those expensive toys your friends provide?"

"A man named Levi makes all kinds of toys for me," she said. "Most of them aren't as harmless as this drone."

It was an opening, and I followed her lead. "Randolph thinks you might be dangerous. He thinks you murdered three men in Lisbon."

She shrugged. "They weren't good people."

"And you get to decide that?" I asked.

She gave me a dark look. "How many people did you kill in Afghanistan?"

"More than three," I admitted. "But that was a war, and they had just murdered a group of school children."

"You were ordered by your superiors to stand down, but you chose not to. In the eyes of the military, it was murder. Which is worse, Cain, killing all those children for an ideology, no matter how vile and twisted we think it is, or killing them for money?"

I shrugged. It was a rhetorical question, and she wasn't looking for an answer. It was the first time I'd seen her truly angry. She turned to me again. "I don't care what Randolph thinks, but I want you to know that children were dying in my war too. When that happened, I lost it, same as you. Tell me, Cain, which of our murders was worse?"

Chapter Twenty

She took the controls after that and neither of us spoke until the rolling hills to our west pushed their way into the clouds. Most of the snow remaining on the Catskills was man made, but the March sun was gathering strength as it made its way north, driving moisture from the ground and creating an impenetrable ground fog. The Gypsy saw me looking down at the haze and anticipated my question.

"The compound is still fifteen miles north of here. It's lower ground and the snow has been gone for weeks. It'll be clear up that way."

"What are we hoping to find?"

"I can't tell you that," she said quickly, then laughed at my expression. "Not because it's a secret, but because I'm not sure. It's a private gun club on the site of an old farm. Maybe they're all just good old boys, but I'm told some of the people there are dangerous."

"Told, by Randolph?" I asked.

"I've never talked to your friend Randolph, and I don't plan to. Odds are he'd lock me up if he thought it would work to his advantage." She had turned north and we were losing altitude.

"I think he likes you," I offered, "and I know Jenny does. They have coffee all the time and talk about you."

She gave me a twisted smile. "Jealous? I like Jenny. Too bad you couldn't make that work."

I smiled back. "Then I wouldn't be able to spend all this quality time with you. I will say I feel used, I'm just not sure if it's you or Randolph that's doing it."

Her smile grew. "I'm a lot more fun than Randolph."

I nodded. "I bet you could be."

The flirting eased the residual tension and we fell back into easy conversation as we flew north. After another ten minutes she turned us west again, pointed to our left, and handed me a pair of binoculars.

"I'm just going to make one pass at a distance, then use the drone. This was a very successful farm back in the day. I found newspaper articles archived from the early thirties about this location, with pictures. They raised cattle and hogs and slaughtered and stored the meat right here. That was before there was any decent commercial refrigeration."

To the north, beyond a stretch of dense pines, I could see water. A sizeable lake. "They probably cut ice from that lake, like they used to do at Rockland," I said. I'd seen it done with a chainsaw when I was a kid living in Buffalo. Those people had been building ice sculptures, not supplying a growing city with T-bones.

She nodded. "The building to the north is what used to be the processing plant. They packed lake ice in sawdust and kept everything below ground to keep the meat cold through the summer. The structure to the south is a newer pole barn. You can see the outdoor range to the east, and some sort of a training ground. They must do active shooter drills and things like that. The whole acreage is fenced and they have a gated entrance."

"Do they do any concealed-carry training, or shooting events for the public?"

"Members only, and it's not easy to get an invite. Jenny's brother is a member and so are a lot of the people that work for him."

"Are those more deduction, or do you have a spy?" I asked. The Gypsy was peering down at the compound and didn't favor me with a response. "It has to be the same compound Randolph was talking about," I said. "He had pictures too. He's hoping they'll invite me to join because of my time in the Rangers."

"That will make you Randolph's spy," she pointed out. "I'd think twice about signing up for that. How many vehicles do you see?"

I did a quick count. "Thirteen. Not a very big club."

"There were fifty or sixty here last weekend. I flew over once, but I didn't have the drone and didn't want to attract attention. It's hard to know how many people come here, because some might be parking inside. That's part of the reason we're here, to get a body count."

The compound disappeared behind us. The Gypsy eased back on the throttle and pushed a small lever on the console between us. "Flaps," she explained. "We're going to stay behind the tree-line, and I want to make as little noise as possible. With the flaps partially extended we can fly at half throttle and half speed."

"And I'm going to do the flying?"

She nodded. "I didn't bring you along for conversation. I have to operate the drone. Keep us at three thousand feet and don't let the airspeed drop below seventy-five miles an hour, ever. That's the outside set of numbers, just so you know. I'll put us in a slow turn, one round every four minutes or so, and all you'll need to do is keep the attitude indicator in the same place. Easy."

I knew three thousand feet was from sea level. It didn't look nearly that far to the treetops below. Still, far enough to kill us if we went down. "What happens if the airspeed drops?" I asked.

"If it does, drop the nose, and I'll tweak the power. The stall warning will start sounding if you screw up, and I'll correct the rudder if I feel a skid. If we went into a spin at this altitude, they'd be scraping us off those rocks. "

"You already mentioned that," I grumbled. "And then you said this thing flies itself."

238

"Keep the airspeed steady, that's all you have to worry about."

When we were a sufficient distance from the compound the Gypsy banked slightly and explained which instruments I needed to watch, then started fussing with the drone. She reached back into her bag again and produced a controller. It had several levers, buttons, and a small screen that lit up when she turned it on. Next, she pulled an extendable aluminum rod from the bag and pulled it out to about four feet. It had a u-shaped hook at the end. I took my eyes off the instruments long enough to see that the drone had two wire hoops protruding from its back, or what would have been its back had it been a real bird.

I shared my opinion. "That looks pretty damn primitive."

She grinned. "I know. This ought to be interesting." She turned a switch on the drone and I heard a growling noise. "Gyros," she explained. "I'll start the drive motors after it's in the air."

Before I could ask any more questions, she opened her door and leaned out with the drone in one hand. Granted, she had her seatbelt on, but the action made my stomach turn. "Steady, Cain," she called above the rush of the wind. I turned my attention back to the instrument panel.

239

She popped upright suddenly and grabbed the transponder from the console between us after pulling her door shut. The screen came alive and she chuckled gleefully, like a kid winning at Mortal Combat. "Levi is a genius. He told me it would fly on just the gyros, but I didn't believe him. Keep circling. I'll get some altitude, then put it out over the compound."

Power didn't seem to be a problem for the device. As I watched from the corner of my eye, it matched our speed, then started to climb almost straight up until it had nearly disappeared. The Gypsy stared down at the screen and gave me updates as she extended the wings and put the drone into a sweeping turn that carried it out of sight beyond the trees. "Levi," she mumbled, "I love you so much." She glanced in my direction. "Not that way. I love his wife too."

"Never asked," I responded, "but good to know."

We stayed like that for twenty minutes, suspended in four-minute turns while I watched the gauges, and she watched the screen, taking pictures with the drone. I wasn't watching the gauges all whole time. She caught me looking at her and gave me a quick wink.

"Keep it in your pants, Cain. Remember, we're doing this for Mickey."

"He'd approve," I said. "It never was about the popcorn."

She smiled at the memory. "He seemed like a sweet guy. I wish I would have had the chance to get to know him."

"He was, and you're right. Finding out who sent those shooters is the important thing."

"Then what? Will you go after them?"

"Much as I'd like to, I'll probably never get the chance. Do you think it could have been Frank Mercer?"

"Frank's done some things that he should pay for, but he wouldn't send shooters after Jack. What does Randolph think?"

"He doesn't share his theories, and he's hoping you'll tell me who did it."

"Is that why he hasn't brought me in for the incident at the Exotic?"

"First, he'd have to find you. But a lot of innocent kids died that night, and I'm sure Randolph doesn't like that anymore than we do. I don't think he's trying too hard to hunt you down."

She nodded, studying the screen as she maneuvered the drone. "He knew I'd find you."

"And why is that?" I asked. "I'm beginning to think you like having me around."

"Son-of-a-bitch!" she objected loudly, then looked up quickly. "An eagle, or some kind of bird just slammed into the drone. It's not responding. If it falls into that clearing and they find it..."

A soft moan started sounding from the dash. The Gypsy lifted her hand quickly and pointed down. I checked the airspeed and pushed the yoke forward.

"You worry about your bird, I'll worry about mine," she snapped. "I have it leveled off and responding again. Hopefully the wings will retract or I'm going to have to put it down somewhere."

I risked a question. "If the wings don't fold in, we can't fly slow enough to retrieve it with your little hook, right?"

"Exactly," she shared. "It'll do ninety fully charged and trimmed. The plan was to bring it right up beside us and hook it, but honestly, I've never tried this before. This is the first time I've had a partner." She glanced up quickly. "Someone to fly the airplane."

I grinned at her. "Glad I could help, partner."

It took another ten minutes to get the drone back to our location. The Gypsy spent the time staring at her screen and swearing occasionally while I kept us flying. The terrain below us was covered with trees, broken only by short patches of rock-strewn hillsides that looked useless for anything but a hiking trail. From trips to the Catskills I knew there were a few twisting paths through the countryside going north, but from our vantage point I couldn't see any sign of people. There would be no one to witness what we were attempting. A video of something this crazy would probably go viral.

"Alright, the wings are tucked and it's closing in on us." The Gypsy tossed her headset aside and pushed the door open. "Keep it steady."

I could hear the howl of the drone's motors above the wind as the she brought it closer. She had the controller in her left hand and was using it to fly the contraption, while reaching out with her right. I cringed when she reached back and unbuckled her seat belt to be able to reach further out the door. Finally, she flipped her legs up over the seatback, put her head down, and slid forward through the opening, reaching out with Levi's idiot-stick. Her right foot was hooked around the headrest of the seat and it was the only thing keeping her from plunging headfirst out of the airplane.

Suddenly her legs shifted and her body lunged forward. I was sure she was going headfirst into the trees below us, so I grabbed an ankle and pulled back as hard as I could. She swore loudly again and I heard a rending sound, followed by what I took for shredding metal. Then, just the rush of the wind.

"Gypsy," I yelled, still trying to keep the airplane level, "are you alright?"

"Pull me in," she called. "I almost had it!" she said as she spun around in the seat.

I took that as an accusation and responded loudly. "I thought you were falling out!"

"I was. Nice catch," she acknowledged. "Luckily, the drone is lodged between the wheel skirt and the strut, and it's probably hooked on one of the catch wires. Unfortunately, it's upside down, so the hook is worthless. I'm going to climb down and grab it."

"Are you kidding me? Let's just land somewhere. Can't you download the pictures on your phone and just scrap the drone?" The idea of her climbing out of the airplane a thousand feet above the rocky terrain below us made me feel sick, again.

"If it could send pictures, it could be hacked. And landing the plane would probably demolish it. That thing is worth a small fortune and Levi will kill me if I wreck it. Don't worry, I'll hang on this time. Just don't hit any bumps."

I didn't appreciate the levity. I tried to keep my eyes on the gauges, not the yawning opening and the long drop as she pushed the door open and reached out for the wing strut.

"That's not going to work," she complained. "I can't reach the strut with the door in my way. Keep circling, I have another idea."

After a couple of attempts, she pulled enough seatbelt free to take two wraps around her wrist. "Couldn't fall if I wanted to," she said

244

confidently. She pushed the door open with her leg, then braced it with Levi's retrieval stick and started sliding through the opening. I was holding our airspeed and watching her simultaneously. Despite the brace, the passenger door was pounding against her shoulder as she slid down onto the wheel skirt, straddling the broken drone and the wheel. If she had fallen, there would have been nothing I could do. Briefly, I wondered how I would get back on the ground by myself, then pushed that aside.

Wounded though it was, the aerodynamics of the drone made it want to fly once she dislodged it and turned it upright. She fought the drone and the wind for a minute, then shook the seatbelt free from her left hand. She slid down, straddling the wheel skirt while using both hands to fight with the drone. An especially strong gust of wind slammed the door against her shoulder, and I could see she was struggling to stay upright. My instinct was to reach out for her, but the stall warning started again and I shifted my attention back to the controls.

Finally, after considerable wrestling, she pushed the wounded device up through the open door and onto her seat. The gyros were still buzzing noisily, and the battered mechanical bird twisted in my hand as I tossed it, none too gently, onto the deck behind me. Then I reached out for her free hand and pulled her back up through the opening.

She slid into her seat and pulled the door shut, then looked at me. "I hope that didn't hurt your shoulder?"

"Never felt a thing," I replied, "but I may have shit myself."

She laughed and grabbed the controls on her side of the airplane. "Okay, I'll take us out of here."

She added power and flew north to avoid being seen from the compound. After a minute she looked over. "You're not looking so good," she pointed out.

"Just so you know," I said. "I am never going flying with you again."

Chapter Twenty-One

The sun on my shoulder and the roar of the prop did their damage and lulled me into a dreamless sleep. The bump of the wheels on the runway woke me an hour later. That was not the plan. I was hoping to talk more.

"Wow, sorry," I said. "I spent half the night painting. Now what are we doing?"

"Doing?" she asked. "I'm going back to Boston, and I would imagine you have more painting to do."

"I'm hungry. Should we grab a bite? I still have questions."

She nodded as she put the drone in the back of her Jeep. "I knew you'd try to trick me into telling you all my secrets."

"I'm not that smart," I admitted, "and I only want a few of your secrets."

"Follow me. There's a little burger place up the road."

It was a quiet afternoon at Percy's Pub. Half a dozen men in their fifties and sixties, farmers if I was going to guess, sat at the bar watching a baseball game. A tall, dour-looking woman with an apron sat with them but stood when she saw us. Seven pairs of eyes followed our every move as we walked to the far end of the room. We took a spot past the pool table with a window and a view of the parking lot. The waitress dropped menus on the table and we each ordered a beer. She brought us bottled beer and asked if we'd like glasses, then said she'd be back. She returned to the farmers and started talking, casting furtive glances in our direction. Before long, all six of the men and the waitress were staring at us openly.

"I don't think they see many people like us around here," I offered.

The Gypsy looked over at the group. "What?" she asked loudly, to everyone and no one in particular. They all turned back to the game, and she grinned at me. "I love small towns. They're probably all wondering if we bought the old Johnson place, and if our kids are old enough to play football."

"I don't think that's what they're wondering," I said. "You're being too generous."

"Look at us," she said, waving a hand between us. "We would have very large, very athletic children. Our daughter would play professional basketball, and the twins would both be tight ends for the Giants."

I went along. "Three professional athletes in one family, that is impressive. And of course we'd have the biggest house in town, because you'd make us a fortune in the stock market."

"Undoubtedly," she said, inspecting the bowl of taco chips that was sitting between us. "Sadly, after the kids were gone, you'd take up golf and leave me alone in our mansion. I'd get desperately lonely and have an affair with the mayor. He and I would run away together and join a commune."

"Damn that mayor," I objected. "Does nothing ever last?"

"Nope," she said sadly.

"Is the commune a nudist colony?"

She shrugged and took a drink of her beer. "If that makes it better for you."

I shook my head. "I hate to disappoint the local football team, the Giants, and especially the mayor, but I don't think I'm quite ready to put a ring on it. Since I've met you, I've been shot twice, harassed by the FBI, run out of Las Vegas, and dumped by my girlfriend. I'd prefer to think you're just bad luck, but I'm starting to wonder. Who, or what are you?"

She grinned again, "I'm just a girl..."

"Stop it," I muttered. "I'm being fairly serious right now. I don't know what to make of you. Right now you seem relatively normal. You're laughing and flirting and drinking beer as if you didn't just almost fall to your death an hour ago while taking infra-red pictures of a para-military compound that might be a training ground for terrorists."

I could see the mischief in her eyes. "You thought that was flirting?"

"Gypsy, come on. I'm going to work for Jack Mercer next week and I need to know what I'm getting into."

"Jack seems like a good guy," she said.

"You can do better than that," I argued. "I need to know who I'm dealing with, and I'm not talking about Jack and Frank Mercer. What is going on with you? You stop bank robberies, you kill hitmen, and you shoot like no one I've ever known. And when you almost fall out of an airplane, you act like it's just another day at the office."

She shrugged. "I grabbed the wheel strut. I might have lost the drone, but I wouldn't have fallen."

"That's not my point. It's not normal behavior."

She started pulling nervously on the label of her beer bottle. "It's normal for me."

"Come on, Gabriel." I caught her look and started over. "Okay, Gypsy, how is it that you're better at practically everything than even the most talented people are at one thing? It's trivial, but I doubt I could fly that drone with two hands if I practiced for a year. You did it with one hand, while dangling out of an airplane a thousand feet off the ground."

She was studying her beer bottle, still pulling at the label. "I should have just held the door open with my foot and flew it into the cabin. But those rotors are like razor blades."

"Gypsy!" All the farmers looked over. I lowered my voice. "Just tell me something that's real. Anything. I need to know who you are if I'm going to trust you."

She looked up quickly. "You don't trust me?"

"I do, mostly," I admitted. "You saved my life, so I owe you. But like I said before, I feel like you and Randolph are pulling all the strings and I'm the guy doing the dance. I don't trust Randolph, but I'm doing my best to trust you."

She raised her bottle and motioned to the waitress. "One more, Cain? Two is my limit."

"Mine too." I acknowledged the waitress, then returned my attention to the Gypsy.

"For what it's worth," she said, "I'm much more normal than you think. Boring, most of the time. And I trust you completely, Adam."

"Good to know," I said. When Randolph used my first name, I figured he was trying to con me. When the Gypsy did it, I wasn't as sure. "Why?" I asked.

"When Mickey went down, you stood over him and returned fire. That wasn't the smart thing to do."

"What else would I have done?" I asked.

"See? That's why I trust you." She left that hang while she picked up one of the chips from the bowl, tasted it, then tossed it down. "Gross," she mumbled, then started telling me the truth, or at least a small part of it.

"Gabriel Luca, my grandmother, trained me. The family calls her Gabby, but sometimes I still call her Grandmama. It's a habit from childhood, so don't make fun of me. She is still training me, or trying to. Lately, that isn't going very well. I've said that she is a spiteful old tyrant and I stand by that. I love her, of course, and I would die before I'd let anyone hurt her. But lately she expects too much. There are things that I refuse to do that she considers part of the job."

"I know you're an investment counselor. What else?"

"There's more to it, obviously. Suffice it to say I work with a group of people that try to make a difference, in a good way. They point me in the right direction, and my grandmother has spent years teaching me what to do when I get there."

"Like that night in Vegas? So basically, you're a vigilante?"

"No," she said quickly, then shrugged. "Maybe. Sometimes. I think of it as being like the FBI, only without all the red tape and opportunities for corruption. Granted, the line gets blurry from time to time, especially when my grandmother is involved."

"Still," I cautioned, "you're operating outside the law."

She chuckled. "As if the FBI and the NSA are doing so well."

"How does something like that stay a secret?" I asked. "Randolph started paying attention because you're always showing up when there's trouble."

"He has to realize that I have help."

"I'm not sure that he does," I said. "But what about the Mercer family? How is Jenny's family involved in all of this?"

"That's part of the problem I have with my grandmother. Her last marriage was to a man named Patrick Codona. It wasn't a warm relationship, and he was gone on business most of the time, but she claims to have loved him dearly. He was in business with Frank Mercer and another man. They were doing very well until they expanded overseas."

"Agent Randolph told me some of this, but I'm not sure that he knew who the third man was. He said he just disappeared one day."

"Patrick's body showed up in a morgue a few days after his disappearance. Randolph needs to read his emails."

"But Randolph must know who your grandmother is?"

"He might know she's Patrick's widow, but he doesn't know who I am or that we're related, so what does it matter?"

"And the Belgian?"

"Rafael Mertens. Some people say he's a ruthless killer, but I'm not so sure. My grandmother doesn't care which partner did what, she wants them all dead. I'd prefer they went to prison."

I shook my head. "Sounds like a lot of cloak and dagger. And dangerous. I thought you'd be more fun than Randolph."

She grinned and hoisted her new beer for a toast. "I still could be."

"And your Grandmama," I asked. "When do I get to meet her?"

"You don't," she said sharply.

Suddenly it was awkward. "We're working together, sort of, so I just thought..."

Her voice turned cold. "I appreciate that you helped me today, Cain, and what you're trying to do. But let's not make more of it than it is. You want the man responsible for Mickey's death, and I want Frank Mercer and his friends in jail."

I tried to save the moment. "Okay, but someday the twins are going to want to meet their great-grandmother."

She didn't return my smile. "That's never going to happen. Sorry, but you wouldn't like my grandmother, and she wouldn't like you. Let's just leave it at that."

Chapter Twenty-Two

The slender bespectacled man pushed his wire-framed glasses up with an index finger, straightened his bow tie, and read the sign on the bakery door. He was late, but the shop was still open. A bell rattled from above the door as it swung shut behind him. He walked up to the counter and stood looking down at the glass case with a shy smile on his face. The pair of young women behind the pastry case stared at him curiously. One held a broom, the other a spray bottle. Both stopped what they were doing and stepped up to the case, laughing and pushing at each other playfully.

"Are these fresh today?" he asked, pointing down at the pastries.

Charity Luca gave her sister a gentle shoulder nudge and turned away. The man was not unattractive, but he sounded like a tourist. Not worth fighting over, even if it was a mock battle. She was past the point of one-night stands. Her sister was not.

Patience smiled and nodded. "Of course. My father would rather die than let us sell day old turnovers. Everything was made fresh this morning."

"They look incredible. Does your father do all the baking?"

"He does most of it. He and my mother own the bakery." She laughed and pointed at her soiled smock. "My sister and I are just his indentured servants."

"You look alike, you and your sister," the man said. "And your mother too." He was looking over her head at a family portrait on the wall. "You're all very attractive women."

"Thank you. I'm told we take after my mother. Short like her, unfortunately."

The man smiled again. "I would say that taking after her has worked out pretty well for you. Very well, actually." He looked away quickly, blushing, and fumbling with his words. "Is it okay to say that? I didn't mean any disrespect."

Patience shrugged and offered an awkward smile. "You can say it, if you want."

An aluminum tray rattled against the tile, and the young woman's sister snickered loudly as she retrieved several powdered doughnuts that had tumbled to the floor. She gathered them up in her apron and picked up the tray with her free hand, then backed into the opening behind her.

"Just so you know, sir, it's five minutes until closing." She started to turn away, then stopped. "Not that we're in a hurry. My sister seems to be enjoying your company."

Patience glared at her back. "Damn it. She loves to embarrass me."

The man continued to fumble. "I'm sorry if I gave her the wrong impression. Not that she had the wrong impression. I like your company too. Not that I would really know, because we've just now met, but I can already tell I would like your company. Crap. Now I'm embarrassing myself." He dropped his head and stared down at the case, mumbling again. "What's good here? I need some bagels to take home, but I'm not going to buy those today."

"Is this your first time in Boston?" the pretty brunette asked. "You don't sound like a native."

"Just visiting for now, but who knows? I've been thinking about relocating to the east coast. I have some contacts out here, and I'm considering a new job."

"Boston is okay. It's probably better if you haven't lived here your whole life, but mostly I like it. How long will you be staying?"

"I'm not sure. It might be just a week, but I have no reason to rush home. Maybe I'll stay longer and see the sights. But I should order, so you can close up on time. How about two of those strawberry creampuffs. I'll eat one tonight, and one for breakfast."

Patience gave him her warmest smile. "They're the best. I'll be sure my father makes more of those in the morning, in case you want to come back tomorrow."

He nodded and stuttered out a reply. "I'll be back, for sure. For sure. Will you be working tomorrow afternoon?"

Her smile widened. "Every day except Sunday."

"Maybe you could help me decide where to go in Boston, if I decide to stay and see the sights?"

Patience bit her lip, then stumbled on. "Or maybe, if you'd like, I could just show you some stuff. If you'd like." They both heard a snort and laughter from the kitchen. Patience frowned. "I'm going to kill my sister."

The man chuckled. "Please don't. You wouldn't look nearly this pretty in prison orange."

Patience reached for the pastries with a set of tongs. "My father leaves at four, so come in after that. I'm twenty-three, but he still thinks he can tell me who to date. You're not an axe murderer, are you?"

"No. I promise. I'm always a perfect gentleman." There was another guffaw from the back room and a small wince from Patience. The man looked up at the family picture again. "Your father's a big man. I don't think I'd want him mad at me."

Patience handed the man the small bag of pastries and made change, then extended her hand. "No, trust me, you would not want him mad at you. I'm Patience. That's my name, but

I'm not patient at all. You can ask my sister about that tomorrow when you come back, if she lives through the night. My father calls me Patty sometimes, but I like Patience. Sorry, I'm babbling."

The man took her hand and shook it slowly. "Patience. That's a great name, and I'm really looking forward to having a tour guide. My name is James. James Olson. But you can call me Jimmy. I'll see you tomorrow, Patience, same time."

The bell over the door clattered again as Jimmy left, and Charity Luca burst from the back room. "Good Lord, you tramp! Two minutes and you're volunteering to show him stuff? I know what you want to show him. What was with all the stuttering and blushing? I thought I was going to have to hose you two down or drag you off of him."

Patience giggled. "He's a little old for me, but he's so cute. I wonder if he'll really come back?"

"He was babbling like an idiot, and he never took his eyes off your chest. He'll be back. And believe me, he's going to want to sample more than Daddy's creampuffs."

Patience slapped her sister's arm and laughed. "Whatever it is Jimmy Olson wants, I think he's going to get it, and then some."

Darius Luca settled into the leather chair in front of his sister's desk. She was upset with him and was avoiding his gaze. The door had been unlocked, and he hadn't bothered knocking. It was a breach of protocol that he repeated frequently. The woman sat with her back to him staring out the window. Finally, she spoke.

"She defied me again, Darius. She does it more often than not these days."

"Is this about the kidnapping?"

The elder Luca spun her chair back to face him. "Somehow she managed to spirit the child away without any violence."

"And how is that a bad thing? Did any money change hands?"

"No, the delivery was to be made the next day. I was surprised that the child was still alive, frankly, knowing who was involved."

"Do you know it, or is that just your hate telling you what you want to believe?"

"I can't be absolutely sure, that's true. The facts might indicate otherwise. My husband's partners don't usually leave witnesses to their atrocities, even seven-year-old girls."

"And what is it that Isabelle did that upset you?"

"It's what she didn't do. She did nothing to the men who took the girl other than report their whereabouts to the police. I told her specifically that they needed to be dealt with. A life only to save a life, she said, or we are as bad as the people we fight. We argued and she walked out. I am losing her, Darius."

"You will, if you don't see beyond your hatred. I know what you've lost, Sister, and I will be there to help you get your pound of flesh when the time comes. But this isn't Izzy's fight. She isn't a weapon you can dispense as you see fit, she is your granddaughter. You owe her an apology."

"The day her parents died, she came to me and begged me to teach her. She swore an oath to be the person her mother was. Someone who would stand up to people willing to kill to line their own pockets. People like Frank Mercer and the others."

Darius softened his tone. "Her mother was like neither of you, Gabby. I know the guilt you feel, but your daughter made the choice to go into the tower that day. You couldn't have known what was going to happen, no one could."

"She knew," the old woman said quietly. "Somehow she knew, and she thought they would be able to help people get down."

"There was no way to know. Not that it would be the Twin Towers. We knew New York was a likely target, but not the exact day, not the exact place."

"She knew," the old woman repeated stubbornly. "And Izzy has her gifts." She waved a hand at her brother's expression. "I'm not suggesting the mystical. I'm just saying that my granddaughter has the same sort of mind her mother had, analytical, always processing every scrap of information that comes her way, be it from the group or from her own observations. Her mother was good at it, but Izzy's abilities astound me."

"Which is why you should trust her judgment," Darius scolded. "Our people in the field need to have the freedom to react. Izzy can't be bothered wondering if you'll approve of her every decision when she's in the middle of a fight. You know that better than most."

"Of course. But there is something to be said for experience. The three men she let go might return someday and do something even more vile. Dead men don't commit crimes, Darius."

"And they have no chance for redemption. No matter how vile, killing them when there is an option amounts to murder. I agree, Tyrel Davis doesn't deserve your mercy, or hers. I'm not sure about the other two, but each man deserves to be judged on his own merits."

The old woman lurched to her feet, turned her back on her brother, and walked to the window. "Ambassador Grant is a good man, and a good friend. If they had killed his granddaughter, I would have found them myself. He did his best to persuade my husband to come home to me when things went to hell over there, but Patrick felt obligated to stay because of his friendship with Frank Mercer. He thought he could stop what the other two had started. Now Patrick is dead and Frank's in hiding."

"Do they know that Isabelle is your granddaughter?"

"They would come for me if they did. They think I'm just a grieving old woman with no power to hurt them. Izzy has caused them plenty of trouble and cost them a great deal of money in the last couple of years. And if I were the horrible grandmother you seem to think I am, she would have cost them a lot more. I've only sent her in when it was absolutely necessary, and I try not to put her in danger when there are other options. She didn't have to get involved in Las Vegas, but she chose to. In my view, Jack Mercer was expendable. His father is no innocent, and the apple never falls too far from the tree."

"Fortunately for Izzy, and for a lot of people that were at the club that night, sometimes it does."

The old woman spun and nodded toward the door. "Go to hell, Darius, or back to your pies and cakes where it's warm and cozy. I've asked for your help as many times as I'm going to. Sooner or later, they will learn about our little organization, then none of us will be safe."

"I'll be ready, and there are others who will be with us if we need them. Don't let this consume you, Gabby. Your life is a long way from over and you need to make the most of it. Come to supper. I'll make sure the girls are there, and perhaps a German torte will sweeten your disposition."

"Feed it to my dead husband's partners, Darius, and lace it with cyanide. That would do wonders for my disposition." Darius stood quietly at the door, waiting until she looked up at him. Her features softened and she managed a laugh. "I know. I am a bitter old woman. I will come to supper and make nice with your wife and daughters. Perhaps by then Isabelle will have forgiven me and join us."

Chapter Twenty-Three

"I give it a week. She'll cool down and think about it, then you two will work it out."

Jack Mercer had spent the first ten minutes of my employment trying to cheer me up and convince me that his sister's departure was temporary. I knew better. Some people find love easily. Not because they're lucky, but because they can love and be loved easily. Jenny was that kind of person. I was not. That was my failing, not hers, and I said as much to Jack.

"Truth be told, she deserves somebody better than me, Jack. She's warm and caring and generous, and I'm none of those things. She finally gets it. I don't think this break-up is temporary. I hope she'll be able to talk to me once she cools down, but I'm not going to beg her for another chance. That wouldn't be what's best for her."

He shrugged it off. "I think you're being too hard on yourself, Cain. I like you, and I'm a good judge of character. Give it some time."

"I still need a job," I said. "I just don't want to get it under false pretenses." There were false pretenses, just not the ones he thought I was talking about.

"Fine, we'll keep Jenny out of it. You're a big guy with plenty of security experience, so I would hire you anyway. And Cap would be upset with me if I didn't bring you on after everything I told him about you."

"Cap?"

"Captain Gregory. I mentioned him before. He'll go through all our company policies and rules with you, so you don't get us sued. He's a gun nut like me, and I told him you were a shooter in Afghanistan. He goes up to the club every other weekend and runs things. He loves shooting and talking about it. And talking and talking. He's a good guy, but he really likes the sound of his own voice. He's the president of the club, so he can grease the wheels and get you a membership if you want. It's not for everyone, but half of the people that work here are members, so it would be a good way to meet the other guys."

I nodded along. "Sure. I wouldn't want to disappoint Captain Gregory."

Matt Gregory looked to be about sixty. Except for the color of his buzz cut and the lines around his eyes, he could have passed for a thirty five-year old drill sergeant. And he talked like one.

Jack introduced us. "This is the guy I was telling you about, Cap. He worked security at a casino in Vegas, so he knows the basics. Eventually I want him on one of the bank trucks, but he'll start with Conrad."

"Come on, Jack! Ten years in the trenches and he gets to be a glorified bouncer?" He grabbed my hand and pumped it enthusiastically. "Matt Gregory, and thank you for your service, Soldier. Jack told us about what you did in Vegas. Good work there too."

"Thanks, Matt, but I didn't do that much."

"Cap," he said, thumping himself in the chest with a fist. "Three years in the Navy, a lot of years ago, and I was no officer. If I had it to do over, I'd have gone Army, like you. How many tours did you do?"

"Three. But my dad was in the Navy and he liked it. Must have, he was always gone."

"Bunch of pussies, no offense to your father. Adam, is it?"

"I'll call you Cap if you call me Cain."

"Cain it is then, and I don't really think that about the Navy. It's just that I always regretted not joining the Marines or the Army. That's where the real action is. Ever go hand to hand over there? But what am I talking about? A guy your size, they had to know better."

"I need to get back down to the office," Jack said suddenly and sent a wink in my direction. "Cap, don't wear Cain's ear off the first day."

Cap started right in on me. "I'd like to hear about Afghanistan, if you're okay talking about it. Jack tells me you were a shooter." He tipped his head and repeated himself. "If you're okay talking about it."

"Maybe we should talk about the handbook first, since I'm on the clock." No one who asked about Afghanistan ever wanted to hear what I was willing to tell them, and I didn't expect Cap to be the exception.

Jack was right, Cap talked a lot. We did manage to go over the handbook: Mercer Security's Rules of Engagement. There were a lot of rules. He talked and I listened. He explained what to say to clients when they were being unreasonable, what techniques to use to defuse aggressive behavior, and when it was permissible to use force. Which was almost never. I was glad I didn't plan to make a career of it, because it sounded just as boring as my job at the casino had been. Surprisingly, he didn't bring up the gun club until the end of the training.

"Jack said you might be interested in joining the club. I'm the president, so I can make that happen."

"Maybe," I said. "It's just about shooting? No politics?"

"The way things are these days? You can't stop people from talking about it completely, but it's discouraged. It's grounds for termination here at work, just so you know. That's in the handbook. Probably unconstitutional, but it's in there."

"Suits me. When everyone is carrying a gun, talking politics is just asking for trouble. So this club, what all do you do, and where is it?"

Captain Gregory was enthusiastic. "We shoot, of course, and some of the guys bring their reloading equipment. We do dry fire exercises and synchronized rifle drills, just like the Marine Corps band. We're marching in the parade on Memorial Day in Jefferson Heights. Quite an honor, I think, so we're practicing hard. And every couple of months we set up an airsoft course."

"I'd have to pass on that," I said. I wanted to fit in, but paintball? "Jack said every other weekend?"

"The first and third Saturday of every month, and we added the third Sunday until after the parade. Kind of late for you to get in on that."

"Never cared for marching," I admitted.

"Doesn't matter," he went on, "but you have to show up at least once a month if you want to lead a team. Jack and I were both hoping you will, and team leaders don't pay dues."

"Where am I leading this team?"

"Lead, as in instruct," he explained. "Most of the guys shoot deer rifles, but we all could learn something from you. And you could help us set up realistic shooting scenarios. We have a private range, just over a thousand yards for the big guns. How far can you shoot accurately?"

"No wind, low humidity, that's doable. It gets a lot harder farther out. In training we had all the variables loaded and help doing the calculations."

"Is it okay if I ask how many Taliban you've killed?"

"Honestly, I never had a sanctioned kill." That much was true. The Army hadn't sanctioned my nighttime excursion against Rahimi, and I wasn't about to volunteer any information about that little soiree. "I did put a few trucks and motorcycles out of service with my Fifty, just to slow them down and get their attention."

"A lot of the guys just like to hang out, and they'd love to hear stories about stuff like that. It's meant to be social, but there are a few hard-core shooters. We have guys with M82's, one 338 Lapua, and even a few Denels."

"Serious guns. I didn't know you could buy a Denel in this country," I said. "Why spend that kind of money just to punch holes in a target half a mile away? There are plenty of cheaper options that are almost as accurate."

"Henrik Mauer and his bunch live and breathe guns. Mauer owns the property and leases the range back to the club. He and some of his buddies meet more often in the old slaughterhouse. They take themselves pretty seriously. Too seriously, if you ask me."

"Politics?" I asked.

"Yeah, and Henrik isn't wrapped too tight. Nuts, if you want my opinion."

"Great," I said dryly. "And you want me to teach him to hit a pie plate from a mile away? That'll end well."

Cap shook his head and chuckled. "I'm all for the second amendment, but that idiot shouldn't own a gun. Especially a gun that can kill people from halfway across town."

"That's saying a lot, considering you're the president of a gun club."

"Some things are just common sense. I'm guessing his boys are going to want some tips, but I'd stay away from Mauer if you can. I have a bad feeling about that guy."

I liked Matt Gregory and Jack Mercer, but being Randolph's spy was starting to feel like a bad idea. Often as not, spies got shot.

I started my real training the next day, such as it was. Darren Conrad wasn't the talker Captain Gregory was, or nearly as fit. His Mercer Security jacket barely fit around his middle. He looked disappointed when he saw me, then shrugged and pointed at a white van. "We can't drive our own rigs."

I nodded. "I read that in the handbook. Something about bumper stickers upsetting the clients."

Conrad snorted and pulled his seatbelt around his ample middle, then looked at me again. "You're the guy from Vegas? I heard you got shot out there."

"I did, twice, but I'm pretty much healed up now."

"Won't matter as long as you can stand up. Fancy luncheon for some rich prick that's getting an award. We just have to make sure people are on the guest list and keep the paparazzi away. Not that any paparazzi are going to show up. This should only take one guy, but I'm supposed to show you how it's done."

"Do we each get a list and check people off as they come in?" I asked.

"One list, so I'll let you deal with that. It'll be part of your training."

He started the van and drove out to the interstate, then turned north. It wasn't long before we hit traffic. He sat looking dourly at the cars in front of us without saying a word. Finally, I attempted conversation.

"How far north are we going?"

"Twenty minutes, if it wasn't for this mess. Might be an hour at this rate."

"How far up is that gun club Captain Gregory was talking about?"

"Never been there. I don't trust some of those guys." He eyed me cautiously. "I hear you're buddies with the boss."

"I don't know about buddies, but he asked me to join that club. You don't trust some of the members?"

"There's three or four guys that I don't like to work with, and they're members. Tough guys that like to throw their weight around. I've been on jobs with them, and often as not they end up hurting someone. If some guy comes after you with a broken bottle, fine, mess him up. But you can't beat someone down just for yelling at you."

I grinned at him. "That's in the handbook. And Jack did say that I have to behave myself."

He managed a smile. "I've heard the stories. I'll try not to piss you off."

"These guys you don't like, am I going to have to work with them?"

"They all work on the cash trucks, so probably not at first. They came up from Philadelphia after Frank's accident."

"I suppose Jack needed extra help after that. Jenny told me about what happened to her dad."

"Jenny?"

"Jack's sister. She moved back here with me from Vegas. That's how I know Jack, and how I got this job."

"I didn't know he had a sister. You've heard the rumor about Jack's dad?" For a guy that didn't talk much, Conrad had heard a lot of rumors and seemed willing to repeat them. I already regretted mentioning Jenny. I said that I hadn't heard any rumor about Frank Mercer.

Conrad nodded his head. "Supposedly he's still alive and hiding out from the cops. Of course, the guy that told me that is one of the guys from Philly, so I'm not sure if I believe it."

"I think I'll still give the club a try," I said. Conrad shrugged and clammed up again. We spent the rest of the ride in silence.

The luncheon was in the conference room of a private golf club with two entrances that faced each other, separated by a circle drive and a pair of fountains. While Conrad checked in, I walked around the building. When he came back outside I questioned the logic of security. Anyone from the clubhouse only had to walk around the back of the building to enter the conference room from the rear patio.

Conrad handed me a clipboard and shrugged. "That's where I'll be, making sure no one sneaks in that way. You would think they could just lock the door, but I guess having security makes them feel important. Rich people, right? Just ask their names and check them off the list. If anyone gives you trouble, use your pager. And don't hit anybody."

The guests started arriving shortly before noon. They unloaded themselves from their Bentleys and Jaguars, handed their keys to a pair of eager valets, then announced themselves to me. Most seemed surprised that I didn't know their names, but no one gave me any real trouble. From the snippets of conversation I heard, I knew it was a retirement party for a hedge fund manager. They had decided to throw in an awards ceremony and drink a lot.

By twelve-thirty, most of the names had been checked off my list and I was getting bored. I shifted my position enough so that I could watch the other entrance. There were a dozen sets of clubs in a rack near the entrance to the clubhouse and a college kid was busy with a rag, cleaning and polishing them. One of the valets pulled up in an Escalade and the pair threw four sets of clubs in the back.

Shortly after that, four golfers in their sixties with red faces and round bellies came out, handed the kids more cash than they deserved, and got in the shiny SUV. I could hear them talking and laughing about missed putts, their bitchy wives, and how drunk they planned to get at the next stop. Right then I decided I was never going to take up the game. Unlikely as the scenario the Gypsy had created might be, that mayor was going to have to find another woman to run off with. The Gypsy would never be a golf-widow if I had anything to say about it.

I recognized the next golfer when he walked out of the clubhouse. He was wearing Dockers and a sweater vest. He had a putter in his hand and he was examining it carefully. When he spotted me, he glanced to his left and right, then ambled over and extended the club.

"What do you think? Is this going to make a difference in my game?"

I wasn't happy to see him, but the sweater vest put a smile on my face. "Depends on where I put it, Collins. How did you find me? Is the FBI tracking my phone?"

Collins tucked the putter under his arm. "Randolph has been hoping we'd hear from you."

"He said not to call unless it was important."

"No red flags?"

"I got an earful about the gun club. Some big guns, but nothing illegal."

"And the Gypsy?"

"No sign of her," I lied.

He looked confused. "We had you at an airport in Massachusetts. Are you taking flying lessons?"

"I'll be leaving my cellphone at home from now on. Trust goes both ways, Collins. Tell your boss I don't like being spied on. That's not what I signed up for."

"Might I point out that trust is earned, and that lying to the FBI is a crime."

"I don't remember getting my Miranda rights read to me. Now take that putter and go away before you need to have it surgically removed."

He offered a weak smile. "I can't tell when you're kidding."

"I'm not," I assured him, then played nice. "Just tell Randolph to take it down a notch. It's too early to have any idea of what's going on with Jack, and it'll take me a while to get to know the people at the gun club. My first meeting is next weekend. All things considered, they might not welcome me with open arms. It could take months, and they may never trust me."

"And the gypsy woman?"

"Gypsy. It's her name."

"More of an alias. Does she trust you?"

I liked Agent Collins less every time he opened his mouth. "You'll have to ask her that when you find her."

"Any thoughts on how we can determine her true identity and possibly track her down?"

"She doesn't trust me that much. And she's not the problem, Collins. She's more likely to be part of the solution. Arresting her would be a big mistake."

"I'm sure Agent Randolph has no intention of arresting her. He seems as enchanted by her as you are. He just doesn't like loose ends and not knowing what her motivations are."

"I trust her a hell of lot more than I trust the FBI, and you. And I think her chances of figuring out who sent those shooters to the Exotic are better than Randolph's, or mine. You tell him when I know something about Mercer or that gun club that amounts to anything, I'll be in touch. But don't expect me to rat out the Gypsy, because I'm not going to do that."

"Agent Randolph expects your full cooperation."

"Does he? Or is that just you, trying to look good for your boss? I have your number and I have Randolph's. When I know something, I'll call." From the corner of my eye I saw Conrad coming in our direction. I lowered my voice, took a step closer, and glowered down at Collins. "Now go play with your putter somewhere else, somewhere far away."

"What was that about?" Conrad asked, watching Collins beat a hasty retreat.

"Just some hacker complaining about his slice," I explained.

"Ever play the game?" Conrad asked.

"Never," I said. "And I'm never going to."

Chapter Twenty-Four

"What the hell have you been doing?" Olson cringed and pulled the phone away from his ear. "Three weeks it's been, and not a word."

"I'm being careful, Detective Murdock. You did say Darius Luca had been implicated in a murder. I've met the guy, and he's not someone I want to antagonize. I'm making progress, but it's...complicated."

"I turned you loose with my best lead, Jimmy, and the clock is ticking. The FBI is going to get a subpoena and I'll have to turn over that coat. Before long they'll be knocking on the same doors you are. Any sign of the woman we're looking for? God-dammit, Olson! Do I have to come out there myself?"

"Obviously, Detective, you have no jurisdiction in Boston."

"Don't care. I have plenty of vacation time saved up and I've always wanted to see the east coast."

"No offense, but without any authority, all you're going to do is make Darius mad. And you wouldn't want to that. I'm told he used to be a professional boxer."

"Big tall guy I bet. Black hair like the woman you're supposed to be looking for?" The detective snorted in Jimmy's ear. "I'm sure glad we're not paying you for this."

"He is tall and swarthy looking. Arms the size of most mortals' legs, and hands as big as a catcher's mitt."

"Great visual, Hemingway, but save it for the book. Any mention at all of the woman I sent you out there to find?"

"Detective!" Jimmy's voice cracked, then he calmed himself. "As you said, I'm an unpaid volunteer. Granted I appreciate the lead, but I have to be careful how I approach this. I have made progress. Patience mentioned a woman, and she could be the one we're looking for. She's related to Darius and the girls somehow. Patience says that she travels a lot and has an exciting job, so that would fit."

"Who the hell is Patience?"

"Darius's youngest daughter. He has two girls, Patience and Charity. Both extremely attractive young women."

"Patience and Charity?" Jimmy eased the phone away from his ear again as Detective Murdock went on another expletive-laced rant. "Are you even looking for that woman, or are you too busy getting your dick wet?"

"Settle down, Detective." Jimmy said calmly. "It's all part of the plan. I've been invited to a family dinner this Friday and I'm told Darius's sister and her granddaughter will be there. I'm reasonably sure the granddaughter is the woman we're looking for. Patience said Izzy is very tall and quite muscular. She's actually very jealous of her."

"Ain't that cute," Murdock mocked, then raised his voice again. "Then get a God-damn picture of her!"

"How am I supposed to do that without raising suspicion? Just be patient, Detective. I'll call you next weekend with an update."

"You'd better, Jimmy," the detective growled, "because my patience is running thin, and my charity is about to come to an end. See what I did there?"

Jimmy chuckled. "Very clever, Detective. Don't worry, I will call you."

"I'm not kidding, Olson. I will get on a God-damn airplane, and…"

Jimmy ended the call without acknowledging the detective's further threats. Granted, he had bent the truth, but the detective wasn't his editor, or his boss. He had neither now, and that was liberating. All part of the plan? Any plan Jimmy had formulated changed about five minutes after he walked into the bakery and looked into the brown eyes of Patience Luca. The plan had devolved further after two weeks of unremittent sex and whispered words of affection. There was even talk of love.

Now there was a whole new plan. A plan that had very little to do with discovering the identity of the woman at the Exotic and writing a book about the FBI's involvement. It was possible that after he made a heartfelt confession, Patience would forgive him for his subterfuge. It would have to be a carefully crafted and well-timed confession, lest he found himself on the wrong side of Darius Luca. It was also possible that the subject might never come up.

"Sorry about this," the Gypsy said, sliding the wounded drone onto the work bench. "Our retrieval system failed miserably. Luckily, the hoops got caught on the wheel skirt and I was able to climb down and retrieve it. But it's plenty fast and the wings extended perfectly."

Levi rolled the drone over, making clucking noises as he examined the damage. "I knew it would run circles around anything made commercially. I'll extract the camera and get the proofs ready. I don't know what you're looking for, but the negatives will show hot spots better than anything I can print."

"We can look at them later tonight, if that's alright."

"Dinner with Grandmama?"

"Don't remind me. I wouldn't go, but Patience has a new man that she insists we all meet. He's made it almost a month, so Charity thinks he's the one. Darius hasn't scared him off, so maybe she's right."

"I don't know why everyone is so scared of Darius," Levi commented. "He strikes me as a perfectly gentle man."

"Now. Making donuts agrees with him. I haven't used the knives, but it's been a month. Should we swap them out?"

"Absolutely. The constant movement dulls them slightly. No trouble getting through airport security?"

"None. They never get a second look. Even if they show up on a scan, they get passed over as part of the shoe."

"That's why I insisted on two identical blades and the concave design," Levi said. "The width adds strength. I wouldn't be surprised if they actually make the boots stronger."

The Gypsy rolled her knee to the side and pulled on the loop at the back of her shoe. "The finger-loop makes them easy to get on, but the catch sticks sometimes." She grunted slightly and pulled again, withdrawing an eight-inch plastic shaft that extended down the back side of her boot. She examined the tip of the blade and ran a finger along both edges of the knife's width. "Still fairly sharp, and I was running in them."

Levi frowned as he examined the edges. "Who were you chasing?"

"Being chased," she corrected. She reversed the earlier procedure and handed him the blade from her second boot. "A couple of wannabe muggers, or potential rapists. I'm still not sure which. I didn't hurt them too badly."

"And the footrace? What if they had caught you?"

"Not even close, lucky for them. Just a couple of lightweights. Honestly, I felt bad after the fact, but I'd just been arguing with Gabby and I was in a mood. She makes me want to hurt someone every time I talk to her."

"Still, you should be careful," he scolded. "And how is Adam Cain?"

"Why would you ask me that?"

"You couldn't use the drone without someone flying the airplane. Your grandmother asked me, and we surmised it was him."

"I wanted him to see what he's getting into. And it was nice having someone to talk to for a change."

"Of course, but Gabby's going to ask you about him."

"It's not her business," the Gypsy said stubbornly.

Levi was installing the new blades in the Gypsy's boots. He squinted down at his work through cheaters two sizes too large for his face. "Attractive fellow, this Adam Cain?"

The Gypsy slapped his shoulder. "Stop it. You're too old to gossip, and I don't have time for a man. But yes, he's very good-looking."

Levi handed the Gypsy the repaired footwear. "If Patience Luca can settle down, there's still a chance for you."

"Maybe she's finally found the right person and all the craziness is behind her," the Gypsy offered.

Levi pulled his oversized glasses off and rubbed at his eyes. "Maybe the same could be said for you."

"It would never last," the tall woman said, then changed the subject. "I'm sorry you and Gwyneth are going to miss supper. Everyone will have to be on their best behavior, even my grandmother."

"Someone has to hold down the fort," he said, "and I would much rather tinker here than be caught between you and your grandmother."

"I had a talk with my brother about you," the matriarch of the Luca family said after they had started the short drive to Darius's home. "He thinks I owe you an apology."

"He's always been the sensible one," the Gypsy said dryly. "Why are you apologizing?"

"I didn't say I was," the older woman said quickly, then managed a laugh. "He did point out the fact that you have very good instincts, and that I should trust you more. I would have rid the planet of those three men, but I can accept the fact that you didn't. He reminded me that you're not my personal weapon to dispense when I feel aggrieved." The old woman took a deep breath and let it out slowly while her granddaughter waited. "If I've treated you that way...I shouldn't have."

The Gypsy nodded. "I know that's as close as I'll ever get to a real apology."

"When the law doesn't do its job, Izzy, we have to act."

"Sometimes it's unavoidable, like in Vegas. Killing those bastards didn't bother me in the least. But shooting people isn't always the right thing to do."

"You're sounding more like your mother every day," Gabby said.

"You and I would both be happier people if we were more like her," the Gypsy said, parking the car. She pulled the keys and opened her door, then looked back. "But I don't want to talk about her with you. It never ends well."

James Olson stared down at his plate, ignoring the buzz of dinner conversation, lost in thought. He was very sure that the woman sitting across the table from him, fondly known to her family as "Izzy", had to be the person he'd seen in the video of the shooting. "Way taller than me and crazy good-looking" had been Kyle's description. Izzy was both those things, with waves of dark hair that fell onto her back. A luxurious mane that would easily conceal her face were she to be bent forward and moving across a dimly lit room with a gun in her hand.

Izzy was almost certainly the mysterious woman that Detective Murdock wanted to talk to so badly. Seeing her rekindled Jimmy's curiosity, and thoughts of the story he could write. He had spent a good deal of time and money traveling across the country in pursuit of what could be a career defining moment. None of that mattered now.

Jimmy knew Detective Murdock wouldn't appreciate the irony, and would probably threaten him with bodily harm, but he had found the antithesis of violence and murder in the ready smile and willing body of a woman ten years his junior. Exposing the identity of the beautiful woman dining with them, and the machinations of the FBI, had ceased to be important to him. For the time being at least, the only story Jimmy Olson wanted to write was his own.

Roused from his epiphany by his girlfriend's sharp elbow, Jimmy looked across the table at the grandniece of his host. She was regarding him coldly and he looked quickly away. Could she possibly know what had brought him to Boston, or was it his own guilt that was sending chills down his spine? This was another bit of irony he had hoped to avoid, the time when the pursuer became the prey.

Izzy's grandmother was asking him a question. "Patience tells us you're looking for a job here, Mister Olson."

"Yes," he said, trying to express a confidence he wasn't feeling. "I have a couple of interviews coming up in Boston, but anywhere on the east coast would be great."

"And you're from Los Angeles?" the older woman asked. "What is it you do?"

Jimmy shifted uncomfortably in his chair. He had told Patience what he did for a living, so it was too late for a lie. "I'm a journalist."

"He got tired of writing about trashy celebrities," Patience volunteered enthusiastically. "James wants to work at a serious newspaper and be a serious reporter. Investigate things."

"Investigate things?" Gabby asked. "What kind of things?"

Patience continued speaking for Jimmy, elaborating. "Corruption in the government, crime stories, politics. Important stuff like that."

"Good luck," Charity said. "People are going to believe whatever they want, doesn't matter what they read in the newspapers."

Patience glowered at her sister. "And he's going to write a book."

The granddaughter spoke up. "That sounds interesting. Fiction, academic, or an exposé?"

"Nothing definite, but possibly an exposé," Jimmy offered, meeting her gaze. "I thought I had stumbled onto something important and hard-hitting, but I've kind of lost interest in that concept. New city, I need new ideas."

The woman's eyes bored into him. "But if you're passionate about an idea, you should write about it. Some stories need to be told."

"There are parts of the story that I might continue with," Jimmy said, looking cautiously across the table. He was starting to sweat. "But not all of it. I've recently uncovered some things that could result in a conflict of interest." There it was, Jimmy thought, she would have to know what he was implying. He was rewarded with a warm smile.

"Sometimes the unexpected happens," she said, "and if we react the way we should, life rewards us. And if we don't, it goes the other way."

Jimmy smiled and nodded, aware that what she'd said could be taken as a veiled threat. He slid an arm around his girlfriend. "Finding Patience was unexpected, and I have no intention of screwing that up."

Jimmy did his best to study the senior members of the Luca family as they ate. He had no doubt that Darius Luca might be as capable as his grandniece, given the need. Patience had implied on more than one occasion that he had 'dealt' with unwanted suitors for both his daughters and kept the immediate neighborhood drug free.

Izzy's grandmother, Gabby, was the more complicated of the two. There was tension there, Jimmy was sure, and an effort on everyone's part to appear civil for his benefit. He caught the older woman looking at him repeatedly and couldn't help wondering what secrets her granddaughter had shared with her, and with Darius.

While Patience and Charity cleared the table, Jimmy passed on a drink and announced his need for fresh air. He wasn't surprised when Izzy followed him outside. He leaned against his rental and she sat cross legged on the stoop.

"Nice night," he offered, "but I couldn't breathe in there. Did you eat as much as I did?"

"The food is always good here. My aunt is a wonderful cook. Darius, and the girls too."

"I've gained ten pounds since meeting Patience," Jimmy shared.

"She's quite smitten with you, and very dear to all of us."

Jimmy nodded and smiled. Another veiled threat, but a well-intentioned one. He waited, sure she would give him some confirmation that she knew who he was.

"You know I travel a lot for my job," she said, and continued when Jimmy nodded. "I've spent a lot of time on the west coast lately, and in Las Vegas. Jimmy Olson. That's a name that jumps off the page at you. I saw a couple of your articles about the mass shooting. Good work, I thought. Your human-interest story about the young guy who was traumatized by the shooting at the strip club, and the follow-up about the kids who were orphaned that night; those were both well done. Those were stories worth telling."

"It did seem like the victims were being over-looked," Jimmy said, studying his fingers. "Most of the coverage was about Adam Cain, and about the mystery woman that killed the shooters. That was good work too. The act, not the stories."

The Gypsy shrugged and inspected the toe of her boot. "Finding out who that was would be a big story, wouldn't it?"

Jimmy nodded, then went all in. "I can't imagine the woman involved would thank whoever wrote that story. I wouldn't want to be that person." They both sat quietly for a moment, then Jimmy volunteered more. "I know the local detective on the case, and he's a bulldog, very persistent. Turns out he has that woman's coat, so he has her DNA. It seems likely he'll find her sooner or later. Or the FBI will."

"I would think she expects to be found out, eventually."

Jimmy nodded, sure they were on the same page. "It's a shame though, after saving who knows how many lives that she can't stay anonymous if she wishes. I would never reveal her identity, but I'd tell her to watch out for that Detective Murdock."

The Gypsy rocked to her feet and stretched. "We'd better get back inside or Patience will think I have designs on you. Good chat, Jimmy."

Before she opened the door Jimmy spoke again. "Are you going to tell Darius about me?"

The tall woman laughed. "Who do you think told me?"

Chapter Twenty-Five

It was the first Saturday of the month and I was early. The steel gate was locked, but a small sign said, "Cherry Hollow Gun Club". I sat in my truck looking things over. The hollow in question was considerably flatter than the surrounding landscape and ran the length of the shooting range, well over half a mile according to Captain Gregory. At the end of that distance another rolling hill crossed the property. It had been excavated, leaving a bank of sand ten or fifteen feet high and a hundred feet long. It was the perfect backstop for even the most inaccurate of shots. I could see targets at one-hundred-yard increments, all the way to the sand banks.

From the airplane it had been hard to judge the height of the surrounding hills. They weren't tall, but steep, and covered with fallen trees and brush. The natural shape of the little valley probably helped contain the sound of gunfire, although there didn't appear to be any neighbors close enough to lodge a complaint. North of the range I could see a small pond that was overflowing with seagulls and waterfowl. A surprisingly large stream ran from it and traversed the length of the northern side of the property, ducking behind the older building on that side, then crossing under the road I was sitting on through a large culvert. Its spring-fed water was undoubtedly bound for the lake that the Gypsy and I had seen from the air.

The pole barn where the vehicles had been parked was on my right, its big door shut and locked. The building on my left was an older timber framed structure built from roughly hewn logs that might have been there for a hundred years. The roof had been replaced, but like a lot of buildings in New England someone had gone to the trouble of revitalizing the architecture, chinking the old logs, and replacing some of the timbers. Undoubtedly, it was the same building the Gypsy had seen in the photo archives. Once a slaughterhouse and meat processing plant, its purpose now wasn't clear. There were two windows visible from where I sat, both with heavy steel bars inside the glass. I could see only one door.

It wasn't idle curiosity that had me surveying the property. I'd received more texts. The first was from Agent Randolph reminding me that I had an obligation to the FBI, and that he wanted to meet with me soon. I didn't feel all that obligated, but talking to Randolph was better than dealing with Collins. I had returned his text.

The second text was from the Gypsy. She had disappeared shortly after the day of our flight without explanation and I was sure I knew why. I had pushed too hard to make it personal.

She didn't want personal. I was starting to think I did.

This text was from a different number. She didn't identify herself, but she had spelled it *Cane* again. Our new personal code. Her message was short. *'We need to know more about what's in that old meat plant.'*

I sat in my pickup contemplating my options. Much as I wanted to look in through the barred windows of the low structure, jumping the fence wouldn't be a good way to gain anyone's trust, much less ingratiate myself with the members of a potentially violent militia. I could see security cameras mounted on both front corners of the older structure, and they didn't look like the cheap fakes some people put up to dupe would-be vandals. It was reasonable to presume there were more behind the building that I couldn't see.

I started my pickup and backed out of the short driveway, drove north for a quarter of a mile, then made a U-turn and drove slowly back toward the property. From my new vantage point I could see part of the back side of the building and the stream that ran parallel to it. The ground fell away on that side and there was a rock and cement wall running the length of the building. It looked like the whole structure had a full basement under it. It must have been the perfect place to store ice packed in sawdust and fresh meat bound for the tables of hungry city-dwellers.

I glimpsed a door and another security camera through the trees, then spotted a dust trail in my rear-view mirror. I drove back to the gate and pulled off to the side as if I had just arrived. Anyone inside the building might have questioned my intent had they seen me, but I could always claim that I thought I was at the wrong gate.

The vehicle responsible for the dust trail wheeled up to the gate and a man jumped out quickly, swatting at the dust cloud that filled the air, then rounded the front of his truck and walked over. He had a pistol on his hip, and he slipped the thong off the hammer as he walked up. I dropped my window and put both hands on the steering wheel.

"I'm here for the meeting," I explained. "Captain Gregory said eight."

"You're an hour off. The club meetings start at nine." He looked at me owlishly. "What's your name?"

"Adam Cain." I offered him a hand through the window. "Is there a sign-in sheet or something?"

"I heard about you." He nodded and ignored my hand. "Sniper in Afghanistan, right? Cap talked like you're a big deal."

I grinned at him. "Nope. I didn't see much action, but I can kill a chicken from five hundred yards."

He managed a smile and finally took his hand off the gun. "I guess it wouldn't hurt if I let you in early. You can park along the south wall of the big shed." He pulled a set of keys from his pocket and walked to the gate. He pushed the gate open then motioned for me to drive through. He pulled in behind me and parked beside the older building, then walked over with his keys.

"Sorry, I didn't get your name," I said.

"Cole. Cole Conley. Mauer's out of town on business, so I'm minding the gate and keeping an eye on the Bunkhouse until he gets back."

I shrugged. "Mauer? Bunkhouse?"

"Henrik Mauer owns the property and stays in the old slaughterhouse when he's here. He calls it the Bunkhouse."

"Does it have a bunch of beds, like a hunting camp?" I asked. "I was surprised there's a full basement. I could see it when I drove up."

"You're all kinds of observant," he said dryly.

I nodded at the bars in the windows. "Not much of a view either."

"Mauer isn't the kind of guy that cares about scenery. He's all about security."

"Still, it's a cool old building," I said. "What's it like inside?"

297

"Don't expect an invite. Henrik's pretty careful about who he has around."

"I'm just curious about the way it was built. It has to be a hundred years old, isn't it?"

"I guess," he mumbled, then frowned at me. "You a shooter, or a carpenter?"

"Both," I said. "Painter, electrician, and plumber too. I'm remodeling my dad's old place just south of Poughkeepsie and working for Mercer Security."

"Heard you got shot at that club in Vegas a while back."

"Along with a lot of other people. Do you work for Jack too?"

"On loan, sort of." He leaned against the big door of the steel building and pushed it to the side. "I need to go back and check on Henrik's place," he explained.

"Would it be okay if I take a look inside? I'm curious about those roof trusses."

"No," he said quickly. "Nobody goes in there without Henrik or Vince saying it's okay. They take security seriously, not like this bunch of weekend warriors." He nodded dismissively at the rows of chairs set up on one end of the steel building.

"What's to secure? It's just an old building," I said.

"And it's none of your business," he snapped. When I grinned and shrugged, he relented a little. "The guys in Cap's club like

298

shooting and marching and pretending they're in a war. But when the real shooting starts, they'll shit themselves and run back to their wives."

"The real shooting?"

His frown deepened. "Look, Mister Cain, personally I'm glad you're here. We need someone like you who can actually teach us something about shooting, and someone who's been in a real fight. Word is you got tossed out of the Army for killing too many Taliban, which in my mind was what you were getting paid to do. I would think that would piss you off. If I was you, I'd be pretty unhappy with the worthless politicians that run that show.

"But if you want to fit in with people like Henrik and Vince and me, you can't keep asking so damn many questions and looking to nose around. If all you want is to hang out and drink beer with Cap'n Gregory and his bunch, that's fine too. But it would be too bad, because we could really use you."

I risked it. "Use me?"

"What did I just say?" he growled. "Enough with the questions. Grab a chair and wait for someone to show up. Cap's usually early, so he should be here any minute. There's a big pot and some coffee in that steel cupboard. Make yourself useful."

Captain Gregory came in a few minutes later wearing a pleated Naval uniform and carrying a clipboard. As more people drifted in, he introduced me and explained that I was the new rifle instructor and that I would be taking over the supervision of the range. He winked and called me Lieutenant Cain. One of the other guys explained that all the team leaders were given the rank of Lieutenant. If it wasn't for Mickey, I would have gone home right then. Playing soldier wasn't my idea of fun.

Everyone milled around drinking coffee and talking while they waited for the meeting to start. Cole came back in, followed by four other men. They stood apart from the group and none of the others approached them. It looked like Cole was doing most of the talking and motioning in my direction. I caught their glances and turned my back to them. People continued to pour into the building, and I finally spotted Jack Mercer.

"Interesting club you have here," I said.

He laughed and nodded toward Captain Gregory. "I know, it's a little much. Cap takes himself too seriously, but his heart's in the right place. Did he make you a Lieutenant?"

I nodded. "Fastest promotion I ever got. I guess I'm leading a team."

"It'll grow on you. There are a lot of really good guys that belong, and a good share of them work for me. After we're done shooting we break out the beer."

"Cole and his bunch, do they work for you?"

"Most of them. My dad's old partner sent a few guys up from Philly to help out after my dad was killed." He nodded in their direction, and they all raised a hand.

"They seem to have their own little clique," I pointed out. "I asked about the old building and Cole got defensive right away."

"They stick to themselves, but they do their jobs."

"The Bunkhouse, that's what Cole called that old building. Cap isn't the only one that takes himself too seriously."

He nodded. "Mostly they're okay, but Henrik Mauer is way out there. Vince too. He's a whole different breed of cat. Dangerous, if you ask me. They're both conspiracy theorists, and too political for this group. But they sit in from time to time, and they were both good friends of my dad."

"Just to be clear," I asked, "your father died when that oil rig exploded, right?"

"Yeah," he said. "Just shy of two years ago. Why? Have you heard the rumors?"

"Pretty much everybody I've worked with says he isn't really dead, just hiding from the law."

He shrugged and his smile disappeared. "I hope you won't repeat that stuff to Jenny. I don't know how she'd feel about it."

"I haven't talked to Jenny, and don't know that I will. How is she?"

He frowned and gave me an odd look. "Fine, I guess. I thought I heard her on the phone with you the other night. I was hoping you were patching things up."

"Wasn't me. Tell her I said hello and that I hope she's doing well."

He slapped my arm and laughed. "I wouldn't give up just yet, Cain. She'll come around."

The meeting started and Captain Gregory insisted that I go up front to be introduced. "We have a new member, Gentlemen, and he'll be a valuable addition to the club." He went on and on, mostly lying about my shooting record until it became embarrassing, then called for a vote. Apparently being a Lieutenant in Captain Gregory's outfit wasn't automatic, but no one else wanted the job. It was my first day and I was already officially the new range commander.

"Other than giving people a few pointers, what is it you want me to do?" I asked after the roll call.

"You're the man out there," Cap assured me. "However you want to run the range is up to you. But if there's any shenanigans, or anyone is doing something dangerous, let me know. We take safety very seriously here, and anyone not following the rules faces expulsion. I doubt you'll have any trouble." He glanced at the entrance and waved his hand at someone, then turned back to me. "Vince just walked in. They use the range a lot, but when our group is here they usually stay away. I'm guessing they'll want to join in today, since you'll be instructing."

Vince was a grey-eyed blond man pushing fifty. He was a few inches shorter than me, but barrel-chested and powerful looking. He appraised me with a cold look as we walked over.

"Vincent Carlson," Captain Gregory said. "Adam Cain. He's the one I told you about. Trained sniper, although he tells me he never shot anyone over there. At least not that he'll admit to."

I could see Vince's interest was piqued. He ignored Caps' chatter and nodded in my direction. "Maybe you could give me a few pointers. I have a pair of 82's, and I just bought a converted Denel."

"Nice." I did my best to sound enthusiastic. "I've never shot a Denel, but I've heard they're every bit as good as the American guns."

He nodded. "Henrik has one, so I looked around. It's a lot lighter than the Fifty."

"I'd love to shoot it sometime, if you wouldn't mind," I said. Most men love to show off their toys and Vince was no different. His smile turned genuine, and he extended his hand.

"Good to meet you, Cain. I hear you got tossed out of the Rangers. Sounded like a bullshit deal to me."

"Not part of the plan," I admitted, wondering how yet another person could know about my court-martial. Cole had suggested I should be bitter, and I was, but not because the Army had asked me to leave. I had made that decision before the dust settled in the marketplace that awful day. But I scowled and played the part Vince expected of me. "They should have just let us do our job and stayed in Washington."

"Damn right," he said quickly. The Captain had wandered away, clipboard in hand, and Vince lowered his voice. "How many of those bastards did you really kill?"

"Four for sure, maybe five. I was taking fire and on the run when I took a couple of pokes at the last sentry. Pretty sure the last shot was dead on."

He shook his head. "All those civilians dying, just because the politicians were playing games."

304

I wasn't sure that was true, but I nodded. "Exactly. There was a truce, for all the good that did."

"Damn shame. Those assholes from Washington should have to answer for stuff like that. Drop them off, unarmed, in the middle of Taliban country and see how they do. Am I right?"

"Damn right!" I said.

It was the reaction he was looking for. His smile grew. "Are you headed over to the range now?"

"Shortly, I guess. Cap wants me to go through some safety protocols, then I thought I'd just talk about the basics. A lot of these guys will never take a shot longer than a couple of hundred yards. At that distance, if you don't get buck fever and your rifle is sighted properly, there's no excuse to miss. Over three hundred yards most people need a bench to shoot from."

"Six or eight of my guys want to shoot today, and we're hoping for some one-on-one time with you."

"I don't know, timewise, but we could get a start. I didn't bring my binoculars."

"No problem, we have spotting scopes."

"A lot of it just amounts to practice and knowing your own gun. I hope you have plenty of ammunition."

His early hesitancy had disappeared and he grew more enthusiastic. "Trust me, we have a lot of ammo. We're going to load up and drive Cole's pickup out there. He told me you asked about the Bunkhouse."

It sounded more like an invitation than an accusation. "I thought that was off limits," I said. "Cole said the owner was out of town and that no one is allowed in there. I just wanted to look at the rafters, because it's such an old building."

His mood soured. "Cole's got no say. Henrik and I are equal partners, and if I say it's alright, it's alright. Mostly it's just storage, but Henrik has a living area on the far end. He's here most of the time, but he's got the guys scared to death that someone will get into the arsenal."

"Arsenal?" I asked.

He couldn't help bragging again. "We have over twenty thousand rounds stored in the basement, a dozen anti-materiel guns like mine, a dozen AR's, and enough M1's to outfit a small army." His smile grew. "I even found a couple of rocket launchers."

"Preparing for a war?" I asked.

He nodded. "Don't fool yourself, Cain. It's coming."

The Bunkhouse was a full ninety feet long, but narrow, and built for function. I knew that it hadn't served as a processing plant in at least sixty years, but the steel rails used to hang meat were still attached to the bottom of the rafters. I imagined I could still smell the stench of rotting meat emanating from the basement, but that might have been coming from Henrik Mauer's living area.

Cole and four of the men who hadn't attended the meeting came up from the basement, all carrying ammo-boxes. He nodded to me and pointed at the others. "They came late. It's okay if they shoot with us, isn't it?"

"They can shoot," Vince stated, without looking in my direction. "And Cain said he'd give us some pointers after the others give it up. Right, Cain?"

"Sure," I agreed. I looked up at the rafters, feigning interest. "Those metal rails must have been how they hung the animals when they skinned them."

"Must have been," Vince said absently. "Front to back with a door on either end. Want to see the rest?"

Cole spoke up. "Are you sure that's a good idea, Vince?"

Vince scowled in his direction. "You let me worry about what's a good idea." Cole dropped his head and nodded, then continued out to his truck carrying a pair of metal ammo boxes. The others followed him out the door, then stood beside the tailgate talking to each other.

"I have to remind them who runs the show sometimes," Vince said. "Come on down. We've been stockpiling for years."

The steps creaked under our combined weight and I had to duck my head to pass under the doorframe as we walked into a dimly lit hallway. Someone had rough wired the basement, hanging lights and wires without the benefit of an electrician. There were switches, and Vince flipped one of them. More lights came on and he walked forward, motioning to three small doors on our right as we shuffled down the narrow hallway.

"Ice storage in these, but they did some processing down here too. We picked the corner room because it would be the most bomb proof."

"You think that's likely?" I asked.

He shrugged his massive shoulders. "This day and age? You have to be prepared for anything."

"That's probably true," I said. I didn't mean it the way he had. Cole and his compatriots had relocked the door and it took a few seconds for Vince to unlock the pair of padlocks and turn the key in the deadbolt. I followed him into the dimly lit room. I might as well have stepped into the armory of the 75th. Three rows of rifles lined one wall, and both ends of the room were filled with racks of ammunition boxes. Two RPG grenade launchers hung on the fourth wall, and two long crates sat on the floor. I pointed. "Rockets?"

Vince grinned at me and pulled down a pair of rifles from the rack. "Pretty impressive, right?"

"Better hope there's never a fire," I said.

"That's what makes this basement the perfect place for storage. These walls are a foot thick, poured concrete and rock, and the ceiling is reinforced too. It never gets more than fifty degrees down here, and it stays dry year-round. Of course, if one of those shells ever blew, the whole place would probably be gone. Want to take one of the Fifties, or are you going to use my Denel? Doesn't matter to me. What matters is the training."

"Realistically, what are your goals?" I asked cautiously. "With a spotter, anyone can eventually hit a target. It's being able to do it on the first or second shot that's important."

"Exactly. That's what we want. The goal is to make that first shot count. And I want to know which of my guys I can depend on to do that."

I laughed it off. "Who are you planning to have them shoot?"

He grinned again. "The enemy of course, when the war starts. You know it's coming."

I tried to sound non-committal. "I've had enough war for one lifetime."

He put a rifle in my hands and his smile disappeared. "Just be sure you're on the right

309

side of things when it happens, Cain. You just might live through it."

We each grabbed an ammo box and retraced our steps. I did my best to remember every detail of the place. I couldn't swear Vincent Carlson was planning anything, but he had enough munitions to overthrow a third world country. Maybe he was dangerous, or maybe he was crazy. Probably he was both. But so far, I hadn't seen or heard anything that would tie the people from the Cherry Hollow Gun Club to the shooting at the Exotic and Mickey's death.

The rifle range had six stations and no shortage of people wanting to use them. Captain Gregory appeared again, expounding on my credentials and talking about the importance of following my instructions for the safety of everyone involved. There was no doubt that his little speech was aimed at Cole and the rest of the Bunkhouse Boys, because he never took his eyes off them.

The Bunkhouse Boys. I had amused myself by coining the phrase while listening to our long-winded leader drone on and on. Judging by their disinterest, Cole and his crew didn't take the lecture to heart, and everyone seemed happier when Cap stopped talking and turned things over to me.

After going over the safety protocols one last time, I let the hunters in the group start shooting at the closer targets, answering questions as they came up. I had some experience as an instructor and hitting a target at two hundred yards from a bench-rest isn't difficult. Everyone had used the range before and there were no problems, at first.

By the time we worked our way through the fifty-some shooters that were satisfied with being able to hit the next white-tail they saw, Cole and his troupe were getting bored. They had backed their vehicles up near the far end of the range and were sitting at a pair of picnic tables. The four and Cole sat at one table. Vince was alone at the second talking on his cellphone. I was watching him, wondering idly how he had managed to buy two rocket launchers, when one of the four men sitting with the group stood up. Virgil Grant. I remembered him from an earlier introduction. His hair was long and greasy, like his beard. He had his rifle in one hand and he was pointing with the other.

I followed his line of sight. The pond I had seen before was beyond the range and to the north. I saw the flutter of wings and the flash of white as a snow goose or swan settled into the water. Virgil walked a few steps and raised his gun. He fired before I reached him, then laughed and started talking to Cole. His smile disappeared when he saw me coming, but he turned and lifted the gun to his shoulder again, pointing in the general direction of the birds. I ran a step and grabbed the barrel, lifting it skyward.

He tried to jerk the gun away and glared up at me. "What the hell?" he snarled.

"Hunting season's a long way off, and you're too far away. There's no point in flock shooting."

"Mind your own business and let go of my gun before I shove it up your ass."

Since I had a hundred pounds and the better part of a foot on him, that seemed unlikely. I kept my grip on the gun barrel. "The highway is out beyond that pond. A ricochet off the water could kill someone driving by."

He started arguing again and tried to pull his gun from my grasp. Vince pocketed his cellphone, came to his feet, and walked over quickly. I wasn't sure what Vince had in mind, but Cole must have had a sense of it. He had started in our direction, but when he saw the big man coming, he backed away. I braced myself. Virgil wasn't much of a threat, but Vince looked strong as an ox.

He didn't close his fist, just took a big swing with a meaty hand. He caught the side of Virgil's head with enough force to take the smaller man off his feet and nearly knock him unconscious. Stunned, I stepped back and unloaded the gun, then cradled it in my arm. Virgil stared up at me vacantly, then scrambled to his feet. I could see he wasn't completely sure what had happened, but there was pure hatred on his face.

Vince stepped in front of him and pushed him back before he could gather his wits. "You want more, or are you going to listen?" When Virgil sorted out the fact that it was Vince who had hit him, the fight went out of him and he dropped his head. I almost felt sorry for the guy.

"I had it handled," I said, handing Virgil his empty gun.

Vince turned on me immediately. "Don't tell me how to deal with my people, or you and I are going to have a problem next."

The odds weren't good, but I wasn't going to back down. "Your people, my range according to Captain Gregory." I pointed in Virgil's direction. "Either way, I'm not working with you until you get this mess straightened out. Lesson's over."

Chapter Twenty-Six

Tyrel Davis stood and walked to the window of his office, looking up at the Philadelphia skyline. His security company wasn't nearly as grand as Frank Mercer's operation in New York, and his space was leased. But the small fortune he had amassed in Europe lay ready to invest. There were clients to entertain, bribes to be paid, and a hitman to hire if his current plan didn't work out. If everything went well, if his lackeys did as they were told, he would walk away an incredibly rich man and there would be nothing the Feds could prove. His hired help would take the fall. The phone on his desk lit up and his secretary announced a visitor. The head lackey.

"Memorial weekend, Henrik. It's happening. Everyone will be home for the holiday and there will be speeches to make and babies to kiss. Security will be minimal. Are your men ready?" The older man scratched his scraggly beard and looked uncomfortable. Tyrel raised his voice. "I asked, are they ready?"

"They are. We were hoping for a little more time and a little more training to fine tune things. But I have ten guys that Vince is confident can make the shots. He and I will make it an even dozen. It would be better if we had more time. Vince tells me he has a new guy that might help, a trained sniper..."

"Forget that," Tyrel said quickly. "Adam Cain's a plant. He's involved with the woman I was telling you about."

"The woman from Vegas?"

"God knows where she's from. I'm trying to figure that out."

Henrik scratched again, nervously. "What about Frank? I know the guys would feel better if he was on board."

Tyrel stood and started pacing the room like a caged animal. Henrik waited quietly, knowing it was his best option. Tyrel finally sat down and spoke. "Frank's a problem. I talked to him a few weeks after the oil rig went up, then he went into hiding. Now Mertens tells me Frank thinks we set him up and tried to kill him. He's out to get us both, and I'm afraid he's planning to blow the whole deal."

Henrik shook his head. "Cole and the guys will never believe that of Frank. I'm not sure I do."

"You can't repeat this," Tyrel said, "but I'm told Frank and that woman might be working together. And they have backing, someone with a lot of money. We need to flush her out, Henrik, and Frank too. At the very least, I want to cut her throat myself for all the trouble she's given me. She's our biggest problem right now, her and Mercer. I just found out she brokered a deal with the Feds for the Belgian. Frank might be taking the same deal."

"You really think Frank would sell us out?"

"We have to be sure he doesn't. He hasn't shown his face in well over a year, so where is he? I thought going after Jack in Vegas would bring him in, but it didn't."

The older man frowned. "I thought the senator was the target in Vegas, not Jack."

Tyrel's voice rose again. "But Frank didn't know that! It was supposed to be a demonstration of what we could do, but the men you hired screwed it up. I was lucky to negotiate the deal I did, after that fiasco. Still, you'd think Frank would have something to say if he thought I was trying to kill his kid."

Henrik shrugged. "What can we do to pull him out of hiding?"

"He has a daughter and she's in New York." Tyrel waited impatiently for the man in front of him to reach the obvious conclusion, then spelled it out. "Maybe Frank would come in if we had his little girl."

"We couldn't hurt her," Henrik said cautiously. "I wouldn't let that happen."

"Of course not. Frank shows up, fine. Maybe he sends this Gypsy woman to negotiate, better yet."

"Gypsy?"

"The Vegas woman," Tyrel said impatiently, "that's what she goes by. I don't need a crystal ball to tell her what's going to happen when I get my hands on her."

"But nothing can happen to the Mercer girl," Henrik said emphatically. "Convincing my men that we have to kidnap Frank's daughter is going to be hard enough, without her getting hurt somehow."

"Of course not. Hide her in the basement of the old slaughterhouse. Once we get Frank to cooperate or get our hands on this Gypsy, we'll let Frank's daughter go. Cain, the Ranger you mentioned, he and the woman are tight. Partners, I'm told. If she knows where Frank is, Cain probably knows too."

"War is hell," Mauer mused, "and sometimes difficult choices have to be made. If Frank is dealing with the Feds, I'll kill him myself. The unit would never have to know." He sighed and shook his head. "Frank never was a true believer in the cause."

"Not like you and I," Tyrel agreed readily. "But we don't want any more infighting, and a lot of the guys are still loyal to Frank. Maybe he'd settle for some cash and a guarantee that we'll leave his kids alone."

Henrik shrugged, working it out in his head. "He might have to donate his share. Fifty million dollars will buy a lot of munitions."

Tyrel nodded. "I agree. And we'll need them all once we kill those congressmen. I'm doing reconnaissance, finding the right places to shoot from and picking targets. Equal numbers, just like we talked."

Henrik nodded. "Party doesn't matter, they're all traitors to this great country. That's what this is all about, starting over and building a true democracy. My men know we'll probably suffer casualties, but they're more than willing to make that sacrifice."

Tyrel nodded. "The people will see the politicians for what they really are. You, Vince, Cole, all the men we brought in, you're going to change history. You'll be talked about like Washington and Jefferson."

Henrik's eyes filled. He blinked and grated out a reply. "We're not those kind of heroes, Tyrel, we're just doing our part."

Tyrel bit his lip and said what he knew the man wanted to hear. "You're my kind of heroes, Henrik."

"Thank you," the older man said solemnly.

"Okay," Tyrel continued. "Just remember, no one touches that gypsy. She's mine. If Frank doesn't show up, she will. Hopefully without a small army behind her."

"We can take care of anyone that comes," Henrik said confidently. "It may be the first battle in a long war."

"That's not the play," Tyrel insisted. "We need to keep this quiet until those congressmen are taken care of and we get paid. I want you there making damn sure things go exactly as planned."

Henrik nodded. "I'll do my part."

"Deal with the others as you see fit, but if anyone touches either of those women, I'll kill him myself," Tyrel said again. "And you can tell everyone I said that. We'll hammer out the details next week. I have people watching Jack Mercer. I'm not sure why he was in Vegas that night, but if he gets in the way again, we'll have to get rid of with him. Frank or no Frank."

Henrik Mauer nodded and stood, then extended his hand. "What we're doing is important, Tyrel. We'll all be remembered for this someday."

Tyrel watched him leave before he began to chuckle. "You'll be remembered," he muttered under his breath. "I'll remember you when all that money goes into my Caymans account."

Monday morning I had a note in my box instructing me to report to accounting, something about updating my tax information. Mercer Security wasn't a small company, but the office staff was limited and I knew where to find accounting. I ran the steps to the third floor and walked into the main office. I glanced at the note again and found 312 at the end of the hall. The door was open, but I tapped on it anyway. A familiar voice said, "Come in."

I stepped around the divider. "Morning, Jenny. You're in charge of my tax information? Should I be worried?"

She laughed lightly and smiled. "No worries. I'm done being mad at you. But push the door shut, will you?"

I eased the door closed and sat when she pointed at the chair in front of her desk. "I'm glad to see you, but I'm guessing this isn't about my tax status."

"No, that was just an excuse to get you up here. We haven't talked, and I wanted to clear the air and discuss a couple of other things."

"No need to clear the air as far as I'm concerned. You were right to end it. I don't know what's wrong with me, but it was never about you. Any normal person would kill to be with you."

"Thanks, Adam, but that's water under the bridge. I should have stayed away after the first time I left. But then you got shot, and..."

"And you're too nice?" I offered.

She laughed again, happily, and without bitterness. "I've moved on, just so you know. I'm seeing someone."

"That's great. Really. You deserve someone great." It got awkward for a moment, then she changed the subject.

"I wanted to talk to you about Jack. Have you found anything out? You can't think he was involved in any way, do you?"

"He's too good a guy for that," I said confidently. "But I'm not so sure about some of the people he has working for him."

"Have you shared that with Teddy, or Gabriel? Do you call her Gabriel, or do you call her Gypsy?"

I chuckled. "She hates being called Gabriel."

"How are you two getting along? No, never mind, it's not my business who you're spending your time with."

"I don't spend much time with her."

She chewed on her bottom lip, then spoke. "I guess I thought that maybe you two were…getting close."

"She has as many skeletons as I do, Jenny. Probably not a good match."

"I just wanted you to know that I may have made a mistake concerning her. And concerning my brother."

"How so?" I asked.

"I had too much to drink one night and I was feeling sorry for myself. I told Jack about Gabriel, and everything you told me."

"Most of that came out anyway, when they published the video."

"Except that I told him she was the reason we broke up, and that she followed us to New York to be with you. I told him you two were together."

"You know that's not true, right?"

"I told her that day at the Memorial that I trust her, and I meant it. But she's a beautiful woman, and I was hurting. I'll explain it all to Jack. It really doesn't matter, since he's not involved."

"Probably not. Are you still living at his place?"

"Yes, for now. I'm spending time with someone, but it's just dating. I'm taking it slow this time."

I shrugged. "I wasn't fishing, I just wanted to be sure you're somewhere safe."

"I'm safe, Adam. You stay safe too, okay?"

That was my cue. "Okay, I'd better get to work. Or was there really some accounting to do?"

Teddy, as Jenny liked to call him, was waiting for me when I finished my shift. He had texted the location of a diner a couple of blocks from Mercer Security. He had a spot in the corner and a newspaper spread out on the table. The Times.

"Another crossword?" I asked as I slid into the booth.

He grinned, then folded the paper and tossed it on the seat next to him. "Busted. I'm stuck anyway. Thanks for finally showing up."

I took the coffee the waitress offered and waved the menu away. "Thanks for not sending

Collins again. And I finally have something to tell you."

"I have something to tell you too," he said quietly. "Something of a more personal nature."

I grunted. It wasn't too hard to guess. "You and Jenny?"

"Did she tell you?" he asked. "Or are your detective skills getting better?"

I shrugged. "She said she'd started seeing someone…and there were all those coffees. I got the impression she was jealous of the Gypsy, but apparently not because of me."

"And you're okay with it?"

"Not for me to say, is it. Just try not to hurt her."

"Of course not. Whew, I wasn't sure how you'd react. And how is the Gypsy?"

"Remarkable in so many ways. But I still don't know much about her, personally."

"You don't know much, or there's not much you want to tell me?"

"Both," I said. "She's up to her eyeballs in this mess, and she wants to know who sent those men to the Exotic almost as badly as I do. But there's more to it. She wants to find Frank Mercer and his partners, regardless of who ordered that shooting."

"What's her connection to Frank Mercer? I understand that she thinks there's a connection between Jack being there and the shooting, but what else is going on?"

"There is more to it, but I won't say. She did tell me you should read your emails more often."

He frowned. "What is that supposed to mean?"

"It's like the crosswords, just another piece of the puzzle."

"Funny," he said dryly. "And what about the gun club? Learn anything interesting?"

"Most of the members are hunters or military enthusiasts, marching around and pretending. But I did meet a few of them that should be on a watch list somewhere, if you're allowed to have one of those these days. It seemed like a mixed bag."

"How so?" Randolph asked.

"Why have all those people there? Most of those guys work a nine to five job and shooting someone is the last thing on their mind. They want nothing to do with guys like Vince, and Cole, and Henrik Mauer. Why have any kind of club operating there if you're planning to start a revolution?"

"Cover maybe, or a way to recruit. Money. I do know Mauer almost lost the place before the gun club started. Maybe the dues are paying his taxes. And what's that about a revolution?"

"There are several of those guys that are ready to go to war. They're sure it's coming, and they've been preparing. They have a small arsenal in the basement of that old slaughterhouse. M82's, AR's, even a couple of rocket launchers with plenty of ammo."

Randolph nodded. "And no permits for most of it. I checked. I could shut them down and lock up Mauer for a while just for that. But that wouldn't get us Frank, or Tyrel Davis."

"Or the Belgian," I added. "Didn't you say he's the third partner. The worst of the bunch?"

"I know exactly where he is."

I leaned forward. "And? Is he the bastard that sent those four shooters to the Exotic?"

"No. I'm reasonably sure not. We may have this figured wrong."

"Imagine that. The Gypsy did say that he was probably taking the heat for what Frank and Tyrel had done. If you found the Belgian, why can't you find the other two?"

"Tyrel's in Philly, probably sitting behind his desk right now. We just don't have enough to charge him. I have no idea where Frank is. Ask your girlfriend."

I grinned at him. "Since you're dating my most recent girlfriend, I have to presume you mean the Gypsy."

He laughed. "I do like your sense of humor, Cain. And yes, I meant Gabriel, or the Gypsy, or whatever I'm supposed to call her. What does she know about Frank's whereabouts?"

"Nothing. Or nothing she's willing to tell me. And there's nothing going on between us. We both just want to figure this out."

He chuckled again. "Jenny thinks it's just a matter of time until you two get together. Women's intuition, she said."

"Always the optimist," I said. "Jenny, not the Gypsy. What's our next move?"

"We wait and see while you keep an eye on Henrik Mauer and the other hardcore members of that group. How many of them work with you at the security company?"

"I only recognized a couple, and they're on loan from Philly. But Jack has a lot of people working for him and I haven't seen them all."

"And your next gun club meeting?"

"A week from Saturday. Memorial weekend."

Chapter Twenty-Seven

"What made you think you could go behind my back, everyone's back, and meet with Rafael Mertens? Did you think I wouldn't find out? He murdered my husband for God's sake! Do you really think he deserves our mercy?"

"Yes, I think he does," the Gypsy said. She sat in a chair in her grandmother's office, facing an inquisition. "When I was in Brussels, I made some inquiries and talked to our contacts there. I think Frank Mercer and Tyrel Davis killed Patrick. We've been led to believe all along that it was the Belgian that pulled the others into the sewer with him. It was Frank more than anyone. Frank and Tyrel."

"All this on the word of a murderer?"

"Rafael Mertens is no saint, but his testimony could put the other two in jail for the rest of their lives."

"And how is that justice? A life for a life. You've said that yourself."

The Gypsy shook her head. "A life to save a life. There's a big difference."

"Fine. I will kill them myself," the old woman said coldly, then turned to look at her granddaughter with something approaching hatred in her eyes.

"You have the support of the others, but they didn't train you, they didn't raise you, and they didn't love you. You owe me for that, and it's time to pay your debt. The Belgian doesn't deserve to live."

"I'm sorry, Grandmama," the Gypsy said softly. "But that's not up to you, and it isn't up to me. I could arrange a meeting so you could hear his story. He told me he can prove he didn't kill Patrick, and that it was Frank and Tyrel."

"Put me in a room with Rafael Mertens and I will shoot him in the face," the older woman said. "You've turned your back on me."

"I haven't turned my back on you, but for once you need to listen. Rafael regrets his part in what went on and he's making a deal to testify against the other two."

The elder Luca scoffed. "No surprise there. And you set the whole thing up?"

"With the help of a friend. She knows someone at the FBI."

"I have no doubt Mertens will concoct some story to save his own ass," Gabby said dryly.

"Rafael told me Frank is still in hiding, but that Tyrel is planning something big. Something that would make him rich enough to disappear forever."

"A distraction. Mertens plans to run again."

"He can't run, he's in jail. Help me stop Tyrel and find Frank, Gabby. That's what we do. We can't become assassins or we're no better than they are. Killing them won't bring Patrick back. Wouldn't it be better to ruin Tyrel's plan and give him the rest of his life in jail to think about it?"

A smile tugged at the corners of the old woman's mouth. "That would be satisfying. And I could always have them both killed in prison if I change my mind."

The Gypsy laughed. "Not quite what I was hoping for, but it's a start. Tyrel wants Frank as badly as we do, so I'm going to Philly. I'll keep an eye on Tyrel, and maybe Frank Mercer will come out of hiding while I'm there. I'll talk to Cain and tell him what I'm up to."

The Gypsy's grandmother shook her head. "Obviously you're not going to listen to me, but I don't think trusting this Cain person is a good idea."

"You're right," the Gypsy said as she stood. "I'm not going to listen to you. Not about him, at least." She smiled at her grandmother and walked to the door.

"Izzy?" the older woman said. "I'm sorry about what I said. Raising you was the greatest joy of my life."

Her granddaughter smiled back at her as she opened the door. "Nice, Grandmama. That's how you do an apology."

"What was your name again?" The bewildered receptionist leaned forward and looked closer at her screen. "This damn computer has been acting up all morning."

"Isabelle Daniels, with American Investments? I have a ten o'clock." The Gypsy glanced down at the woman's name plate. Alexa Murphy, assistant to Harold Franks, Vice President of Operations. Alexa's computer problems had been arranged by a shaggy-haired clock maker.

"How'd you manage that?" The woman leaned closer to her screen. "Mister Franks doesn't usually see investment people. He has people who have people for that."

"I met Mister Douglas at a political event last week. He said he'd love to talk more with me, but that I had to speak with Mister Franks first."

The blonde looked the tall woman up and down, appraising her openly. "I'll just bet he did. That's how I got my job. Hey, there you are! I don't know how I missed it. I always go through his appointments the day before, but I didn't see that yesterday."

"Computers, right? Maybe Mister Douglas's secretary scheduled it for me."

"Could be, the bitch." She chuckled and glanced up. "Sorry, that was unprofessional."

The Gypsy grinned down at her. "Sometimes you have to call them like you see them." She glanced down at the plaque again. "Alexa."

"I know, right? She got me booted from the corner office just because I didn't want to talk politics all day, then told Garret I talk too much. Can you believe it? Now I'm doing the same job for less money, and I have no help. Not that she was ever much help."

"Mister Douglas has some interesting ideas."

The blonde looked up quickly. "About Britney-Ann?"

The Gypsy winced. "No. I was talking about his political views. He spoke at the conference I was at last week. He has a lot of fresh ideas, and I thought he made some good points."

"See? That's why I'm stuck in here and don't have that great view anymore. It's always money and politics with Gary. I mean, Mister Douglas."

"He's a very talented investor." The tall woman glanced around. "Obviously."

"Yeah? He's got a screw loose if you ask me. Sorry, that was unprofessional too."

The Gypsy nodded along. "No worries, Alexa. Us girls have to stick together."

"Just because he's rich, he thinks he can take advantage."

"Then don't let him." The Gypsy bit her lip. That had slipped out.

"I guess. But he really had me fooled. He's a smooth talker and charming as hell until he gets what he wants. Like all men, I guess. If you end up meeting with him, be careful. He's slick."

The Gypsy nodded. "And I'll watch out for Britney-Ann."

"Bitch," Alexa muttered. She had lost interest in her computer screen and looked up at the Gypsy. "If you want to know the truth, Mister Franks is the one that really makes the money around here, and he won't try to get in your pants. Do you know what I think?"

The Gypsy sighed and set her briefcase on the floor. "No, please, tell me."

"I don't think Gary's even interested in politics. It's just another way to bamboozle people and make himself feel important."

"But he did seem very passionate when I saw him speak. I guess he might have gone too far on a couple of topics. He implied violence was the answer." Gypsy had a transcript of the speech. Violence wasn't implied, it was called for.

"Screw loose, like I said." She dropped her head and lowered her voice. "And he likes it rough. Really rough."

The Gypsy couldn't let that go. "Then you're better off working where you are. Let Britney-Ann deal with that shit."

The woman's eyes brightened. "Good talk, Isabelle. I'm sorry to dump all that on you. Just give me ten minutes, then I'll get you in to see Harry. I mean, Mister Franks."

The Gypsy backed away from the desk and took a seat. She opened her briefcase and pretended to shuffle some papers around, turned on the listening device Levi had installed in the lining, then sat back to wait.

Tyrel Davis stepped out of the private elevator and pulled the sunglasses from his face. The elevator served two offices, and he walked into the glassed reception area of Garret Douglas's suite. In the distance he could see the Capitol dome and the spire of the Washington Monument. It caught his eye and elicited a rare moment of reflection. New York might be where the money was, but the real power was in Washington DC. Power didn't interest him, but he knew his soon-to-be benefactor lived for it.

The redhead that greeted him was striking, and Tyrel found that amusing. As much as power, beautiful women had always captivated Garrett Douglas's attentions. That would be worth remembering if he ever needed to further ingratiate himself with the man. It was a weakness, and one that Tyrel didn't share. Women could be bought and sold like the loyalties of hitmen and informants.

He didn't wait long. The pretty redhead ushered him to the open door of the billionaire investors office, then pulled it shut as she left. Tyrel dropped into the chair in front of the mahogany desk and nodded. "Nice digs," he said casually.

"Thanks. I try to surround myself with the finer things."

Tyrel knew the man well enough to joke. He nodded his head in the direction of the door. "Like your receptionist?"

Douglas nodded and chuckled. "I couldn't get along without her. She's easy on the eyes and smart as they come. She's made me a hundred times her salary in the last year, and if I ever make a serious run for office, she'll probably head up the campaign. She doesn't know the details, but she knows why you're here. She's fine with it. You took the precautions I suggested?"

"Better. One of my guys colored his hair and threw on one of my suits. He looked pretty damn convincing. He put on the same sunglasses I always wear and took the limo. I snuck out a side door of the hotel and dodged in and out of a couple of shops, then flagged down a taxi. There's no way the feds could have followed me here."

"And the woman you mentioned?"

"She's an annoyance, nothing more. I shouldn't have said anything."

"Could she be a reporter? That's the last thing we need, considering the timing. The stocks are being moved and some of the newspapers watch for that kind of activity. I know your interests don't necessarily align with mine, but I expect you to be careful."

"I'm not the political animal you are, Garrett, but does that matter? And for what it's worth, the people I have lined up to do this share a lot of your goals."

A frown crossed the older man's face. "Listen, I don't want any more unnecessary bloodshed like that catastrophe in Las Vegas. I don't know what the hell you were thinking, but I didn't ask you to slaughter half the people in that club."

"You asked for a demonstration," Tyrel said levelly. "Granted, it could have gone better, but you did say you wanted casualties. You said it had to get national attention. What did you think would happen when four guys opened up with automatics in a crowded club? AK-47's don't have a conscience."

"Kids!" Douglas ranted. "Twenty-eight people dead and who knows how many hurt."

Tyrel shrugged. "Nobody is going to miss a bunch of strippers."

Douglas slammed his hand on the desk. "Bullshit! Strippers or not, that wasn't what I asked for. And the senator walked away unscathed."

Tyrel held his tongue and tried to look contrite.

Douglas continued. "That can't happen again. These shooters had better be good, and they better hit what they're shooting at. Absolutely no collateral damage. Is that understood?"

"I can't guarantee that no one else will be hit," Tyrel objected. "It all has to happen at the exact same time or word will get out and we'll start losing targets. These guys are well trained, but they'll be out several hundred yards, using military grade rifles. Big guns with a lot of power. They could hit their target and kill the person standing behind them. Not likely, but it could happen."

"I'm a businessman, Tyrel, and it all comes down to numbers. I agreed to fifty, ten down now and forty in the Caymans when it's done. But here's my deal. You lose a million dollars for every innocent killed. Two, if they happen to be children."

"No Goddamn way!" Tyrel erupted loudly and shot to his feet, toppling the chair behind him.

Douglas barely reacted, but within seconds the door popped open and the redhead stepped in. "Security, Sir?" she asked.

The man behind the desk waved a hand. "Just a negotiation, Brit. Close the door please." He sat quietly until Tyrel regained his composure and sat down, then continued. "It's no different than any other performance contract. Do your job, fulfill the terms, and you'll get the full amount. Ten people go down with the congressmen, and you only get thirty million. Incentivize your shooters. You could give them an accuracy bonus, and still do very nicely."

"And who's going to keep score?" Tyrel asked.

"I think the press, contaminated as they are, can still count. We'll go by their numbers."

"And if the whole country goes up in flames?"

"That won't happen. But it will disrupt the market and wake some people up. I'll make a ridiculous amount of money and we'll be doing the world a service."

Tyrel's eye narrowed. "And I'll get my share?"

"I've said I'm a businessman, Tyrel, and I have no doubt that you would hunt me down if I tried to cheat you." He smiled suddenly and leaned forward. "I'll tell you what...in the interest of fairness, I'll sweeten the pot and add a million dollars for each one of those congressmen confirmed dead. If it all goes well, you could walk away with sixty-two."

Tyrel nodded and the smile returned to his face. "That seems fair."

"Perfect." Douglas stood and extended his hand. "It's agreed then. It's a pleasure doing business with you."

"Thanks, Isabelle!" The Gypsy flipped a hand at the blond receptionist and walked into the hallway. The meeting had gone about as she'd expected. It was brief. Harold Franks had been confused by her presence, but not immune to her charms. He had spent twenty minutes listening to her talk and then suggested dinner at his apartment that evening. From her research, she knew that he was married and had a two-story in Georgetown. Hopefully Harold would treat Alexa better than her previous tryst. That affair seemed inevitable.

The plan had worked. Levi had studied old blueprints and discovered that the penthouse offices shared a wall. After digging out her laptop, the Gypsy stood her briefcase against that common wall. It wasn't ideal, but the sound sensing technology was directional, and Levi hoped it would be able to pick up a conversation through two layers of sheetrock and insulation. That remained to be seen, and she was eager to get back to her hotel and listen to the recording.

The elevator arrived and she stepped in. Before she could push the button, the only other door on that floor opened and Tyrel Davis walked out. "Hold that, would you?" he called out.

"Got it," the Gypsy said, and put her boot against the stop. After he stepped in, she smiled and pushed the lobby button. "Floor?" she asked.

338

"All the way down, same as you," he said, then tried to make conversation. "Nice, having our own private elevator."

"Very," the Gypsy said, then looked straight ahead. Two strangers in an elevator can be awkward, and normally she would have offered more. Flirting opened doors for her and often led to revealing conversations, but talking to Tyrel Davis was the last thing she wanted to do. He wasn't looking at her the way men often did. There was indifference, then a small frown.

She was dressed for her day job, slacks and a white shirt with a faux tie. Her long hair was piled high, tied with a scarf, and she was wearing glasses. Plain glass, but no one ever noticed. She knew the video footage of her didn't show enough detail for recognition, but she imagined that Tyrel Davis would have watched it by now. The only well documented fact from that night was her height, and there was no hiding that.

"Mind if I ask what you do?" he asked as they neared the main floor. "Garrett is a good account to have, no matter what business you're in."

"Stocks and bonds," the Gypsy replied as the elevator reached its destination. As the door hissed open, she heard Tyrel's phone chime. She stepped out of the elevator and walked quickly toward the main entrance. There was a doorman outside and a security guard stood just inside flirting with a pair of young women.

Tyrel started shouting. "Stop that woman! She has my briefcase!"

The doorman was holding the door open for an elderly man, and the security guard wasn't quick enough. By the time he had disentangled himself from the two girls he was trying to charm, the Gypsy had slipped past him. The doorman made a half-hearted attempt, but she put her shoulder down and bowled him over, then tucked the briefcase under her arm and started running. The security guard shouted a warning, but the sidewalk was crowded. She knew he wouldn't fire his gun and had probably been trained not to. Tyrel's goons were a different matter.

Two black cars sat across the street and the Gypsy heard Tyrel shouting frenzied instructions behind her. She wasn't sure if they heard him or managed to read his body language, but both vehicles pulled away from the curb and spun toward her. The first driver slowed as he neared the curb and she took advantage, running across the top of the vehicle without losing her stride. The second driver, still in the middle of the street, jumped out of his car and brought a gun up.

She dodged as he fired once, then heard the screams as the crowd behind her started running in every direction. He hesitated for a moment, standing behind the car door with it open. She slammed into the door, then swung over the top of it with her briefcase. It wasn't much of a weapon, but she used the hard edge of the side and caught him just above one eye. He went down, but the hardcover case popped open and sent reams of paper cascading down on top of the man. Only dazed, he reached up and grabbed at the case, managing to cling to an edge as she tried frantically to jerk it from his grasp.

A shot rang out and tore a hole in the windshield two feet from them. The tall woman looked back as the shooter raised his gun again, then released her grip on the briefcase and dropped to the ground long enough to grab her laptop. Within seconds she was across the street, running through two lanes of traffic and dodging honking cars. Another moment, and she had disappeared into the scattering pedestrian crowd beyond.

Tyrel Davis stood looking after her, then pulled out his cellphone and made a call. "You have two days to track down the gypsy woman, and I don't want any more excuses. She was here in Washington and she's about to blow the whole deal. You have forty-eight hours, hear me? Find her, or I'm coming after you."

Chapter Twenty-Eight

Regret is a difficult emotion, if emotion is the right word. I guess it is, because emotions aren't rational, and most of the decisions I've regretted weren't made rationally. And like most emotions, my regrets weren't always clearly defined or absolute.

I regretted not spending more time with my mother before she died, but I was too young to know how precious each minute would feel after she was gone. I had the same regrets concerning my father, but less so. And there were times when I regretted joining the Army, because it meant I had to watch a group of school children die and learn what that felt like. And, during weaker moments, I regretted meeting Mickey, because it meant I had to watch him die too.

But if I hadn't joined the Army, I wouldn't have known the wonder of watching those same children laughing and playing hopscotch in the middle of a bloody war. Or been there for my best friend when he needed to get drunk in the heat of an Afghanistan summer because he missed his wife. It's human nature to look for the best in the worst of situations, and regret is seldom absolute.

My current regret was. I regretted ever leaving Las Vegas, ever letting Jenny walk away, and ever going to the Exotic the night of January third. I wanted to hit rewind; go back and remake every decision I'd made in the last five months. I regretted it all in the space of a few seconds, right after my phone rang in the middle of the night.

"Adam, they have Jenny," Jack Mercer said. "When she didn't come home, I thought maybe she was just staying out late and forgot to call. I just got a text. They want to make a deal for my dad."

"Who?" That's when it hit me. The regret, and a cold strangling fear.

"They didn't say. They just said that they have her and that they'll trade her for Frank. That's all I know."

"Who?" I asked again. "Where are you? Did you call the police, or Randolph?"

"No cops, or she dies. Of course they're going to say that, but I have to believe them. It has to be Mertens or Tyrel. Who's Randolph?"

"Where are you?" I repeated.

"In my car, driving north. She's at the compound somewhere. I have twenty-four hours to bring Frank to them. I thought maybe I could make a deal, offer myself instead of her."

"Then they'd have you both. Come get me," I said. "I'm three blocks off the interstate."

"I have your address in my phone." There was a long pause. "We have to talk," he said.

"Just get here as fast as you can. I'll call Randolph, and the Gypsy."

"The Gypsy?"

"Just drive. I'll explain, and I'll be ready."

I called the Gypsy first. She answered on the second ring. "Nothing good ever happens at this time of night, Cain. What's going on?"

"They've taken Jenny," I said, knowing the fear was obvious in my voice. "Mertens and Tyrel. They want Frank, and they want to trade."

"Dammit. I left Philadelphia a couple of days ago and I'm in Washington. I followed Tyrel down here. But it's not Mertens. He's in protective custody, and he's taking a deal to testify against Frank and Tyrel. Why would Tyrel be worried about Frank enough to kidnap his daughter? Something's happening, and it's happening soon."

"I don't care," I snapped. "All I know is that someone has Jenny. We never should have left Las Vegas."

"Try to calm down, Adam. They want Frank, and they won't hurt Jenny until they have him. I'll call Levi and have him pick me up, but it'll still be three and a half or four hours before I can get there. Have you called Randolph?"

"My next call. Why is Levi picking you up?"

"Chopper," she said. "Knowing Levi, he's already at work tinkering with his clocks, and the helicopter is only five minutes away. It'll be

344

faster that I can drive it. Any idea where she's being held?"

"They want to exchange her for Frank, at the gun club." A thought occurred to me. "There's a club meeting today, and Captain Gregory's drill team is practicing for Memorial Day. There'll be fifty or sixty people there by nine o'clock."

"Then you'd better move fast. They would most likely keep her in the old slaughterhouse. If she's in that basement, no one could hear her screaming."

My voice betrayed me again. "Screaming?"

"Sorry. Of course, she'll be calling for help. But they aren't going to hurt her as long as they need Frank. Keep me posted or I'll come in expecting the worst. Memorial Day. Whatever they're planning, they must be desperate to find Frank before it happens. Are you sure you want to call Randolph? If the FBI shows up and starts shooting, it could be bad for Jenny."

"I have to let Randolph know they have her. They've been seeing each other."

"All the more reason not to tell him. He might be as irrational as you are right now."

"Sorry," I said. "But I was lousy to her." My voice broke. "I should have been better."

"It's going to be alright," she said quietly. "We'll get her out of there. And, Cain?"

"Yeah?"

"Try not to get shot again."

By the time Jack Mercer charged into my house I had two guns ready and I was dressed in full camo. I handed him a to-go cup filled with coffee.

"Any more texts?" I asked as we ran to his vehicle.

"No, and no idea where they're holding her. The Bunkhouse makes the most sense, if she's even on the property. Someone is really desperate to find my dad to do it like this."

"Mertens is in jail," I said, "so it has to be Tyrel."

"Then Mauer's probably in on it, and maybe Vince," Jack said as he backed out onto the road. "Cole's all in as far as thinking there's going to be a war, but I can't imagine he would agree to kidnapping Jenny. He thought my dad walked on water."

"Have you called Frank, or has he made contact at all? He'll show up for Jenny, won't he?" I asked desperately. "Randolph thinks that's what Vegas was about, killing you to send a message to your dad."

"Who is Randolph? And you mentioned a gypsy?"

"Randolph is the FBI agent in charge of investigating this whole mess, and coincidentally, the man your sister has been dating since we split up. I say we don't call him, at least not yet. If they said no cops, he would qualify. The Gypsy is Gabriel, the woman that stopped those shooters at the Exotic and saved both our lives."

"They weren't after me," Jack said quietly as we hit the on-ramp and sped north. "They were after Senator Baker. I was his security detail."

"So you did have a gun that night." We both knew the implications of that.

He glanced in my direction. "Not the right time to kick my ass, but I get how you feel. My priority was to protect the Senator, and barricading ourselves in that room was the best way to do it. Getting myself shot wouldn't have made a difference." He paused and took a breath. "There's more, and it gets worse."

"I hate when people say that," I muttered. "What?"

"My dad's not coming."

I closed my eyes. He was right, this was worse. "He really is dead, isn't he?"

"The rumors were only half right. He survived the oil rig explosion and came back to the states. But the lousy bastard never even came home to see my mother and tell her what was going on. She either fell in the pool because she was drunk, or somebody pushed her. Maybe that was a message for the old man too. But after that he went off the deep end. I'd like to think the guilt finally got to him. He called me into the office on a Sunday night a few weeks later. I found him there, dead. Pills."

"So why the charade?"

"I didn't know who to trust or how to protect Jenny. I was sure Tyrel or the Belgian would come after the New York branch if they knew. There were paperwork issues that my dad never got straightened out, and if Jenny and I were dead, the New York branch would have been theirs."

"So you kept Frank alive, more or less."

"I sent emails to myself from him, making sure they found their way around the office. I sent encrypted texts to the Belgian as if I were my father, and I started rumors. I always had the impression that Tyrel and Rafael were afraid of my dad, and they bought the idea that he had faked his own death to throw the feds off his trail. I used that as insurance, but I knew it wouldn't work forever. When Jenny talked about an old friend in Las Vegas, I told her to go away. Put everything behind her and get out of New York." He looked over glumly. "She was safe for a while."

I stifled a groan. "Until I brought her back here."

"That wasn't your fault," he said.

"It feels like it was. The Gypsy told her she was in the middle of this."

"The Gypsy? Gabriel?" I nodded and he continued. "Jenny talked about her, but she always called her Gabriel. How is she involved, and why did she follow you to New York?"

"She didn't follow us," I explained. "She's in the middle of it too. She was looking for your father and trying to get to Tyrel and the Belgian. Just Tyrel now. Rafael Mertens made a deal to testify against the others. Other, since Tyrel is the only one still alive."

"But why is she involved?" he asked again.

"Does the name Patrick Codona ring any bells? I trust you, but that's all I'm going to say about that."

"That's enough," he said as his hands tightened on the steering wheel. "One of my father's regrets. He left a note."

I shook my head. "How the hell did you and Jenny ever turn out so well?"

"My mother was a wonderful person. Now I'm starting to think that maybe she was murdered, and that maybe Tyrel Davis was responsible. If I live through this, I'm going to kill that son-of-a-bitch," he said grimly.

I nodded. "Get in line."

Chapter Twenty-Nine

We drove down the last two miles of gravel with the headlights off, following the ghostly outline of the road in front of us. I glanced at my phone. An hour until daylight, then any advantage we might have would be gone. A few hundred yards from the gun club, Jack turned west onto a bumpy trail, barely an opening in the trees, and followed it back into the woods.

"I'll leave the keys on the front tire," he explained, "in case you and Jenny make it out and I don't. I'd like to think some of these guys would be loyal to me, but there's no love lost between Vince and me. Mauer, he's just plain crazy. He'd kill anyone if he thought it would help his cause."

"Nothing's more dangerous than a zealot," I said. "Afghanistan was full of them."

"I'd like to think it's not the same thing," Jack said, "but I'm not sure there's much difference."

He grabbed a canvas bag from the back of his SUV and we started down the trail back to the road. "What's in the bag?" I asked.

"Paint, bolt cutters, a battery grinder, and a night scope. Oh, and two tear gas canisters."

"They're not going to be happy to see us. If they're keeping Jenny there, she's probably in the basement. I saw an entrance from the road, but I couldn't tell you how secure it is."

"I own a security company," Jack offered, "so I pay attention to locks and cameras. There's a heavy padlock and a pair of dead bolts on the door facing the creek, and one camera that looks too old to be of much use."

"Why padlock it from the outside?" I asked.

"No idea," Jack said. "Two sets of steps going upstairs, so maybe that door never gets used, or maybe they're afraid of their own people stealing from them. If there's a bar inside, we're screwed."

"There's not. Vince gave me the grand tour the first time I was here."

I could barely make out Jack's face when he looked over at me. "Why would he do that?"

"I guess he thinks I'm his brand of crazy. He really wanted me to teach them to shoot."

"Any idea how this is going to go?"

"We can try sneaking in," I said, "but Jenny might not even be there. Lights!"

We had nearly reached the main road and we split up, both plunging into the brush on either side of the trail. Headlights flashed through the trees briefly, then an oversized four-wheel-drive pickup tore by our location, still picking up speed. We waited a minute then walked to the end of the trail.

"That was Vince's truck," Jack said. "I hope Jenny wasn't in it."

"They couldn't make the swap for Frank if they moved her," I pointed out. "It's a good thing, Vince leaving. That's one less person to deal with, and he's probably the most dangerous of the bunch."

"They have to know I'd come for her, even if Frank didn't show up," Jack said, his voice strained. "They know me. I've had beers with these guys."

"The Gypsy thinks that whatever they have planned is going to happen on Memorial Day. She's not wrong very often."

"Our company is supplying security for a dozen events in the city over the weekend, so maybe that's part of it. They want Frank, but maybe they want me out of the way too." He shook his head and his voice broke. "It's my fault they took Jenny. I should go in alone."

"I brought her back to New York, and I let it slip that you have a sister. They might not have known that, so there's plenty of blame to go around. Not that it matters, because you're not going in there by yourself. The paint is for the camera in the back?"

"Yeah. You should be able to reach it. Unless they recently put something up, there are no other lights back there. Henrik is usually here, so they didn't go all out on security."

We walked quickly down the road until we could see the gate. Vince hadn't taken the time to close it, and it stood open. I put my finger to my lips and pointed to the hill that stretched above the stream on the north side of the property.

"Let's work around the back side," I whispered. "We can watch the front from the east end for a while and try to figure out how many of these assholes there are. We need an idea of what we're up against."

He nodded and we abandoned the road, climbing carefully up the steep grade and following the hillside until we could see the front of the Bunkhouse. We huddled down together and Jack handed me the night scope. There was a light shining through the barred window beside the main door, and an occasional flicker of movement when whoever was inside passed close. After about ten minutes the door opened and Cole stepped out with another man behind him. The second man lit up a cigarette and they stood in the dim light of the doorway talking. It sounded like an argument. I handed the scope to Jack.

"Henrik Mauer," he said quietly. "Crazy as they come. It sounds like Cole isn't happy that they kidnapped Jenny."

After another few minutes Henrik stepped inside, then came out with a rifle and handed it to Cole. He tucked it under his arm and climbed into one of the two vehicles that still sat in the yard. There was another brief conversation, then he drove out of the gate and turned south.

Vince had gone north. After he finished his cigarette, Henrik walked out and locked the gate again.

"Any chance Henrik's alone," Jack asked quietly, "or do you think it's a trap?"

"I doubt he's alone, but would he trust anyone else to watch Jenny?" I asked. "Would Henrik hurt her?" I didn't have to elaborate, Jack knew what I meant.

"I don't think so. He strikes me as being too honorable for that, in his own twisted way. Why risk a kidnapping now just to bring my dad out of hiding?"

"It has to be about the holiday, like the Gypsy said. Maybe Tyrel is afraid Frank would try to move in at the last minute and take over the operation or turn state's evidence like the Belgian is doing. Either way, does it matter? Frank's not coming."

"But we could say he is," Jack said, sounding desperate. "Or I could trade myself for Jenny, like I said before."

"How?" I asked. "There's just the two of us, and once they've realized that they'll take me out and have you both. Then what? If they are planning something for Memorial Day, they can't risk letting Jenny go until it's done, Frank or no Frank. And the longer they have her, the less likely it is she'll live through it. We have to get her out of there now. I say we take her any way we can. No deals."

He was quiet for a long moment, then he nodded.

There was only one vehicle left in the yard. A rusty two-door pickup was parked just beyond the light of the window. Only room for three people. That might mean Henrik didn't have a lot of back-up, or that Vince and Cole had left some people behind. It was also possible that they weren't expecting us to come for Jenny as quickly as we had. I wasn't the optimist Jenny was. That seemed less likely.

Jack pointed toward the hill. "Short of going in shooting, our best chance is to try to sneak in through the basement and come up one of the stairs."

"No shooting if we can avoid it," I said as we started moving to the back of the building. "But how are we going to get in?"

"The grinder blades I have will cut through anything, but cutting those deadbolts will make some noise. The lower level is super-insulated, but they still might hear it."

"Unless they're distracted," I said. "I could go back and get your Jeep. Create a diversion."

"Damn," he said. "I love that ride. You're going to wreck it aren't you?"

"I'll run it through the gate, then pull down by the pole barn and fire a few shots. They're itching for a fight, so I'll give them one. How long will it take you to cut the locks?"

"The grinder blades are diamond tipped. Half a minute each, a minute, tops. But..."

"With all the noise I'm going to make, they'll never hear you. Worst case, Henrik stays with her if she's upstairs. If that happens, disregard what I said about shooting and kill him if you can. I'll keep the rest of them busy, but it'll be up to you to deal with him."

"What then? How are you going to get away?"

"When you hear me hit the gate, start cutting. I'll give you one minute each for the three locks, and another three to find Jenny. Three more to get her out of there and run back to the road, and another minute for a cushion. I can keep them busy for ten minutes, then I'll drive back out of there. Get her to the road and I'll pick you up."

"And if you don't make it?"

"I'll make it," I assured him, then hedged. "But if I don't, get her away from here any way you can. There are cabins on that lake north of here. Once she's safe you can call for the cavalry and the FBI."

"It's a dumb plan," he complained, "but I don't have a better one."

"It'll be light in half an hour, and Vince or Cole might come back any minute. We have to move, right now."

I left Jack pressed against the basement wall of the Bunkhouse and hurried back along the hill to the road, then retraced our steps to Jack's vehicle. I grabbed the keys and got in, then opened the glove box and retrieved my phone. I couldn't keep Randolph in the dark, no matter what the Gypsy thought. I had very little signal.

"Dammit, Randolph, voicemail? I'm with Jack Mercer. They have Jenny at the gun-club and they want to trade her for Frank. We're going in after her, right now. They said no cops, but it's Jenny, so I figured I had to call you. I'm ditching my phone so don't bother trying to call me back. Just get here as soon as you can. They're planning something big for Memorial Day. That's all I know." I ended the call, turned my phone off, and tossed it into the woods.

I backed out onto the gravel, then accelerated and cornered into the short drive that led to the front gate of the Cherry Hollow Gun Club. The gate was twenty feet wide, a single piece of aluminum that hung on three pins and was chained at the opposite end. I hit it at sixty miles an hour and the Jeep didn't even slow down. The crumpled aluminum clung to the brush guard for the space of a few seconds, then fell in front of me as I slowed.

I drove halfway to the pole shed, then pulled hard on the steering wheel and spun the vehicle in a circle so that it was facing the road again, perpendicular to the front door of the Bunkhouse. As an afterthought, I touched the alarm button on the key fob. The headlights began flashing and the horn started blowing as I jumped out of the driver's door. The more noise I made, the more noise Jack could get away with.

Bodies started spilling from the building in front of me. Five in all, and I was sure Henrik Mauer was one of them. If our assumption that she was in the Bunkhouse was correct, that should leave Jenny unattended. I still couldn't be sure she was out of harm's way, so my first shot was high. Hitting any kind of a target would have been difficult, considering the poor lighting and the flashing of the Jeep's headlights, but I fired two more quick shots into the old logs to the left of the doorway.

Three of the men from the Bunkhouse ran behind the pickup and I fired two shots in their direction. Another went right and threw himself down behind a pair of landscape timbers that surrounded the crude parking lot. The fifth man, Henrik Mauer, stood behind the heavy door frame of the old building. I could hear him shouting instructions, but the blaring of Jack's horn kept me from hearing what he was saying. On cue, the alarm stopped.

"Who's there?" Henrik yelled from his hiding place. "Come out, and surrender. Lay down your weapon and you won't be harmed.

This unit adheres to the rules of the Geneva Convention."

Jack had said that Henrik was crazy. He didn't sound overly bright either. I stalled, watching the seconds tick away on the dashboard of the Jeep. When it got too quiet, I called back to him.

"What does it say in the Articles about kidnapping innocent women? Give her up and I'll be on my way." Realizing my mistake, I fired a shot, then moved around to the far side of the truck and fired again. Hopefully, they would think they were facing at least two shooters. I bluffed some more. "Frank wants his daughter back safe and sound, then he's willing to talk."

"She's been asking for him," Henrik called back. "I'd hate to see anything bad happen to her. She's a very pretty woman." I knew he was taunting me, but the door was open and I couldn't see Jenny anywhere in the line of fire. I used the hood of the Jeep for an armrest and took my best shot. I heard a yelp and the shoulder that had been my target disappeared.

One of the men hiding behind the truck bolted for the doorway and I fired again. I was trying for a hit now, sure that Jenny must either be in a backroom or in the basement. I heard more shouting and glanced at the clock. Seven minutes, almost eight.

Then I heard one of the shooters calling to the man hidden behind the landscaping timbers. "Get that son-of-a-bitch!"

A barrage of gunfire erupted from three directions, but the bulk of the vehicle protected me. I returned fire, then reached for my second clip. They were talking amongst themselves again, and I heard Henrik shouting instructions. "We have to take him alive. Those are the orders. Go down and get the girl."

Eight and a half minutes. Jack might be on his way out to the road with Jenny, or he might not. I knew I needed to give him more time. I slid into the driver's seat.

The Jeep was still running, and I threw it in gear and pushed the accelerator to the floor. It wasn't far to the front of the Bunkhouse and there wasn't a lot of distance to pick up speed, but the Wagoneer was big and heavy and had plenty of horsepower. Twenty feet from the building, I pushed the door open and rolled out. My gun flew from my hands as I tumbled closer to the building, nearly joining the collision of steel and timber that did considerable damage to Henrik's Bunkhouse and Jack's SUV.

My second roll brought me back to my feet, and on a dead run toward the back side of the Bunkhouse. I knew that at least two men were right behind me, and as I started down the slope near the stream, the third man came running from my right. He was no match for my size and fear induced adrenalin. I grabbed a handful of jacket with my right hand and tossed him in the general direction of the water as I turned the corner of the Bunkhouse. I was hoping to see the back door open and Jack and Jenny long gone, but that's not the way it happened.

Vince Carlson had Jack pushed against the wall, pinning him with one arm while holding Jenny by the hair with his other. I had just a moment to wonder who had been driving his truck earlier and if that had been an intentional ruse, then I was on him.

He turned at the last second, alerted by the crush of gravel as I ran down the slope. Jenny, eyes wide, pulled free as Jack swung quickly, landing a solid punch before I reached Vince. I hit the big man with a shoulder, then hit him again with my fist before we both went down. I swung again, trying to loosen his grasp and get to my feet before the two men behind me could scramble down the hill. The blow barely fazed him, and he grabbed my legs as I struggled to stand.

From the corner of my eye, I saw Jack coming forward. "Run," I called to him. "Get Jenny out of here. Run!"

Vince had a death grip on my leg, but that didn't stop me from lashing out at the other two men who came stumbling down the hill. They both had guns in their hands, and they were looking in Jack's direction. Like my legs, my arms are deceptively long. I stretched out and knocked the first one down with a blow to the forehead, then grabbed the second man and clung to him as Vince rolled my legs out from under me. Overwhelmed, I fought my way to my feet again and managed to get my hands on all three of my assailants at once. I called out to Jack again, begging him to run, then went down under the combined weight of Vince and rest of his men. The last thing I remembered was the flash of blond hair as Jack and Jenny disappeared into the darkness.

Chapter Thirty

Much of what happened in the next hour was best forgotten, and I'm still trying to do that. Although I hadn't seen the room before, I surmised that it had once been used for ice storage, and that I was in the basement of the Bunkhouse. They were calling it the Interrogation Room. Grown men playing at being soldiers.

I was seated on a wooden bench with my legs pulled under me so that I was almost kneeling. At first I wasn't sure what kept me from falling forward, but it only took a moment to realize that my arms had been pulled up and back, and that my wrists were tied with some sort of leather strapping. Falling wasn't an option. Neither was getting my hands on my captors.

Judging by what I saw, I hadn't been unconscious long. Vincent Carlson took the first shot. He didn't close his fist, just hit me with a beefy backhand a few times and bloodied my nose.

"I told you, Cain, you needed to be on the right side of things. You could have been a valuable asset. Being able to kill a man from a mile away is a skill that could have made you a lot of money. But you'd rather be a traitor and work for the FBI."

"It's better than licking Tyrel's boots," I said.

He grinned and slapped me again. "I'm not going to hurt my hand on your thick skull. I'm going to need to be able to squeeze a trigger in the very near future. But don't worry, the fun's just getting started. Virgil will be back with my truck in a couple of minutes, and he's looking forward to making you talk about Frank Mercer and that girlfriend of yours. We're closing in on her and that meddling family of hers. They'll all pay."

"More women and kids to murder? I've heard you're good at that." It struck a nerve and enraged him. This time he used his fists.

After a while I lost track of the repeated questions about Frank Mercer, the Gypsy, and her family. And I lost track of who it was inflicting the pain. At some point, Vince was replaced by another man I'd seen before but couldn't identify, then Virgil took his turn. He was still holding a grudge for the humiliation at the gun range. His attack was personal and especially vicious. The questions were fewer and it was more about inflicting pain.

Then Henrik Mauer stepped up, leering at me with a part of an axe-handle in his usable hand. "Just as well I loaned Cole my Denel, Cain. Because of you I won't get to join the party when it starts. I'm going to show you how we treat spies in my regiment." I took some satisfaction from the fact that his other arm was wrapped in a fresh bandage and managed a lopsided sneer. A scratch, he said, then swung his club.

***

I tried to shake the cobwebs from my head as I heard the latch click and the overhead light came on. I desperately wanted to talk to the Gypsy again. I couldn't remember when they had brought her in, and I hadn't heard the story of her capture. Having her, they would still want Frank, and probably intended to beat that information out of her. Frank was never coming, and I wanted to share that fact with her. That, and a number of other things, given the chance.

Having the Gypsy meant they no longer needed me. They would kill me sooner than later, unless I was able to stop them. I tugged at my bonds, trying to assess how much strength it would take to free myself, then slumped forward and closed my eyes, watching them through narrowed slits. They were laughing and taunting the Gypsy. I waited, unsure of how my body would respond when the time came to move quickly. I needed them to be close.

Virgil walked over first, pulling a handgun from its holster. Henrik followed, smiling smugly, then turned back to the Gypsy and the third man. "Last chance, Miss Gypsy. You've had some time to think about it. Where is Frank

Mercer holed up? Tell us, or Virgil is going to put a bullet right between Cain's eyes."

"I told you I don't know where Frank is," she insisted. "I can't tell you what I don't know."

Henrik stopped and looked between us. "Maybe you're not that important to her, Cain, but I know someone who is." He was grandstanding and enjoying himself, all the while moving closer to me. He stopped and turned back to the Gypsy.

"Patrick Codona. Does that name ring a bell? Or Gabriel Luca? But I would imagine you call her grandmother. Vince is on his way to pay her a visit right now. Tell me where Frank is. Maybe I can still stop him."

The Gypsy's voice gave her away. It was plaintive. "I don't know where he is!"

I was afraid she would react too soon, lunge at him before I could get my hands on Virgil and possibly get shot by the third man. "Frank's dead," I said loudly. "He's been dead for almost two years."

Henrik walked back to me and put his face inches from mine. "Bullshit! Everyone knows that's not true. It's you who's about to be dead, Mister Cain. We don't need you anymore. Virgil?"

Virgil stepped closer. Close enough. With a surge of effort, I yanked my left arm free and grabbed a handful of greasy hair. I pulled down hard and drove his bearded face into my knee as

I snapped the strap holding my right wrist. His gun went off as I circled his neck with my right arm and stood quickly, twisting as hard as I could until I felt the vertebrae snap. He died quietly.

Henrik Mauer stumbled away from us and fell onto his back, frantic, forgetting his wound and clawing at his shoulder holster. Virgil's gun was close. I swept it up and fired three times. It might be true that I couldn't hit a shooter from the length of a strip club, but Henrik Mauer was eight feet away from me. The first shot killed him. The next two were for Mickey.

As I swung the gun in his direction, I heard a strangled gasp come from the third man and saw the surprise in his eyes as the Gypsy withdrew her knife from under his arm. She pushed him away with a look of disgust and smiled grimly at me. "Our combined futures are looking better now, Cain, but we need to hurry. They had to hear those shots from upstairs." She pushed through the door and started running down the hallway.

"What time is it?" I asked. "There are fifty or sixty guys in the drill yard and they're all on our side."

"Are they prepared for a firefight? That would be a blood bath. Hear those sirens? Jenny must have found a phone and called Randolph. They'll deal with whoever is left."

367

"That's a good thing, right? We can warn your grandmother and the cops can stop Vince."

"That's not the way we do things, Cain. No cops. Run!"

I followed her, running as hard as I could in the knee-deep, icy water of the spring-fed stream that paralleled the backside of the Bunkhouse. The wail of sirens grew. The stream passed under the road through a large steel culvert that had been oversized for spring flooding and we dove into it just as three squad cars rumbled overhead. In the distance I could hear the thumping of helicopter blades.

"Is that Levi?" I asked.

The Gypsy continued to the far end of the pipe and sat down. "No. That one's bigger. It sounds like an Army troop carrier. I'd say Randolph is done playing nice and he's going to clean house. Levi is refueling east of here and waiting for my signal."

"He left you?"

"He has his job and I have mine. Besides, he's useless in a fight."

"How did you know they had me?"

"The locks had been cut and the basement door was hanging open. I was doing a little recon, and they caught me."

I didn't buy it. "Or you let them catch you to get to me."

She shrugged. "It worked didn't it?"

The steel tube we were hiding in was six feet in diameter, big enough to sit with our feet braced above the water while we caught our breath. The Gypsy reached up and pulled a magnetic box from the ceiling of the culvert and removed what could have been a garage door opener. "I left this tracker and a few things in here on my way in."

"Is there a cellphone in that box?" I asked.

"No phones. If we hadn't made it out, they might have found it. No phones, so there are no numbers to trace."

"You didn't know if we would make it out?" It was a revelation to me.

"No," she said, "I didn't know."

"But you're the Gypsy," I argued. "You always know."

"I don't always know," she said, shaking her head. "Things happen and people die. I don't always know."

"But you knew the shooting was going to happen in Vegas. You knew I was going to come to New York," I insisted. "You knew being here would make Jenny happy, and you knew that seeing you that day at the Memorial would end it for her. I think you even knew about her and Randolph somehow."

"But..." she said, her eyes suddenly wide, her voice suddenly shrill. "I didn't know about you."

I blinked, not sure what she meant.

She looked up at me and there were tears in her eyes. "I didn't know if I could get you out of there alive, or if they would beat you to death before I had the chance to try."

I shrugged. "But you did. I'm a little worse for wear, but very much alive."

It surprised me that her tears came faster, and that she was angry. "But watching them do that to you, I didn't know if you would live through it," she insisted loudly. "And I didn't know how afraid that would make me. I didn't know how terrified I'd be of losing you. I didn't know that! And I never expected to feel this way."

She didn't give me time to respond. Suddenly she was on top of me, straddling me with her feet dangling in the cold water. She pushed against me roughly, tears running down her face, both hands tangled behind my head, pulling me closer. It wasn't a gentle kiss. It was raw and desperate and painfully intense. My lips already ached from the beating, but I didn't care. This was what I'd wanted since Vegas.

It was over as quickly as it began. She slid away from my grasp and spun back to a sitting position, then spread her legs and dropped her hands into the water.

"I have blood on my hands," she said dully, "from the knife. I always have blood on my hands when I use the knife."

"I'm sorry you had to do that," I said.

Her voice shook. "I wonder sometimes if I'm any better than the people I hunt."

"You are nothing like Mauer and Davis, Gabriel. They murder people. You fight because they give you no choice. I'd be dead if you weren't willing to do that."

"Still, I hate it," she said, continuing to scrub her hands together. "I hate watching people die, even the worst of them." She shook her fingers dry and stared down into the water. "I hate never being at home." She paused, and her voice dropped to a whisper. "And I hate always being alone."

"I'm right here," I pointed out.

She drew a shuddering breath. "I was afraid in there. I'm never afraid."

"I'm right here," I repeated. "You don't have to be afraid, and you don't have to be alone."

"But maybe I do," she said softly. "I was never afraid until I met you." She gave me a bleak look, then motioned for me to hurry. "We need to move if you're able. There's a trail that goes north and a clearing where Levi will pick us up. He'll have a phone. Your friend Randolph will clean up here. It's going to be a long day at the Cherry Hollow Gun Club."

I glanced over my shoulder as we ran into the woods. A large helicopter had landed just beyond the pole barn and twenty real soldiers were spilling out, joining the growing contingent of law enforcement. The drill team was already on their knees with their hands clasped behind their heads. I could only imagine what Captain Gregory would have to say Monday morning, if I ever returned to Mercer Security.

Chapter Thirty-One

Twenty minutes later a small helicopter came in from the north. It barely cleared the treetops, then dropped onto the only piece of level ground within sight. It had taken the best part of that time for us to get to the small clearing a mile and a half north of the gun club. I hadn't realized that Virgil's bullet had torn through my calf until it started throbbing. The Gypsy produced a roll of medical tape from her hidden stash and wrapped it quickly, murmuring something about my getting shot again, but not meeting my gaze.

I wasn't sure if the spontaneous burst of affection had been just that, or simple relief at finding me alive. Either way, her sudden withdrawal was confusing. I chose to ignore it and asked the more practical question. "Why not talk to Randolph? He can make sure Vince doesn't get to your grandmother. And what did you mean, that isn't the way you do things?"

"My grandmother likes the police even less than she likes Tyrel and the Belgian, if that's possible. And the group as a whole avoids that kind of exposure. How long have you known about Frank Mercer?"

"Jack told me on our way out here to find Jenny. He's been playing Frank for the last two years, communicating with the Belgian and spreading rumors to keep Tyrel at bay." I grinned at her. "Hard to believe I knew something you didn't."

She nodded. "Yeah, hard to believe."

I caught the trace of a smile. "You knew?"

She shrugged and pointed as the helicopter settled to the ground. "Levi's here. I have to warn the others, then we'll talk."

We ducked under the wash of the blades and the man inside pushed the passenger door open and handed the Gypsy a cellphone. She motioned for me to climb into the front seat. "You're too beat up to sit in the back. I'll be just a minute."

I climbed in and the sandy-haired man in the pilot's seat handed me a headset. I reached out a hand. "Adam Cain. I take it you're Levi?"

"I am. Glad to finally meet you. Izzy mentioned you, but getting any details out of her is impossible. She did say you're a natural when it comes to flying."

"Not because I like it," I said. "And I like helicopters even less than airplanes."

He chuckled. "Then you might want to close your eyes, because I'm going to get every bit of speed I can out of this bird going east. The family is in lockdown mode, but Izzy's going to want to get there as fast as we can."

"Izzy?" I asked.

He looked over at me. "I hope you're not calling her Gabriel. She hates that."

"So I've been told," I replied. "I call her the Gypsy."

He shrugged. "She has many names, depending on where she is and what job she's on." Levi looked beyond me as the door was pulled open and the Gypsy scrambled in quickly. He applied power and the helicopter jumped off the ground. "With only three of us on board we should make good time, but I have to avoid the airspace around that compound. Cops everywhere, and they have air support."

"How are you?" The Gypsy reached forward and put a hand on my shoulder. "I know that was rough, but I've seen you go through worse."

"The drugs were better in Vegas," I shared. "Got any Tylenol?"

"This is a full-service flight," Levi said and motioned to the seat behind him. "There's a medical bag back there and plenty of bottled water. What the hell happened? You look pretty beat up."

"They're making their move," the Gypsy said from the back seat. She handed me the Tylenol and more tape for my calf. "Tyrel Davis is calling the shots. They almost had me in DC, and Tyrel has had his fill of me. Somehow, they put Gabby and me together, and probably Uncle Darius too. Tyrel would like us all dead, and soon. It has to be about Memorial Day."

"Jack told me that he was never the target in Vegas," I offered. "He said the shooters were after Senator Baker." I turned in the seat to look at the Gypsy. "Or did you know that too?"

She grinned at me. "You manage to be useful at times, Cain. I didn't know that for sure, but it isn't surprising. If Tyrel wanted to get someone's attention and negotiate a higher fee, killing a couple of dozen civilians and a US senator would do it. Killing Jack Mercer would have been a bonus, although if things go his way, I'm sure Tyrel plans to disappear permanently. He'd have no use for Jack's company if he skips the country."

"Jack thought Tyrel would try to kill him to take the New York branch," I said for Levi's benefit. "That's why he kept the rumors going that Frank was alive. Maybe if Tyrel goes away, Jack will be safe. And Jenny."

"He won't go quietly," the Gypsy said from the back seat.

I thought I already knew the answer, but I asked the question. "Any idea what they're planning?"

"We have Tyrel Davis, a man whose only allegiance is money; Garret Douglas, a sadistic and politically active billionaire; and you, training a group of long-range shooters," the Gypsy mused. "When you throw in a bunch of politicians making speeches on Memorial Day, it adds up to an assassination attempt. Possibly, multiple assassination attempts."

"Fortunately, I didn't get as far as the actual training," I pointed out. "But if they go after a bunch of politicians and manage to kill even half of them, partisan as things are, the whole country will go to war."

"And because it's my nine to five to know these things," the Gypsy said, "I can tell you that the stock market will take one of its biggest hits in history. Anyone who knew it was coming could make billions in the matter of a few days."

Levi tracked north a few miles as we climbed, then leaned the copter toward our destination. I knew less about helicopters than I did airplanes, but I could tell we were going about as fast as the chopper would fly.

"Gabby said to tell you that she sent Gwyneth to her parents' house," the Gypsy said to Levi. "I don't know what my grandmother is thinking. She said she plans to deal with whoever is coming herself, and she locked up the store."

"Why wouldn't she go to the bakery with Darius and the girls?" Levi asked.

I could hear the resignation in the Gypsy's voice. "She's too damn stubborn. Even after working with Darius for all those years, she refuses to admit she needs his help. She insisted she can handle it alone. She said that it's what she's used to doing."

"Don't let her do that you, Izzy," Levi admonished. "She's playing you. She would have you be like her. Old, bitter, and alone."

"I have no intention of doing that. But it's too much to ask of another person, living like I do."

Levi continued flying perfectly straight but turned in his seat to glare back at her. "Dammit, woman! Do you hear yourself? You already have one foot in her shoes as it is. Live, Izzy. Let yourself be happy. It's alright to want something normal."

"It's too hard," she mumbled. "How can I live a normal life?"

The chopper rocked wildly as Levi expressed his frustration. He jerked his head around again and pointed a finger in my direction. He was shouting. "Start here. The solution is right in front of you." He shifted his gaze to me. "Literally, the answer is sitting in the seat right in front of you." He turned back to the controls, still cursing under his breath.

I turned so that I could see them both. "You both know that my headset is working, right?" Levi chuckled. The Gypsy looked out the window.

I twisted around and stared at her until she turned back to me. "I did offer," I said quietly.

"You have no idea what's involved," she muttered. "And we barely know each other."

I grinned at her. "It's been pretty interesting so far, and I bet I can handle it. But tell me, what's involved? Start with Darius and the bakery, because I'm lost."

She gave me an eyeroll. "Darius is my great-uncle. He started working with the group when he was still in high school, then he brought my grandmother in. He retired after his girls got old enough to understand how dangerous it was, and his wife insisted. He runs a bakery now, but he still dabbles and keeps his ear to the ground."

"This group," I asked, "what's their deal?"

She exchanged a look with Levi, then spoke again. "I'll give you the short history. It started years ago when my family first came to this country. Several families actually, and they settled in New York City. Because they were new, they were easy targets for the gangs and crooked cops, not to mention the loan sharks and dirty politicians. At first it was just our family and a few others sharing information, telling each other who to trust and who not to trust. Then they started organizing with more people in the neighborhoods, shutting down the loan sharks and running off the gangs. When the gangs demanded protection money and became more violent, so did the group. There was a lot of bloodshed."

"Your group sounds a lot like the Mafia," I pointed out. "But that was a long time ago. Right?"

"Years ago, and eventually it got better. Some good people took over and cleaned things up. But the concept of looking out for one another has lasted all this time, and it keeps growing. We have people all over the country, and contacts in Europe. These days it's run more like a business, well-funded and diverse. There are people in my investment group making sure we have operating capital, people with connections in Washington digging up information on crooked politicians and organized crime, and kids on the street corner telling us who's selling drugs." She gave Levi a crooked smile. "We even have people that build high-tech drones and fly helicopters." Levi glanced in my direction and raised his thumb.

I turned back to her. "And people that are good at what you do?"

She nodded. "Sometimes it isn't enough to know that people are planning something terrible. Sometimes you have to stop them."

"Mitigate," I said.

The Gypsy nodded. "When all else fails, I mitigate. But my grandmother would have me punish, and that's like going back to the old ways. I'm not doing that."

I turned back to face the eastern skyline. "I get that," I said, "but I think I'm going to like your grandmother."

"Olson. Olson! Over here."

Jimmy was a dozen paces from the Luca Bakery. He stopped and retraced his steps to the doorway of the recently shuttered jewelry store that was next door. A ragged looking man in a tattered coat sat in the doorway of the vacant building. He had a dirty scarf covering half his face and a grimy felt hat pulled down to his eyebrows. A brown paper bag sat between his legs and the neck of a bottle protruded from it. He looked homeless, but Jimmy knew the voice.

"Detective Murdock." Jimmy grinned. "Down on your luck?"

"Funny, you little prick. If you would have done what I asked you to do, I wouldn't have to be sitting here right now. I'll admit, except for the fact that my ass hurts, it's kind of fun. I haven't worked undercover for twenty years."

"It's an interesting costume. Is there anything in that bottle?"

"Of course. It's cold here compared to Vegas."

"It'll get colder if Darius sees you. He won't take kindly to you sitting right next door to his business."

"Nice guy, actually. I've been here for three days and he's been feeding me scones. He said he was fine with my sitting here, as long as I don't panhandle and chase his customers away. Before I leave town, I'm going to buy a bunch of pastries to take home with me. I've given up on you bringing me bagels."

"What can I say, Detective? Is finding the mystery woman really this important to you? Why not just let it go? She saved a lot of lives that night. I've moved on and you should too. I'm staying in Boston, and I'm getting married at the end of June. Who knew chasing that lead of yours would result in my meeting the woman of my dreams."

"Good Lord," Murdock grumbled and took a swig from his bottle. "You're absolutely worthless. You're of no use to me or yourself. I was starting to like you, Jimmy, but you've turned into a love-starved middle-schooler with a crush. That must be some ass you're tapping to make you forget about writing your book and nailing the FBI."

"Be nice, Detective. Patience is a wonderful woman."

"I'm sure she is, Jimmy. You're the one that's lost his marbles. But don't worry about me. I'll sit out here and do my job, burn up my vacation time while you're in there canoodling with the help. Never mind that your little girlfriend might be in the line of fire now that the shit's hitting the fan. I'm sure she'll be fine.

She's probably a secret Ninja or something, like that cousin of hers."

"The shit's hitting the fan?" Jimmy asked.

"The whole east coast just went on the highest alert possible. I get those memos. There's an imminent danger of a terrorist attack, believed to be domestic, as of about fifteen minutes ago. It's active right through Memorial Day. They're shutting down everything. No parades, the Vice President can't visit, and no fishing trip for the Governor. It's all been canceled."

"I doubt that has anything to do with our case. Your case, I mean."

Murdock tipped his bottle up again. "I'm not sure about that part, but I do know there are some rats on the loose and I'm planning to catch one of them."

"The only thing you're going to catch is pneumonia, Detective. How much of that bottle did you drink? There's no story here and no one is a terrorist."

Murdock pulled the dirty sleeve of his coat across his lips. "Okay, Scoop. But don't say I didn't try to cut you in on the story. Now you'll have to read about it in the newspapers like every other schmuck, or watch the little girl on the five o'clock news tell the story you passed on. Go away now. You're going to blow my cover."

"I knew this was going to happen," the old woman said to herself as she pulled at the last strap holding the vest in place. "Too much exposure and too many video cameras around these days. Izzy should have stayed out of it and let them kill Jack Mercer and that Senator. No great loss to the world," she mumbled, "either one of them."

The eldest Luca pulled a sweater around her shoulders and turned to examine her profile. The sweater hid the vest and the shoulder holster. She hadn't fired a shot in over a year, but she had every faith in her ability with a gun. And the small shotgun standing beside the doorway into the workroom didn't require accuracy. There was another handgun stashed beside the shotgun. The back door was deadbolted and the security bar was in place. They would have to come at her through the front door of the shop, and she would be ready for them. It was almost ten o'clock. Time to open.

"I told her," she mumbled, "these people don't deserve second chances. I won't hunt them, but they're only going to get one chance to kill me. She can't fault me for defending myself, and the cops can't either." She snickered as she turned the key in the front door. "Poor old woman like me? I'm just trying to keep my business from being robbed. Self-defense in any court in the country."

She hadn't been open long when James Olson walked through the front door. He looked confused. "I was told to push the buzzer because you wouldn't be open. Darius sent me to bring you back to the bakery," he said. "I'm supposed to tell you that Izzy is on her way. In a helicopter?" Jimmy shifted uncomfortably under the old woman's gaze. "And Darius said to tell you there's strength in numbers."

"Did he lock up his bakery? Is he going to hide under his bed and not face these assholes?"

"No, but he sent the girls to a safehouse somewhere. Mrs. Luca refused to leave, so I volunteered to stay instead of her. I don't understand why you won't just call the police?"

"That isn't the way we do things, Jimmy. They wouldn't show up anyway. No crime's been committed yet. But from what Izzy said, Tyrel Davis has put a price on all our heads. He put it together somehow, Izzy being the girl in Vegas, and her being my granddaughter. If he knows that much, he knows about Darius too. And I presume he already knows what happened at the compound. His little army is shrinking in a hurry, and he can't be happy about that."

"Shrinking?" Jimmy asked.

"Izzy and that Cain fellow saw to it. Three dead, and the FBI is shut down the rest of the gun club operation."

Jimmy's eyes widened. "Dead? They saw to it?"

"Yeah, Jimmy, dead. This isn't one of your celebrity stories, this is getting real. You need to go back to the bakery. I'll come over there as soon as my granddaughter gets here. Do you have a gun?"

"A gun?" Jimmy wiped his sweaty hands on the front of his jacket, then held them up as evidence. "I don't have a gun! Do you?"

"Of course I have a gun," Gabby snapped, "several of them. How else am I going to rid the world of these reprobates? I don't know if Darius has a spare, but you need a weapon. I have one in the back."

Jimmy felt sick. There was a wedding to plan and he wanted to live to see it. Shaking, he followed Gabriel Luca into the back room and looked at the handgun. "I don't know how to shoot one of those," he explained. "I'll be less than worthless. What if I shoot Darius by mistake?"

Gabby slid the small Glock from its holster and opened the breech. "It's loaded. Just point and shoot; put some lead in the air. It might distract them and give Darius a chance. You'd be surprised how intimidating it is to have someone shooting at you."

"I would not be surprised," Jimmy said as he took the gun, "not surprised at all."

Before they had moved from the dim light of the backroom, they heard a soft rap on the back door, then a pause and a louder knock. There was another long pause, then the knocking grew louder, easily loud enough to be heard from anywhere in the store.

Jimmy sighed and a smile appeared. "Izzy's here."

"Dammit," Gabby said in a hushed tone. "No. There's a special knock. They made fun of me, but now it's not so funny, is it? Don't worry, there's no way they can break through that door without explosives."

Jimmy's voice broke. "Explosives? Is that likely?"

Gabby didn't answer right away, and they both heard the chime as the front door opened. "Hide," she said quietly.

"Can I call the police now?" he whispered desperately.

"Too late for that. Stay out of sight. Maybe they're just doing recon and waiting for Izzy. But if anyone other than me comes through this door, start shooting like your life depends on it. Because it will."

There was another series of loud raps on the back door, and for a moment Gabby had second thoughts. Izzy would never forget to use the special knock, Darius might. But he would call out, and no one had. She slid her handgun from its holster and stepped back into the

387

display room. The mirrored panels on the back side of the jewelry case were tall enough to hide the gun at her side if the door had only chimed to signal the entrance of Mrs. Appelbaum or one of her other regular customers. If not, the plated steel panels would do more than reflect the glitter of the diamonds on display.

It wasn't Rosemary Appelbaum who had walked into the store.

The men split up and the bigger of the two strolled casually along the wall lined with clocks. The smaller man took the opposite wall, peering at the arrays of crystal and reconditioned lamps. Rarely, men would come in looking for something special for their privileged wives. They were generally wealthy men, wearing Rolexes and silk shirts. These two were not particularly well dressed.

"Can I help you?" Gabby asked the taller of the two.

He smiled at her, but she caught the look that passed between the pair. "Maybe. Is your name Gabriel Luca?" When she nodded, he continued. "I knew your late husband. He died rather easily."

Gabby recognized the distraction. The taller man had expected his taunt to pull her attention away from his accomplice, or maybe they thought she really was just a helpless old woman. She put two bullets in the chest of the second man before he could fire a shot, then ducked down behind the display case.

Surprised by the resistance, Vince dropped to one knee and crouched behind a massive grandfather clock, waiting. He didn't have to wait long. The knocking had stopped on the back door, and Gabby was keeping one eye on the front, expecting a third assailant. There was a third assailant, but he was behind the wheel of Vince's one ton pickup. He hit the back door hard enough to loosen the hinges and break the lock. Daylight spilled around the edges of the steel door, but the bar held. Dimly, Gabby heard the truck back up and race its engine for another run.

The eldest Luca glanced into the shadows behind her, searching for what she hoped would be her backup. No Jimmy. She knew she needed to end it before whoever was in the truck breached the back door and she was caught in a crossfire. Taking a risk, she stood quickly and fired a pair of shots into the big clock. But in the space of time that it took her to glance back, Vince had moved. He fired three times. The force of one of the shots slammed Gabby into the wall and she crumpled to the floor.

Vince charged forward, wanting to be sure of his kill. He would put one in the old woman's head to reinforce the message, then move on. He heard an engine roar again and cringed when he saw the corner of his new pickup push into the opening in the back of the store. Vince wasn't the true believer Henrik Mauer was, but his pickup was an acceptable loss. He knew if he found the Gypsy and collected the bounty Tyrel Davis was offering, he could buy a dozen pickups.

Vince didn't bother walking to the far end of the showcase, he vaulted over it, intent on making sure the old woman was dead. He didn't see the slight man with the wire-rimmed glasses until it was too late. And he didn't see the shotgun. When he realized his mistake and started to lift his gun, Jimmy pulled the trigger. Vince was five feet from the business end of the gaping barrel of the twelve gauge. He died violently.

Jimmy rolled to his feet and checked the gun. It was a side-by-side, and there was still the man driving the pickup to deal with. He had heard more shots coming from outside, but after glancing down at the bloodied body just a few feet away, he was feeling weak and disoriented. He didn't feel sick to his stomach anymore, but he knew he would when he had to tell Darius about his sister. For now, he just wanted to stay alive. He hunkered down in the dark and waited. Then he heard a voice he recognized.

"Grandmama! Olson! Where are you?"

"Here," he croaked out, and dropped the shotgun. "We're in here."

The woman he now called Izzy plunged through the small opening between the front of the pickup and the shattered door. She ran past Jimmy and fell to the floor beside her grandmother. Adam Cain squeezed through the opening next and Jimmy shouted a warning to him. "There's another one out there somewhere."

"Not anymore, Jimmy," Cain replied. "Is that her grandmother?"

Izzy was leaning over Gabriel Luca, stroking her forehead and talking softly to her.

"Is she dead?" Jimmy whispered.

She smiled up at him through tears. "No. She's alive. She was wearing a vest, but the impact must have done some damage. She has a pulse but it's weak, and she's unconscious. She needs an ambulance."

The old woman's eyes fluttered open. "I'm alright. I think. Holy Christ, and Judas Priest, that hurt."

Jimmy opened his phone and started dialing 911. Cain knelt down beside the two women and handed Izzy a chair cushion he'd found in the workroom. Gabby laid her head back on the pillow, then turned to look at the gruesome body of Vincent Carlson. "What happened? I don't remember doing that."

"I used the shotgun," Jimmy said. "I've never shot a handgun, but I hunted quail when I was a kid."

Gabriel chuckled. "Good job, Olson. Maybe you do have the stones to handle Patience. I had my doubts."

"I have to go, Gabby," the Gypsy said. "Jimmy can wait here with you for the ambulance and I'm sure the cops are on their way. Cain and I have to get to the bakery. Tyrel has more men. I don't think this is over yet."

"Cain?" The old woman's gaze shifted. She searched the big man's face then squeezed her eyes shut. "Oh, Izzy," she muttered. "Not another one."

Chapter Thirty-Two

"Not saying you're wrong, but why would they go after Darius?" I asked as we jumped back into Levi's car. "I can see Tyrel thinking that your grandmother was out to get him because of what he did to her husband, but you said Darius is a baker now."

"He is. But he used to do what I do, and he was old school. Violent. He didn't just retire and buy a bakery, he went into hiding. He made a lot of enemies back in the day. There's a bounty on him too."

"Too?"

"As of an hour ago, Tyrel put a price on my head. Both of us, actually, although yours is substantially less. My uncle has been dodging hitmen for a long time. Years ago he shut down a group of drug runners and killed three of them. One of those men was the brother of the man that's hired Tyrel to do all this. He's the same man that stands to make several billion dollars if Tyrel manages to kill a few politicians and start a civil war."

"And you know all of this because of the group you work for? The same rich people who let you use their toys and have a heliport on their roof?"

"Them, and what I found out when I followed Tyrel to DC. They nearly had me down there and Tyrel saw my face."

"I thought you left town because of me," I admitted.

She grinned. "Narcissist." The banter was back. Banter was good. Banter was normal.

"That had to be dangerous," I said, "being there alone. That group needs to hire me as backup."

"Careful what you wish for, Cain."

"Substantially less?" I groused. "That's insulting."

She grinned. "Ten percent. Tyrel must really hate me."

"Does your uncle know we're coming?"

"I'm sure Jimmy called him by now. Darius isn't as stubborn as my grandmother. He closed the bakery and locked everything up. Anyone trying to kill him is going to have their hands full."

"I hope he realizes I'm on your side," I said. "I don't want to get shot by friendly fire."

"He knows who you are," she said. "I may have sent him a picture."

"Is this flirting?" I asked. "Because I don't want to presume."

She chuckled as we turned into the alley. "Just don't get shot again. I'm starting to like having you around. Maybe Levi is right. Maybe I can have a normal life."

She slowed the car and we dropped the windows, creeping down the narrow alley. It was eerily quiet, other than the shrill singsong of sirens from the direction of the clock shop. The only sign of life was a homeless man with a shopping cart picking through a garbage can. He turned his back to us.

"No casualties on our side so far," I said quietly. "But it would be nice to have a cellphone. I'd like to be sure Jenny made it out alright and talk to Randolph."

The Gypsy pointed to the glove compartment. I pulled the phone out and dialed Jenny. Hers was the only number I knew by heart. She answered cautiously on the second ring. "Hello? Who is this?"

"It's Adam. I just wanted to check in."

"Thank God! Dammit, Adam, there are dead people everywhere, and I thought sure you were one of them. We thought maybe they killed you and threw your body in the woods. Teddy said there was blood everywhere in that basement and that he had no idea where you were. You or Gabriel."

"They had us both, but we managed to get away. With no help from the FBI, I might add. I left Randolph a voice message before Jack and I came to the compound for you. Your boyfriend needs to check his voicemails once in a while."

"He knew you called, but the message didn't come through. When Jack and I got away, we found a farmer and borrowed his landline. As soon as Teddy knew what was going on, he called in the Guard and the local cops. Are you and Gabriel both safe?"

"Safe as we can be until this is over. It's bigger than anyone thought. We think they mean to kill a bunch of politicians, and some of the guys involved are working for Jack. He needs to clean house."

"He knows, and Teddy is going to help him do that. There's a major terror alert and they're talking about martial law."

"I can't talk now. Gypsy's grandmother was shot, but she's okay. There are more bodies, but none of them ours. We're checking on Gabby's brother right now. They might be going after him too."

The Gypsy stopped the car and put it in park. "This is the back door of the bakery," she said as she opened the door. "I'm going to look around."

"I have to go, Jenny," I said quickly. "We'll talk, if I don't end up in prison for the next hundred years. So far I can plead self-defense, but that might change."

The back door of the bakery opened, and a big, heavy-set man stepped into the alley and greeted the Gypsy. She turned to me and motioned. I had just stepped around the front of the car when I heard the hiss of a bullet, followed by the crack of a high velocity cartridge tearing a hole in the air. The Gypsy went down. I felt that strangling fear again, and the surety that I was about to lose her. Then, before I could reach her, she lunged to her feet and threw herself against the side of the car.

I fell to my knees, and she smiled up at me. She was already trying to sit up. She'd been hit high in the left shoulder, high enough to tear a hole in the muscle, but miss the bone. I pulled a sweatshirt from the backseat of Levi's car, wrapped it around the wound and under her arm. "You scared the hell out of me," I admitted. "Are you okay?"

"Not great," she gritted out, "but it could have been worse. And here I was worried about you getting shot again. It must have been my turn."

"Stay there," I admonished. "You're the one he wants, but he can't shoot what he can't see."

Darius Luca crossed the alley and put himself between his niece and the shooter. He opened the driver's door and rested a handgun on the opening as another round clipped the window frame close to his head, then fired three shots. "I'm guessing," he admitted. "I couldn't be sure where those shots came from."

Fortunately, the car was sitting at an angle which limited our exposure. Another bullet howled close but missed both metal and bone. I moved in front of the Gypsy and spoke to her uncle. "Higher up, I would imagine," I said. "A shooter always looks for the high ground. I don't see anything close, but he could be on the roof of that building on the next block."

"That's five hundred yards," Darius said skeptically.

I nodded. "Good thing she was moving. If he's any good at all, he'd have put one right through her heart." Another shot rang out and the mirror beside Darius' head exploded. "Got him," I said. "Two story at this end of the next block. I saw movement on the roof. Do you have a rifle?"

"I'm a baker," the big man snapped, then smiled sheepishly. "I have a scatter gun and three handguns, but no rifles."

"The police have to have heard this," the Gypsy said. She had ignored my advice and was leaning against the back door of the car. "Just stay down and we'll wait it out until they get here."

"And have him come back for another try?" Given the seriousness of the moment, sarcasm wasn't called for, but I couldn't help myself. "That's not the way we do things, Gypsy."

I nodded to her uncle. "See that air conditioner on the roof? He's on the right side of it. Shoot at the AC unit if you have to, but make some noise. I'll make a run for it. There are no windows on this side of the building, so if you're going to miss, miss low. I'll get on that roof and take him out."

"There's a roof ladder on the south end," the Gypsy said wincing, then managed another grin. "But aren't you afraid of heights?"

"Just your flying," I shot back.

Darius Luca laid his Glock on the ledge of the open car window. It was a ridiculously long shot for a handgun. Hitting the building seemed doable, but just hitting the air conditioner would be a good shot. There was virtually no chance he'd hit the shooter, even if he was as good with a handgun as his niece. When he opened fire, I bolted, running a zig-zag pattern until I got to the end of the block. The homeless man I'd seen stepped out of my way as I passed. "Watch your back, soldier," he called after me. His voice sounded strangely familiar.

Once I cleared the side-street I breathed a sigh of relief. The shooter wouldn't be able to see me from the roof unless he walked to the edge. If he had taken cover when Darius started firing, he might not even know I was there. Smaller, older buildings like the two-story he was shooting from didn't require a roof access from inside. The only way onto the roof was from a ladder that was bolted to the wall. To keep kids from trying it, the bottom of the ladder was ten feet in the air. I took a two-step running start and grabbed the second rung, then pulled myself up and started climbing.

When I reached the crest of the roof, I heard the gun go off again. It sounded like a Denel, which identified the shooter for me. Henrik Mauer had given Cole Conley such a rifle, and there weren't that many around. Of the Bunkhouse Boys, Cole was my favorite, but that wasn't going to stop me from killing him if I had to. I raised my head up over the parapet and risked a quick look. He was standing beside the AC unit, using it as a shooting bench and getting ready to fire another round. I reached for my gun, but it was gone.

I'd lost my Glock during the melee at the compound and borrowed a replacement from Levi after the helicopter ride. A Glock 19. The smaller, lighter version of the reliable handgun I usually carried. Apparently too small and too light to stay in my holster where it belonged. I waited on the ladder. When Cole fired again, I made my move.

I slipped onto the roof quietly, but like many flat roofs, it was covered with tar and gravel. Gravel is noisy. I took three steps before he heard me. He stepped away from the air conditioner and spun around, trying to turn the rifle on me.

If Cole had used a proper stand, he would have killed the Gypsy with his first shot. Denels are anti-material guns and meant to hit targets at a considerable distance. Because of that, they're heavy and relatively long. Long and cumbersome. Cole swung the gun around in an arc that he wasn't quite able to complete before I hit him at a dead run. I grabbed the barrel and dropped my shoulder, then just kept pushing. Unfortunately, I had misjudged how close we were to the far edge of the building. Cole's feet caught on the twelve-inch parapet, and he went off the roof backwards, holding on to me with one hand and the Denel with the other.

In jump school we were told that the resulting impact was similar to jumping off a roof. They had to have been talking about a single-story roof, because after doing both, I much prefer the parachute. One story is roughly nine feet. The ledge we went off of wasn't quite twenty feet from the ground, but it was close. I had the luxury of seeing the sidewalk coming and managed to gather my legs to roll. Cole did not.

He landed nearly upside down on the concrete that paralleled the building with most of my weight on his lower body. I don't know if the collision with the ground broke his neck, or the collision with the sidewalk crushed his skull. In either event, by the time I gathered myself and limped back to where he lay, he had stopped breathing. Another casualty of a war that was looking less and less likely to happen.

I picked up the Denel with one hand and started walking back toward where the Gypsy and her uncle waited. When I saw the black sedan sitting behind the bakery, I broke into a run. Suddenly a whole lot of things started to make sense to me.

Agent Blake Collins was standing over the still form of Darius Luca. He had a gun in his hand and it was pointed at the Gypsy. I started to lift the Denel.

"Put it down, Cain," Collins said, "or I'll kill her right here."

The Gypsy eyes shifted from her uncle and turned to me. "Don't try it, Adam. He flashed his badge and Darius let his guard down. He's not dead, Collins, but he needs a doctor. It's not too late to stop this. Take me with you and turn me over to Tyrel. There's no reason to kill them."

I put the Denel on the ground and stepped back. "How long? You're the one who released the original video, aren't you? You knew the Gypsy would find me if I came back to New York, and then you'd find her. And you killed Gainey."

"He's been feeding Tyrel information all along," the Gypsy added.

Collins was fidgeting. He hadn't expected to have to kill the Gypsy himself. He was stalling, and he started talking. "Gainey knew who was really in charge and he kept trying to squeeze more money out of him."

"Tyrel?" I asked.

Collins snorted. "A man who could buy and sell Tyrel Davis with the change in his pockets. It doesn't matter now. Things are on hold, thanks to this bitch and her meddling friends."

"The money means that much to you?" I asked. I had no plan, but talking was good. Talking was keeping my partner alive.

Collins' voice rose and he looked in my direction. His nerve was failing him, but the gun never wavered. "Years in an Ivy League school, top of my class and a fortune in debt. All for what? To make pennies and be lectured to by Randolph? Tyrel is offering a fortune for her, dead or alive, and he's promised to get me out of the country if I bring her to him. I'll find a nice beach somewhere. Mauer's right. There's a war coming to this country and I'm getting out while I can."

"War?" a gruff voice said.

The homeless man I'd seen earlier had wandered up. His head was down and he was muttering to himself. He had a brown bag in his left hand. He tipped it up and took a long drink.

Collins' face twisted and his voice climbed. "Jesus, old man, get the hell out of here!"

"War?" the drunk repeated into the scarf covering his face. "Vet-Nam was bad. Terrible bad." I could swear I knew that voice.

"You'll see terrible bad in a minute," Collins said as he waved his gun at the vagrant. "Now go away!"

The man turned around, still mumbling, and started to shuffle off. Collins turned his gun back toward the Gypsy. I knew I had to risk something, desperate as it might be, before he worked up the courage to either shoot her or force her into his car. Then I heard the sound of breaking glass.

"Sum-bitch," the drunk mumbled.

Collins turned back again, exasperated. He had lowered his gun and was looking nervously at each of us in turn. I could see the indecision on his face. He didn't have the stomach for the cold-blooded murder of a woman, and he knew what Tyrel would do to the Gypsy if he turned her over. I'll always wonder if he would have made the right choice on his own.

Collins lifted his head and stared stupidly at the disheveled old man who had turned back to us and pulled the scarf from his face. Too late, recognition flashed across Collins' face. There was a gun in the homeless man's right hand, and this time there was no mistaking his voice.

"I'll give you just one chance, you pompous little prick," Detective Murdock snarled. "Maybe I don't have jurisdiction out here, but I'm betting your boss will cut me some slack if I have to kill you. Now drop the gun."

To his credit, Agent Collins was no idiot. He dropped the gun.

Detective Murdock pulled the oily hat off his head and tossed it on the ground next to the scarf, then handed me a cellphone. "Call an ambulance, Cain. And you, Mister fancy-pants FBI guy, put your hands behind your head and get on your knees."

I made the call, then went to help Darius. He was conscious, but definitely in need of medical attention. The Gypsy crawled over and cradled his head in her lap while I held a compress to his wound. Detective Murdock finished cuffing Collins, then turned to us.

"Ma'am?" he asked politely.

"Yes, Detective?"

"You owe me a statement, and I'd prefer not to have to chase you all the way across the country again to get it. Are you going to cooperate, or should I ride with you to the hospital?"

She smiled up at him. "You'll get your statement, Detective. I think you've earned it."

Collins glowered in Murdock's direction. "What tipped you off?"

Murdock returned the appraisal. "You subpoenaed my DNA evidence, but when I called Randolph to give him hell about it, he had no idea what I was talking about. I would have figured it out anyway, but someone put a bug in my ear. She told me honest cops were hard to

405

come by and she was pretty sure you weren't one of those."

"She?" I asked and looked over at the Gypsy.

She shrugged with the shoulder that wasn't wrapped. "Must have been Jenny."

"I'd bet not," her uncle said. He managed a weak grin and insisted on sitting up.

From down the alley I could hear the welcome warble of an ambulance as they turned the corner. I slid to the ground next to the Gypsy and put my back against the wall of the bakery. I hurt in places I didn't know existed. But I was alive, and so were the important people in my life.

The Gypsy looked over at me, bemused. "Had enough fun for one day?" she asked.

"If this is normal for you, count me out."

She managed a grin. "Come on, Cain, you and I are just getting started."

Epilogue

Healing takes time. My latest gunshot wound was minor. No bones were broken, but I was still carrying around the pain of Mickey's death and the knowledge of what some people are capable of. I'd seen too many innocent people die in the last year and a half, and I wanted to put that violence behind me. The Gypsy spent one night in the hospital, then went to stay with her grandmother for a week. She said they could help each other heal. She wasn't talking about gunshot wounds.

The country, wounded as it was and still is, survived the attempt by Tyrel Davis and his billionaire backer to start a civil war. It was a quiet Memorial Day with very few speeches made. No one seemed to mind. Agent Randolph and the FBI stepped in to jail or deport most of the men willing to follow Henrik Mauer and take orders from Tyrel Davis. I still didn't trust Agent Randolph, but I was starting to like him. For the time being, Tyrel was free to plot his next scheme and continue to pick the pockets of the wealthy.

On a sunny day in the middle of June, the Gypsy and I met Randolph and Jenny in the park for a picnic lunch. Jenny's idea. After lunch, Randolph asked for a moment, and took the

Gypsy aside. It gave me a chance to talk to Jenny.

She was smiling. "I'm moving in with Teddy."

"That's great," I said, and meant it. "Right time and the right guy?"

"He thinks we have a future together."

"I get why you want that," I said. "Maybe I'll get there someday."

"Some things last, Adam. I'll always believe that."

"Never change, Jenny," I said. "The world needs people like you in it. I never deserved you."

"I was just the wrong girl, but I know you cared about me. It wasn't quite the way I hoped, but you risked your life to save me. That says a lot."

I looked over her head at the tall woman talking to Randolph. "She's done that for me, more than once."

Jenny shrugged. "That should tell you everything you need to know."

"What did Randolph have to say?" I asked the Gypsy as I walked her to her Jeep. Mercer Security wasn't far away, and I had another interview. Maybe a fulltime position, maybe not. And, Agent Randolph had dropped a hint about future employment. I still didn't trust him.

"He wants to collaborate and share information. I told him I'd have to talk to the higher-ups. As a rule, they don't like working with law enforcement. My grandmother, especially."

"Why does she call you Izzy?" I asked. "Levi does too. How many names do you have?"

"Izzy is short for Isabelle. My mother's name, and my middle name. No one in the family calls me Gypsy. You can if it works for you."

"You'll always be the Gypsy to me," I said. "I'll save Isabelle for special occasions, like when we're in bed."

She smiled ruefully and fumbled with her keys, then opened the door and climbed into the driver's seat. It seemed like the rules had changed, but I wasn't sure.

"Would it be weird if I kissed you?"

She lifted a brow. "It is now!"

"Speaking of weird, what's up with your grandmother? She already hates me."

Her smile grew. "You look a lot like my father. He was a good-looking black man too."

"And she didn't like him?

"Not even a little bit. But she'll come around. She'll have to, being a Giants fan."

"I know you're kidding about that."

"About the twins?" The smile never left her face. "Nothing lasts, Cain. Isn't that what you always say?"

I looked across the park at Jenny and Randolph. They were sitting on a bench feeding the pigeons. Jenny had her head on his shoulder and was laughing happily. I turned back to the Gypsy and risked that kiss.

"There's a chance I'm wrong about that."

Tyrel Davis walked into his office and dropped a file folder on the desk. His phone was going crazy, but he had ignored it all morning. The plan now was to lay low and wait for the professional to do his job. With the Belgian dead, there would be no evidence to bring charges against him. He would wait it out, regroup, then take another run at ridding the world of the Luca family. Without their interference, there would be plenty of opportunities to make money. There would be more lackeys to hire and more billionaires to dupe. He would land on his feet as he always did.

As he settled into his chair, he noticed a small square stuck to the plate glass window that faced the Philadelphia skyline. It was held to the interior of the glass by one small piece of tape. He stood and walked to the window and pulled it from the glass. It was a faded Polaroid, the kind of picture he hadn't seen in years. He looked at the image. A very tall black man in a weathered uniform had one arm around a shorter man with sandy-colored hair. They were both holding up beers and smiling, posing for the camera.

Tyrel rolled the picture over and squinted at the writing on the back. *"His name was Mickey Cooper, a casualty of your war."*

Too late, Tyrel Davis realized his peril and looked up. There was a click as steel pierced glass and a small hole appeared above the spot where the picture had been taped. Tyrel heard the click and saw the hole, then everything went dark.

Half a mile away, Adam Cain stood up and disassembled Henrik Mauer's Denel so it would fit in the cockpit of the waiting helicopter. He climbed in and the shaggy-haired chopper pilot lifted off.

"Feel better?" Levi asked Cain as they turned north and left the city behind.

"Not really," the big man said, "but I will. The world's a violent and dangerous place, Levi. I wish I knew how to change that, but I don't. I just know how to fight back."

Levi glanced in his direction. "You and Isabelle, you can do that together."

"If she'll still have me. I had to do it, Levi. She's safer with Tyrel Davis dead. A life for a life, or a life to save a life. Either way, he had to go."

"Maybe, but she's not likely to thank you for this." They flew in silence for a few minutes, then Levi spoke again. "Ironic that he died the way he did, the long shot. The same way he planned to kill all those congressmen."

"Yeah, ironic," Cain said. "But not in a funny way."

"Still," Levi muttered, "she's not going to be happy."

The big man frowned. "She doesn't have to know, does she?"

Levi shrugged. "I won't tell her, but she'll know. She always knows."

Cain shook his head and chuckled. "Yeah. How does she do that?"

END

I hope you enjoyed The Gypsy. Amazon has recently made the review process much easier than before, and it takes just a few seconds to share your opinion with some stars. Please do. Better yet, a written review tells me what you liked, or didn't. Your opinions are valuable to me, so please share your thoughts.

Sign up for updates at www.tjjonesbooks.com or email me at tjjoneswtr@outlook.com if you'd prefer. Your email address will never be shared.

AND DON'T MISS ANY OF THE SLATER MYSTERIES

"My Sister's Detective" Eric Slater partners with his old flames' sister to investigate the death of an old friend. Mystery, Romance, and Murder on the Florida coast.

"My Sister's Fear" The romance takes off, and so do the investigations. Slater and Maggie take on organized crime to stop the trafficking of young girls on the Florida coast.

"Slater's Tempest" A missing heiress, a curious shark, and Slater thinks he's seen a ghost.

"Slater's Vendetta" Slater takes on a street gang and makes a new friend. He's ten.

"Slater's Game" People are dying at Hidden Fairways, and it's not from Covid. Looks like Slater is going to have to fix his slice.

Printed in Great Britain
by Amazon